A Rainbow
Murder Mystery

Praise for *Murder on Easter Island*—

"This engaging novel held my complete attention from start to finish. Daniel Fishinghawk is a terrific detective—rich, complex and real. I particularly enjoyed the historical information woven into the mystery and the exotic location. Highly recommended."

—William Bernhardt, author of *Primary Justice*

"In *Murder on Easter Island*, Gary Conrad creates a mystery of the rarest order when Detective Daniel "Hawk" Fishinghawk is sent to Easter Island to investigate a series of cannibalistic killings. Conrad's writing is never more powerful or his imagination more sweeping than when he delves into the dark mysteries of the universe in this way, and it is the readers' delight to be invited along for the journey."

—Sheldon Russell, author of *The Hanging of Samuel Ash*

"In *Murder on Easter Island*, Gary Conrad blends suspense, a love story, history and a keen understanding of the human soul in a masterfully told story that grabbed me from page one."

—Joan Korenblit, Executive Director, Respect Diversity Foundation

"This Who-Done-It takes some unusual, daring and even glorious twists across time, cultures and ethnicities. Conrad's story evokes feeling as well as inspiring you to figure it out."

—Ken Hada, author of *Spare Parts* and *Margaritas and Redfish*

continued

"Gary Conrad has done it again. Much like *The Lhasa Trilogy*, he takes us on another quirky adventure through a wonderfully exotic landscape. *Murder on Easter Island* is a gruesomely delightful journey through the culture and history of Easter Island. His research, visits and descriptions of the scenes in his book are like a travelogue to a time and a place to which few of us ever get access. Well worth the read!"

—D. Franklin Schultz, author of *A Language of the Heart*

"Of the numerous novels set on Easter Island, Gary D. Conrad's book is the first to effectively weave both history and fact into fiction. A highly engaging murder mystery that aims to educate."

—Associate Professor Ian Conrich, University of South Australia,
curator of the exhibition "Easter Island, Myths and Popular Culture"

"This book is an engrossing combination of the history of Easter Island/Rapa Nui and a contemporary murder mystery. The author's use of an engaging literary device . . . allows the reader to enter the world of ancient Rapa Nui and explore this society's culture, myths and spirituality. As such it works well as both an introduction to the world of the Rapanui, both past and present, and yet is also a gripping page-turner as we follow 'Hawk' in his pursuit of a gruesome and prolific serial killer."

—Roy Smith, Ph.D., Programme Leader,
MA in International Development,
Nottingham Trent University, UK

8/28/15
To Anna-
A fellow spiritual seeker, and a
wonderful friend. Best.
Gary

Murder on
EASTER
ISLAND

GARY D. CONRAD

Gary D. Conrad

Rainbow Books, Inc.
F L O R I D A

Library of Congress Cataloging-in-Publication Data

Conrad, Gary D., 1952-
  Murder on Easter Island / Gary D. Conrad.
    pages cm
  ISBN 978-1-56825-179-0 (hardcover with jacket : alk. paper) -- ISBN 978-1-56825-180-6 (trade softcover : alk. paper) -- ISBN 978-1-56825-181-3 (epub ebook)
  1. Easter Island--Fiction. 2. Mystery fiction. I. Title.
  PS3603.O5555M87 2014
  813'.6--dc23
                                    2014021206

Murder on Easter Island: A Daniel "Hawk" Fishinghawk Mystery © 2015 by Gary D. Conrad

Hardcover ISBN: 978-1-56825-179-0
Softcover ISBN: 978-1-56825-180-6
EPUB ISBN: 978-1-56825-181-3

This is a work of fiction. Any resemblance of characters to individuals living or dead is coincidental.

Cover image of the Ahu Ature Huki by Murray Foote (MurrayFoote.com).
Author photo taken in a grotto, high in the Wichita Mountains, by Chris Corbett.

Book divider page images by the author:
Book One: Moai on Rano Raraku, a dormant volcano and the site of the quarry from where the moai were carved.

Book Two: Cave en route to Mount Terevaka.

Book Three: Rano Kau.

Published by:

Rainbow Books, Inc.
P. O. Box 430, Highland City, FL, 33846-0430
Telephone: (863) 648-4420 • RBIbooks@aol.com • RainbowBooksInc.com

Author's Website:

GaryDConrad.com

Individuals' Orders:

Amazon.com • AllBookStores.com • BN.com

Permissions:

Metraux, Alfred. "The Woman with the Long Arm" & "The Child Changed into Nanue."
In *Ethnology of Easter Island*. Honolulu: Bishop Museum Press, 1940.

The paper used in this publication meets the minimum requirements of the American National Standard for Information Sciences—Permanence of Paper for Printed Library Materials, ANSI Z39.48-1984.

First Printing 2015
19 18 17 16 15   7 6 5 4 3 2 1
Produced and printed in the United States of America.

To Betty Wright
1924–2013
My editor, mentor and friend

Murder on
EASTER
ISLAND

Prelude

Circa 700 CE, Mangareva, Polynesia

Piercing screams echoed through the village.

The old shaman Haumaka covered his ears with his hands in vain as he sat on the ground outside his thatched hut. Five of his clan's best warriors lay dead, stretched out on the island beach, punctured many times over by spears and beaten with clubs nearly beyond recognition.

As the naked corpses awaited being wrapped in barkcloth and placed in a nearby cave, a large group of women and children writhed in agony around them. Between wails they swatted at the flying insects that buzzed around and onto the soon-to-be-rotten flesh.

Haumaka was saddened because, as an elder, he had known all of the dead since they were little boys, when they played and frolicked in the sand of their small beachside community. He had seen them grow to be strong young men, the best of the best.

And now they were dead.

The youth should never die before the elderly, he bitterly thought. But that's the way life is. There are no guarantees — ever.

He shook his head. This was the third battle over the past fourteen days with a neighboring tribe, and they had lost each clash in spite of the bravery of their warriors. The others had simply overwhelmed them with numbers.

This location was no longer safe.

So it came as no surprise when only a short while ago the chief of his clan, Hotu Matu'a, had asked him to dream and find a new island to move to. The thought of moving dampened his spirits even more; he loved his home. He was born and raised here and knew every special place — and there were many.

Tired of listening to the persistent screams and knowing there was work to be done, he stuffed some taro root and baked chicken in his bag, stood and walked barefoot deep into the island forest. The thick calluses on his feet warded away injury from rocks or thorns.

When Haumaka chose to dream, he often went to the base of a hidden waterfall, deep in the jungle — and he headed there now. Only a few knew of its location, as its secret was well kept by the shamans who preceded him. Only when he had advanced far enough in his learning was he taken there.

And there was a reason for that.

It was a place of visions and only for ones whose minds were prepared. He knew of those who had stumbled onto this location, meandered for a while and, upon returning, were stark raving mad, wild-eyed, screaming and seeing things no one else could. The only choice the villagers had was to tie them to a palm tree. After a day or two of wallowing in their excrement, they invariably came to their senses.

Following a half day of hard walking, Haumaka smiled as he heard the roar of the waterfall. He parted the foliage that stood in his way and knelt by the edge of a small lagoon at the cascade's base, inhaling deeply of the mist that gathered around his face.

He bent over, scooped crystal-clear water into his mouth and looked up to see his favorite place for dreaming: a large, flat, moss-covered rock. He sat down on it, realized he was hungry and pulled the food from his bag.

While he ate, he began to listen to the sounds around him: the waterfall, the soft breeze blowing through the trees and the chatter of jungle birds.

The taro root and chicken devoured, he focused on his breath and moved his consciousness inside himself. The noises around him began to fade, and before long the part of him that was spirit left his body and flew into the air and out over the ocean.

While Haumaka had done this many times in the past, he now directed his mind to focus on finding their next island home. He looked at the sun and measured carefully the direction he took.

He accelerated over the water and, using his spiritual sight, saw a lush green isle far in the distance. He covered the span within the blink of an eye. As his consciousness hovered over the small island, he liked what he discovered. It was densely forested, thick with palm trees, and streams of fresh water spilled from the high grounds to eventually empty into the ocean below.

As he looked in all directions, there was no other land to be seen.

This place is isolated, far from the eyes of anyone else, but it is not inaccessible, he thought, pleased with his find.

He was not a seaman by any stretch of the imagination, but guessed the distance between his home island and this one could be sailed in under a month.

And most important of all, it was uninhabited.

Perfect.

When he returned to the village, he would report to Chief Hotu Matu'a, who would send a scouting party to explore the island before he made the decision to move there. While he trusted his shaman, the chief was not one to take chances.

Haumaka smiled as he floated above his new home, and he wondered what the future held for his clan there. Like any good shaman, he had the ability to see into the future, yet knew he could see only the waves of probability — no future was predestined. He closed his eyes and scenes unfolded before him.

As he had predicted, the search party sent by the chief indeed found the isle to be suitable for habitation, and two large canoes containing Hotu Matu'a and a number of his kinsmen set out to sea and successfully landed. Haumaka noted he was not in either of the boats. He grimly nodded to himself.

Death approaches sooner than I would have guessed . . .

In spite of this unexpected revelation, Haumaka was pleased to see how his people flourished on the new island and was awed by the beauty of the statues they constructed. But as the window of time quickened, there was deforestation, and the trees vanished.

He frowned.

He saw conflict among his people, shortage of food supplies, and the statues toppled over. He witnessed as slave traders and diseases devastated the population to a fraction of its previous size. Then there was a period of relative calm, accompanied by population growth, and the placement of many of the statues back to their upright position.

All seemed well again.

Haumaka sighed in relief.

He started to bring his consciousness back to the present when a dark, dense, red-tinged cloud formed over the island of his dream, obscuring it from the light of the sun. He felt revulsion at what was easily the most evil manifestation he had ever perceived and was surprised to find himself becoming fearful.

Suddenly Haumaka knew that the evil force was aware of his presence, and large black, clawed hands reached out from the cloud for him. He screamed and immediately found himself back in his body, sitting upon the mossy rock, sweating profusely.

He leaped from the rock and washed his face frantically with cold water. He jerked his head from side to side and nervously looked around — no further sign of the apparition.

Calming himself, he looked to the sky and felt the late afternoon sun on his face. He had to depart soon or he would be at the mercy of the night jungle.

Haumaka thought deeply. Was he sending his beloved people to a place of doom? Perhaps, but it was the only choice. The immediate future demanded they leave, and leave soon.

But the evil was the strongest he had ever seen. Was there a good strong enough to oppose it?

That was a question for the future.

He picked up his food pack and walked back down the trail, anxiously glancing at any sounds or shadows.

Would the black hands come back for him?

While he knew he had not long to live, he would rather not die in the clutches of evil. He quickened his pace and rushed down the jungle pathway as quickly as his aged legs would carry him.

Book
One

Chapter 1

"Oh, God, this one's even worse."

"You can't mean it."

Detective Dockendorf stumbled from the kitchen of the small apartment as pale as a ghost and holding a handkerchief over his mouth. To his partner, he managed, "Have a look for yourself."

Dockendorf plopped down on the living room sofa, doing all he could not to vomit. The chili-cheeseburger and onion rings he'd had for lunch made a return visit to the back of his throat. He swallowed hard and choked them back down again.

Detective Anderson wiped the sweat from his brow and headed toward the kitchen. Why are these crime scene investigations always like working in an oven? he wondered.

"Dockendorf," he said with a look of disgust on his face, "you are such a gutless fool. Why couldn't the chief have given me a partner with more backbone?"

Anderson entered the small kitchen and the smirk on his face quickly faded into a look of horror. Before he could stop it, a high-pitched scream erupted from his throat, and he fell back through the doorway — ending up next to Dockendorf on the sofa.

A uniformed NYPD officer, who stood guard outside the door to the apartment, cracked it open and peeked inside. From the hallway loud conversation and camera flashes entered the room.

Anderson thought: The press — shit — why don't they just leave us alone?

The policeman asked, "You guys okay?"

Dockendorf answered sarcastically, "Yeah, we're just taking a siesta."

"I'm sure," the officer responded. "When you're finished with your nap, you might actually do your job and investigate the scene." He shook his head and snapped the door shut to keep the press at bay.

Anderson turned to Dockendorf and asked incredulously, "Did you see what I saw in that kitchen?"

"You mean the guy tied to a chair with his head cut in half by a meat cleaver? The one with the empty bottle of Jack Daniel's at his feet?"

"No, you idiot, I meant his cute, pink IZOD shirt," Anderson retorted as he rolled his eyes.

Dockendorf stared at him blankly, "I thought the last murder we investigated was bad —"

"You're not just a kiddin'. His head was nearly taken off with a butcher knife."

"Yep, that's the one."

"The chief says we better get to the bottom of these killings fast," Anderson said. "Now the press has gotten hold of this and has started calling them the Culinary Murders, because each one was killed with something from the kitchen. This guy will make the seventh. The press might not want to admit it, but the worse this gets the happier they are. Those scum suckers are selling a shitload of newspapers over this deal."

"Fuck the press," Dockendorf said, "and the chief can screw himself. How do you solve murders when there aren't enough clues?"

The ringtone of Anderson's cell phone started playing "Three Blind Mice," and he pulled the phone from his coat pocket and answered, "Anderson here — okay, Chief Kelly — right — will do." The conversation ended and he dropped his cell phone back into his pocket.

"Hawk's on his way," Anderson said. "Kelly wants him to have a look around before the rest of the gang gets here."

Dockendorf sighed. "You talkin' about the new guy, from Oklahoma of all places, Daniel Fishinghawk, the crime scene genius? What do you know about him?"

Anderson answered, "Rumor has it that his background is Cherokee Indian — though you could never tell by looking at him. I've heard he's smart as hell — could be in Mensa if he wanted — a speed reader who digests over five books a week —"

"I'm sick of that guy," Dockendorf interrupted. "He makes the rest of us look bad. So he's gotten lucky on a few cases. So what?"

"The ladies in the office can't keep their eyes off him," Anderson added. "Tall, slender, dark hair — they all think he's hot stuff."

Dockendorf threw up his hands in exasperation. "I don't give a shit about how good looking he is." Then he grinned and said, "But this case will kick his ass — just like it's kicked ours. I can't wait to see the chief's new golden boy go up in flames."

Hawk arrived wearing a black suit, a black dress shirt without a tie and black Merrell hiking shoes.

"I'm Detective Fishinghawk. Just call me — Hawk," he said. His trimmed black hair was neatly combed into place, and his piercing dark eyes were bright and alert, as if all seeing. As he extended his right hand, he remarked, "I've seen you both around the office. Good to see you again."

Anderson and Dockendorf stuck out their hands and Hawk shook them.

Hawk asked, "What do you know so far?"

Anderson and Dockendorf glanced at each other before Anderson spoke. "This is the seventh murder over the past four months, and they have several things in common. First, as you know, they have all been killed with a kitchen utensil. Number one victim was murdered with a wine corkscrew, and this one a meat cleaver. Each time it was something different, but always something from the kitchen.

"They have all been men and were all tied to a chair with rope. The killer wore gloves, so there have been no fingerprints. And all of the victims let the murderer into their apartments — like they knew him. And, for a coup de grâce, after they were killed, each and every one of our victims was anointed with a bottle of Jack Daniel's."

Fishinghawk's dark eyes blazed. "How do you know it was a him?"

Dockendorf answered. "There's been so much blood at the scenes we were able to check the shoe tracks. All were the same Nike tennis shoes, men's size six and a half. Must be a little guy."

"I see," Hawk said warily. "Have you found any connections between the victims? Education? Jobs? Clubs? Prisons? Any common history — any at all?"

"Nope," said Anderson.

"Let me look over the scene," Hawk said.

Dockendorf and Anderson ushered Hawk into the kitchen.

Hawk slowly walked around the area, nodded, and led the way back into the living room.

"Was the window AC turned on when you came in?" he asked.

"No," said Anderson. "What of it?"

"How about the other murders? Was the air conditioner turned off at those scenes as well?"

"Come to think of it — yes," confessed Anderson.

"Don't you think it's a little odd, in the middle of summer, for it to be off?"

"Maybe the guy that lived here liked it hot," Anderson guessed as he nervously loosened his tie and unbuttoned his collar.

"No, I believe his killer liked it hot. Look at the on-off dial."

Dockendorf and Anderson both stepped over and stared at it. A small smudge of blood was smeared on the dial. They groaned and reluctantly turned to face Fishinghawk.

"Gentlemen," Hawk said, as he folded his arms across his chest, "I'm no doctor, but I do know that cold intolerance is often associated with glandular disorders, especially hypothyroidism. The killer turned off the AC because she couldn't stand the cold."

"What do you mean she?" Dockendorf exclaimed. "We told you that he was wearing men's shoes. We matched it up."

Hawk shook his head, "*She* meant for you to assume that. That's why she made the tracks so obvious. She's actually a woman's size eight, but she wore men's shoes to confuse you." Then he looked off thoughtfully and concluded, "Our suspect is a woman who is really angry with men — hard to say why, though off the top I might guess it's because she has been around too many who are alcoholics. Besides, women are many times more likely to be hypothyroid than men. It's a dropkick — it's a woman."

Anderson protested, "But —"

"I have a hunch, gentlemen — could be right, could be wrong — but it's worth a shot. I want you to check on the past medical records of our dead, and I believe you'll discover that they all saw the same endocrinologist. What are men usually seen for in an endocrinologist's office? In our group of victims, I'd bet my bottom dollar that they were being treated for impotence.

"If you check the appointment schedule, you'll find that there was a woman who had a hypothyroid condition who happened to be in the waiting room at the same time. I believe she let each and every one of her victims know that she was willing to help them with their problem. Little did they know what they were getting into."

"You can't be serious," Dockendorf said, dismissing the idea with a wave of his hand.

Hawk ignored him. "Oh — one more thing, once you discover her name, I believe you'll find she is a new resident of New York City, probably lived here around four months, and in the place she has lived before there were a number of similar unexplained crimes."

"Hawk, I think you've gone off the deep end," Anderson said, shaking his head. "This is the wildest thing I've ever heard of. There's no way anyone could connect these dots. Are you crazy?"

"Crazy is as crazy does," said Hawk as he shrugged and his handsome face broke into a friendly smile. He nodded, bid them a good day and departed.

Chapter 2

August 20, 2014, Catskill Forest Preserve, New York

Daniel Fishinghawk dared not make a sound.

His weathered moccasins, given to him many years ago by his grandpa, moved silently across the moist earth. Years of yoga, combined with strength training and aerobic exercise, allowed him to move his toned body across the rugged landscape as quietly as a wraith. The sun began to dip below the wooded horizon. He was about to run out of time.

Just a little farther, he thought.

He had arrived in the Catskill Forest Preserve five days ago and had but one goal in mind: Track and find the eastern cougar, which had been pronounced extinct over three years ago by the U.S. Fish and Wildlife Service. Daniel was aware of numerous previous sightings, all of which had been pooh-poohed by the Service. The ploy used to discredit these viewings was to make the finder look like a complete moron.

"Oh, you must have seen a house cat," they would say. Or giving the discoverer just a little more credit, ". . . a bobcat." You'd have thought that by the disdain the Service had for such accountings, someone had said they'd seen Sasquatch.

They just don't want to be wrong, Daniel guessed.

Daniel had been here nearly every weekend over the past three months. He had discovered tracks he was sure were those of the eastern cougar, but his two-day weekends weren't enough time to accomplish the task of finding one. At long last the chief reluctantly gave him a week off, and now he was certain that, just over the wooded ridge, one was feeding on its favorite prey, the white-tailed deer. He heard the sounds of ripping flesh and hoped the animal was distracted by its meal.

As he rounded the top of the ridge, he crouched and carefully concealed himself behind some brush. As he peeked over the top, he saw a huge tan cat, around eighty pounds — probably a male — the eastern cougar.

Daniel squatted back down for a moment and listened. When the noise of eating stopped, and he was certain the cat was finished with its meal, Daniel stood, intentionally cracking a twig.

The cougar pricked up its ears and intensely stared at him, unafraid. The two locked eyes for a few seconds, then the cat ambled away, not bothering to look back.

Daniel watched the cat until he was no longer visible. He had brought no photographic equipment — nothing to record this moment — because it wasn't necessary. His mind worked like a camera, and once he saw something it was tucked away in his memory forever. Some called it an eidetic memory, others, a photographic memory. Whatever they chose to name it, all Daniel knew was that he remembered everything he saw in the minutest detail. For that moment, all he wanted was the image of the cat in his mind, and he had it.

He sat down by the brush, pulled a water bottle from his belt clip, and said a silent prayer of thanks to his grandpa, Hunter Fishinghawk, who had raised him since he was two years old and had educated him on the skills of tracking. He had taught Daniel the subtle things that could never be found in books. Because of him he was able to experience this moment.

God rest his soul . . .

Daniel grimaced as he brought up the memory.

Not so many years ago, when Daniel was attending classes at Northeastern State University (NSU) in Tahlequah, Oklahoma, his grandpa was killed one morning by an intruder who entered their humble home in the countryside. Daniel, who still lived with him, found him that evening on the front porch with his throat cut, wild dogs and vultures fighting over his body.

After Daniel shooed them away, he was horrified to see that large portions of flesh had been eaten away from his legs, arms and face. Daniel turned his head away, knowing he would not forget. Still, his grandpa was larger than life, and that was a memory he'd not forget either.

Grandpa had been tall and strong with his salt and pepper black hair tied behind his head in a small ponytail, wearing his buffalo nickel belt buckle with one coin in the middle, depicting a proud Native American, surrounded by six more coins showing buffalo in a circular pattern. That was his grandpa, yes, larger than life.

And so Daniel took heart and stepped into the house to make a call to the police. That done, he warily walked through the ransacked home, checking every dark nook and cranny, revenge on his mind — but as he suspected, the intruder was long gone. A quick glance around the rooms proved the only thing of value, his grandpa's collection of rare Indian arrowheads, had been stolen.

As a young boy, Daniel loved to look at all the arrowhead colors — waxy shades of black, white, green and brown. He was especially fond of one large green one, razor sharp with a brown area in the center, which had all the appearance of an engraved hawk. Daniel was sure there was none like it in the world. Given his last name, he hoped to keep it forever in memory of his grandpa.

It was not to be.

But at least the belt buckle was left behind, and Daniel kept it propped upright on a coffee table in his New York City apartment where he could see it often.

Per his grandpa's wishes, Daniel had him cremated and several days later solemnly scattered his ashes in the nearby Illinois River, three miles east of Tahlequah. His grandpa was an only child, as was Daniel, and there were no other living family members. All that was there was a pair of red-tailed hawks circling overhead.

It was just as well, Daniel thought. He and his grandpa were both loners.

It was then that Daniel made the decision to be a police officer. If he could keep just one person from losing a family member prematurely, then it would be all worthwhile. After getting his undergraduate degree at NSU, he attended police academy in Tulsa and, after three years of beating the streets as a police officer, took the necessary courses and became a detective.

In the years that followed his career change, violent crime in the city of Tulsa plummeted to a nationwide low, creating quite a buzz in the national media. A visiting investigative reporter from CNN determined that the primary reason for the dramatic improvement was the work of Tulsa's newest and brightest detective, Daniel Fishinghawk. No one wanted to break the law there; the risk of being caught was far too high.

Shortly after word got out, Daniel was recruited to the Big Apple. He wasn't sure he wanted to leave his beloved Oklahoma hills, but when he heard of the proximity of the Catskills and the Shawangunk Mountains, both less than a three hour drive away, he had a change of heart. New wilderness areas to explore struck at his Native American roots.

Since in New York, though, Daniel had made an unnerving discovery. He had been here only three months and already, as hard as it was to believe, at twenty-eight years of age, he was getting burned out. All those years of seeing grisly murder after grisly murder had finally taken its toll, and he wasn't sure how much longer he could go on in his current employment.

Daniel sighed.

He fondly recalled the days when his grandpa took him to the woods around the Illinois River. During those adventures his grandpa taught him respect for Mother Earth and how important it was to be close to the land. City living, he told Daniel, took one away from the rhythms of nature, and he made Daniel promise that wherever his life led him, he would take time to commune with the great outdoors. In this way he would always stay linked to his Cherokee beginnings — and his grandpa.

Daniel loved his grandpa almost as much as he despised his parents, who he never knew. When Daniel was only two years old, his father and mother, Daniel senior and Jenny, who were both crackheads and unable to stay off the bottle, were high as kites one late night when they had a head-on collision with another car on a narrow country road just outside of Tahlequah.

Both were instantly killed. But miraculously enough, little Daniel, who was unrestrained in the back seat of their beat-up brown Chevy Impala, was found unharmed at the scene by the police. It was odd, they said, that the little child in the devastating wreck never cried a lick, but smiled when his grandpa arrived at the hospital to pick him up. Since that time, his grandpa called him not only by his given name, but also "A-da-do-li-gi," Cherokee for "blessing."

It was all for the better, Daniel reasoned as he sipped his water. What would he be like now if he had been raised by two druggies? He didn't want to think about it.

Daniel was disgusted by what he knew of his parents. For that reason, he never used the abbreviation, "Jr.," at the end of his name. His father deserved no credit for what Daniel would become in life.

No credit at all.

The sun now fell below the tree line and was invisible. All that could be seen was a hazy glow as nightfall approached. Daniel clipped his water bottle back onto his belt and turned to find his backpack, which he had dropped off around a hundred yards to the east. He hadn't wanted the sounds of moving fabric to notify his prey.

Daniel returned to his camp, a thirty minute walk away, and bedded down for the night. The sound of tree frogs filled the air, and his mind was peaceful — until he remembered in three more days he had to return to work. No doubt, by that time, in such a large metropolis as New York City, there would be more murders to solve — lots more.

He couldn't bear the thought.

Chapter 3

August 23, 2014, New York City

"Hawk, you ol' son of a bitch, how in the hell did you do it?" Daniel Fishinghawk had just sat down across the desk from his detective chief, Kip Kelly. The smell of cheap cigars lingered in the air around him. "I mean, c'mon, tell me. I'm all ears."

"Chief Kelly," Daniel insisted, "it wasn't that hard. The clues were all there."

"What in the hell are you talking about? I had two of our best men at the scene, Anderson and Dockendorf — seasoned veterans who had worked all these murders — and they couldn't come up with a damn thing."

"Well, chief, I —"

"Don't 'well, chief' me," Kelly said as he stood at his desk, veins bulging on his forehead. "Now I get it that you found the smudge of blood on the air conditioning on-off switch, but for Christ's sake, Hawk, from that point on you made one leap of faith after another. If you'd have made one goof on any of your assumptions, you'd have been up a creek without a paddle."

Kelly sat back down. "But the irony about this whole mixed up case is that you were right — you hit the nail right on the head! What the fuck? We did medical background checks on the victims, and, just like you said, they all had the same endocrinologist. And yes, the killer, Miranda Oberstein — isn't that a helluva name? — put the moves on them while they were sitting in the doctor's waiting area. And, I can't believe I'm saying this, all had trouble getting their dicks up — every fucking one!

"Now, about our murderer: She used to live in San Francisco, and before she left, there were a number of similar unexplained killings. After we arrested her, she confessed to all the crimes without the slightest bit of remorse. Seems her father was an alcoholic who beat the shit out of her at least once a week while she was growing up. And — get this — she then married an alcoholic who did the same thing. After divorcing him, he was her first victim.

"You can't help but feel bad for her, but the truth is she is one sick lady — she'll never go to jail, but she'll be in the nuthouse for the rest of her life."

Kelly shook his finger at him. "Okay, Hawk, time to fess up. Are you psychic? Have you been using the fucking psychic hot line?"

Daniel laughed. "No — let's just say I have a way of putting two and two together."

Chief Kelly stared at him, doubt in his eyes. "It's more than that. You see things that no one else can, and it turns out you're right — always! You haven't missed a case since you've been here — how long has it been?"

"Three months," Daniel answered.

"Commissioner Walsh has you on a par with buttered bread. If you weren't so damn good in the field you'd probably be taking my spot, and I've been in this position over twenty years!"

"Chief, you don't have anything to worry about. As a matter of fact, I've been thinking about —"

"Hawk, stuff it for a sec. I didn't have you come here on a Saturday morning just to tell you how wonderful you are. There's something that's come up — an international deal — and I've got strict orders to give it to you. Your country needs you."

"Me?"

"Yep — you. We have to send our best man to handle this one, and as much as I hate to say it, I'm afraid you're the guy."

"What's going on?"

"How's your geography, Hawk?"

"Not bad, why?"

"Have you ever heard of Easter Island?"

"Of course. Isn't that the place way out in the middle of nowhere with all the statues?"

"Yes, and because of that, lots of tourists," the chief said. "That's what makes this deal so sensitive. I'll tell you straight. There've been a number of murders down there, and each and every one has been tourists. Easter Island is part of Chile, and recently the State Department got a call from Santiago asking for help. The Chileans have been investigating these killings for the past six months without any success. Yesterday the commissioner got a call from the secretary of state himself, asking us to take it on."

"Why us?" Daniel asked.

The chief looked at him like he was crazy. "Because we've got the best fucking detectives in the world! Didn't you know that?"

Daniel said, "I —"

Kelly interrupted, "Listen up, Hawk, this investigation has to be hush-hush. If any word gets out about these murders, their tourist industry will be shot to hell and, with it, the local economy. Chile's cash cow will be dead."

"How many have been killed?"

Chief Kelly's watery blue eyes narrowed. "Brace yourself."

"Yes?"

"Twenty-four and counting."

"Twenty-four? How have they kept this under wraps? I haven't seen anything about this in the news."

"Let's just say that freedom of the press, on this issue at least, isn't happening. Any reporters who have gotten wind of this have been told in no uncertain terms to keep their traps shut." Kelly took a deep breath and added, "Another thing: When you enter their country you'll be under their command. Whatever they say goes — within reason."

Daniel shifted in his chair uncomfortably. "Chief, there's one big problem. How long would it take for a boat to get down there?"

"Fucking forever," Chief Kelly said. "Hawk, what's the problem with you getting on one of those things called an airplane? You can be there in just two or three days."

"I drove a rental truck here from Oklahoma, not just to move my belongings, but also because I don't fly. I don't like heights," Daniel confessed.

"Why?"

"I don't want to talk about it."

"Listen, Hawk, I want you to get to a shrink pronto and get yourself right. I've already promised the commissioner you'll be on a plane next week. And, if worse come to worse, that's what drugs are for. Take two milligrams of Xanax at the start of your flight, and you'll wake up when you're landing."

Daniel felt dizzy just thinking about it. "Well —"

"Oh, by the way," Kelly interrupted, "what did you want to talk with me about?"

"It was nothing," Daniel answered as he stood to leave, cracking open the office door. "I'll get back with you, Chief Kelly, in the next few days."

As he departed, he heard stifled laughter from a desk to his side. He didn't turn around, but he got the joke.

I'm a Native American and I'm calling my boss — chief.

Daniel grimaced and walked on.

Chapter 4

August 29, 2014, en route to Santiago, Chile

Daniel Fishinghawk woke in a cold sweat; his green plaid Patagonia hiking shirt was soaked with perspiration.

He glanced nervously at his watch. He had at least one more hour before he landed in Santiago; he was on his way to Easter Island.

After his meeting with the chief six days ago, Daniel had finally come around to dealing with his problem — the plane ride. If he could just buck it up and hang in there, it wouldn't be a bad thing to get away from the hubbub of the city for a while. Easter Island had a population of around 5,000, a microcosm by comparison.

As he thought about the upcoming case, Daniel couldn't believe that twenty-four murders had been swept under the rug. But it didn't matter now. With any kind of luck, he'd sniff out these killings and be back in a week or so, which would give him plenty of time to figure out how to tell the chief he was quitting.

The State Department had arranged everything. They'd sent a guy from D.C. carrying a first class plane ticket, his passport and a properly filled prescription for Xanax. He wasn't accustomed to taking medicines, but this was more than a convenience, it was a necessity.

He had seen the shrink — he had to for the prescription. But he wasn't about to open his mind to anyone; just like he would never open his heart. It was just too risky. Look what happened when he loved his grandpa. He didn't dare take the chance.

At the moment, though, he was in the plane watching the sun rise through the window beside his seat.

Why couldn't the Xanax have lasted till I landed?

He would have felt a heck of a lot better if it had. Now he held a puke bag to his face and felt like the plane was spinning around like a top out of control.

He thought about taking another pill but decided against it. He couldn't see how he could navigate the airport without being fully alert, especially since he spoke not a word of Spanish.

He would be in Santiago for a few days, just enough time to get his bearings, and then he would take the nearly five hour flight to Easter Island, located in the southeast corner of Polynesia.

How did Chile get possession of a place so far away? Daniel wondered. He hoped to eventually learn and understand. But for now, it was all he could do not to scream at the top of his lungs and run up and down the aisle like a wild man. He hated that he was this way, though given the circumstances, it was understandable. He remembered all too clearly the day it began — after all, he did have an eidetic memory — a happy Saturday gone bad.

Daniel was in the sixth grade when he made the decision to climb the tallest tree he could find along the Illinois River, a giant cottonwood well over a hundred feet tall. He snaked his way to the top where the thinness of the branch barely supported his weight. He was on cloud nine as the tree limb gently rocked back and forth in the light breeze.

Daniel was about to climb down when an unexpected thunderstorm hit. Lightning struck all around, and high winds whipped the tree from side to side. It was then that the hail came down, golf ball sized spheres of ice that rocketed from the sky, pummeling the little boy that he was. After many minutes of sheer terror, he was hit square between the eyes with a large hailstone.

In spite of being knocked completely unconscious, he was still clinging to the tree when his grandpa found him. Even now, he could hear his grandpa's voice:

"A-da-do-li-gi — A-da-do-li-gi — can you hear me?"

"Grandpa," he cried as he shook his head and tried to remember where he was, "is it you?"

"Yes, little one. Everything is going to be okay. I need you to shimmy down to the limb I am standing on. The branch you are on is too small for me to climb."

"I'm scared . . ."

"I know you are — I am too. But together we are strong. Come down to me, and I'll carry you the rest of the way."

Daniel sobbed, "Grandpa, I can't move — I can't . . ." He looked down and saw his grandpa smile at him.

"Daniel, just come down an inch at a time, and before you know it, you will be in my arms. I love you, Daniel. Let the strength of my love draw you down safely."

"I love you too, Grandpa."

Daniel slowly worked his way down the tree. He felt a surge of strength when his foot at last touched his grandpa's outstretched hand, and when his grandpa finally held him tight, he knew he could make it back down. When he did, he swore he'd never lose touch of Earth again, and he would never forget his grandpa's words. "Daniel, always remember that when you find yourself in trouble, just like today, I'll be there for you — always."

Now as a man, whether he was in a plane, or looking out a window of a skyscraper, walking over a bridge or even on an escalator, he once again became a helpless little boy.

Like now . . .

Will I ever get over this? he asked himself.

Something inside said he'd better, sooner than later.

Daniel caught his breath as the plane began to descend through the smog-filled skies of Santiago.

It couldn't touch *terra firma* soon enough.

Chapter 5

August 29, 2014, Santiago, Chile

Daniel's three-day stay in Santiago went without a hitch. All of his expenses were covered by the Chilean police, including a cozy hotel in one of the better districts.

On the drive from the Santiago airport to his hotel, though, he had seen the slums from the highway. Since Chile was known to have one of the lowest poverty rates in South America, he would have hated to have seen countries that were worse. Beggars came like clockwork to his sidewalk café every evening, and he couldn't help but give each one an American dollar or two. After he saw how some of them lived, it was the least he could do.

To Daniel's chagrin, as he had noticed from the plane, the air quality in Santiago made that of New York City seem as pure as the driven snow. He had done some checking before and had found that the air pollution in Santiago was the third worst in the world, ranking only behind Beijing and New Delhi. He felt like holding his breath the entire time he was here.

When he left Santiago, he was glad of it, even though he was scared to death of getting on another plane. Like before, he took one of his trusty Xanax tablets, and when he roused from sleep, the plane was circling over Easter Island.

Curiosity replaced his fear as he saw the city of Hanga Roa, nestled in the far southwest corner of the island next to a large volcanic crater. He looked at his map and discovered the crater was called Rano Kau. Water had collected at its bottom, which was covered with greenery. Just looking at the cliffs of the crater — and how they hung over the ocean — made his heart rate skyrocket.

After landing, he picked up his luggage and was greeted by a sandy-haired man holding a sign with *Fishinghawk* on it. The man was dressed in brown shorts and a short-sleeved tan patterned shirt, and he looked to be in his late sixties.

Daniel guessed it was Jack Daldy, a New Zealander who, along with his Rapanui wife Alame Koreta, was a co-owner of the centrally located Te Manutara Hotel. Daniel planned to stay there for the duration of his visit.

" 'Iorana!" Jack said in his lively kiwi accent as he shook Daniel's hand and grabbed his suitcase.

"What?"

" 'Iorana," Jack said again. "In Rapanui, the local language, it means hello."

" 'Iorana," Daniel repeated as they walked toward the hotel van. "Are you Jack?"

"That's me," Jack confirmed with a grin. "Business or pleasure?"

"Business."

After they had loaded into the van, Jack said, "I thought so. When the Chilean police made your reservation, they told me to hold your room indefinitely." Jack paused for a second and asked, "Are you here to investigate the murders we have been having?"

Caught by surprise, Daniel blurted out, "I really can't say anything about why I'm here. I hope you understand."

Jack replied, "No problem," as he started the van and pulled out of the airport parking lot.

"Anyway," Daniel added, "you should know that I'll likely only be here for a week or so."

Jack stopped the van at an intersection, turned his head and looked him directly in the eyes. "Mark my words, young man, you'll be here a helluva lot longer, I guarantee you."

"How do you know that?"

"I just do. And one more thing — the murders all happen during the night. So watch your step after dark; nowhere is safe on this island for outsiders. Not even our hotel."

Not encouraging, thought Daniel. "I'll remember that."

"Oh, one more thing — did you bring a weapon with you?"

It was just too much trouble for Daniel to bring his Smith & Wesson on a plane and into a foreign country. He chuckled softly. "What kind of weapon?"

It's nobody's business what I do or do not bring into the country, he thought.

As far as Jack was concerned, Daniel might as well have said nothing. "When you meet with the police, make sure they give you one, okay?"

"The island certainly is beautiful this time of year," Daniel remarked, trying to change the subject.

"It is always beautiful," Jack added.

They kept their silence until they arrived at the hotel. As they unloaded from the van and entered the check-in area, Jack again said, " 'Iorana."

"What?"

Jack repeated, " 'Iorana. It also means goodbye."

The following morning Daniel sat in the waiting area at the police department and bided his time. He was informed by the over-perfumed secretary that the Chilean police detective, Alejandro Gomez, with whom he had an appointment at ten, was out investigating yet another of these puzzling murders. She said, in broken English, that it shouldn't be more than a few minutes, and that was two hours ago. Daniel had already learned, though, that the entire place ran on "island time," and no one was punctual for appointments anyway.

It was after two p.m. when Daniel heard a door slam, and an overweight, sweaty Chilean entered from the outside, cigarette hanging loosely from his mouth. He looked like he hadn't slept in months, with large dark-blue bags under his eyes. He sported a well-trimmed black moustache, wore dark brown slacks with a blue-striped shirt, partially pulled out from the front of his pants. A loosened tie hung from his neck.

He stopped in front of Daniel, sucked on his cigarette, pulled it out and exhaled smoke from his mouth and nose. "You Detective Fishinghawk?" he asked.

Daniel stood and shook his hand, "Yes. Please call me Hawk. You must be Detective Gomez?"

"The one and the same. Hawk, follow me into my office," he said as he walked back through a hallway to an unmarked door. They entered and Gomez sat down at his desk, motioning Daniel to sit in the chair across from it.

"My first name is Alejandro, but everyone here just calls me Gomez. I normally live and work in Chile, but due to the serious nature of what's going on here, they've flown me in until this case is solved. I'd like to think I was chosen because I was the most qualified for the job. You see, not only do I speak fluent Spanish, Rapanui and English, I have also studied the culture and have over twenty years in the detective branch."

He stubbed out the last remains of his cigarette in a blue ash tray shaped like a dolphin, folded his arms together, leaned back in his chair and asked, "Do you know how many murders there have been?"

"I hear there have been twenty-four."

"Brace yourself," Gomez said. "Victims twenty-five and twenty-six were discovered this morning on the beach near Akahanga, about a half hour drive from here. Forensics thinks the murders occurred around ten last night, though they weren't discovered until this morning. I just came from there."

Gomez lit another cigarette, using a silver lighter with the initials *AG* on it, pulled out the contents of a manila envelope sitting on his desk and pored over the pages. "Hawk, looks like you come pretty highly recommended. Trust me, we need all the help we can get."

Gomez threw the papers back on his desk. "Okay, let's start from square one. Has your boss told you anything?"

"Not much."

"Good. I told the State Department I preferred to tell you most of the details myself. Over the past six months there have been twenty-four . . . I mean, twenty-six murders. These killings all have several things in common. First, they have all been tourists. No one who lives on the island has been targeted. Second, all have been killed during the nighttime. There have been no sightings of the murderer —"

Daniel interrupted, "Only one killer?"

"Only one."

"How do you know that?"

Gomez answered, "Only one set of fingerprints, the same set, have been found at each of the scenes."

"Are there any matches?"

"None. We have fingerprinted every person who lives on this goddamned island and anyone else who has entered, whether by plane, boat — whatever. As far as we can tell, our killer does not exist. You'd think with this many murders there would be a match of some kind. It's as if our killer comes from nowhere and disappears to nowhere."

Daniel found himself staring at Detective Gomez. He knitted his brow in frustration. None of this made any sense.

"Now, Hawk, brace yourself for the most bizarre information of all. Our victims were tied up before they were killed, and all were cannibalized . . ."

"What did you say?"

"You heard me — cannibalized. And here's the worst part: a number were cannibalized before they were murdered —"

"What?" Daniel interrupted as he leaned forward in his chair. He was rarely shocked, but this was one of the most horrible things he had ever heard.

"All were gagged, so no one could hear them scream. And it seems our killer had two different techniques: Sometimes he used a knife to peel the skin and muscle off, but, more often than not, he ate the flesh right off them. We've checked the bite marks and they all match."

Daniel ventured, "This guy has to be crazy. Have you done a check for mental cases that have a history of cannibalism?"

"Come on, Hawk, we're not amateurs here. Of course we have. Every known person in the world with such an illness is either dead or put away for life.

"Okay, Hawk," Gomez said as he stood and tucked in his shirt, "enough talk. Let's head to the scene. My top man here is Detective Tepano, who is still there looking things over. Let's go check it out. By the way, are you armed?"

"No."

Gomez pulled open a drawer on his desk and slid a holstered Beretta .45 pistol and a box of bullets over to Daniel. "Just so you know — it's loaded, and I hope you don't need it. Everyone who lives on the island is scared shitless, and I don't believe there's anyone who is not packing heat. You'll more likely need it to protect yourself from these trigger-happy lunatics than the killer himself. At least, I hope so."

Daniel picked it up, checked it to be sure the safety was on and clipped it to his belt. He nodded and followed Gomez from his office.

His mind buzzed with all the information Gomez had given him, and, for the first time in his career as a detective, he was baffled.

He didn't like the feeling — not one bit.

Chapter 6

September 2, 2014, Easter Island

The two detectives rode in silence to the scene of the crime. Daniel had yet to take a tour of the island and was stunned at the beauty of the undeveloped countryside. When the road turned alongside the black volcanic beach, the view took his breath away.

It was without doubt the most spectacular vista he had ever seen. The deep blue ocean pounded the shoreline, and thundering waves produced showers of sparkling droplets. In the distance, though, he could see a group of cars parked around an area next to the beach demarcated with bright yellow police tape.

Gomez pulled his police car into the area, and, as he and Daniel got out of the vehicle, they were approached by a trim, Polynesian, early twenties man wearing sunglasses. He had on grey slacks and a long-sleeved blue dress shirt.

Gomez asked the man, "Any news?"

"Nothing you don't already know." He glanced at Daniel and added, "You must be Detective Fishinghawk?"

"Yes," Daniel said as they shook hands.

Gomez put in, "He goes by Hawk for short. Hawk, this is Detective José Tepano."

"José, nice to meet you. Tepano . . . isn't that a Rapanui name?"

"It is, and I'm proud of it. I was born and raised here but got my police training in Santiago so I could come back and serve my people. Currently I am the only native Rapanui policeman on the force."

Gomez groaned, "You might like it here, but when these murders are solved, if they ever are, I'm not spending a second longer on this shithole island than I have to. I'm going back to my home in Valparaíso where I can have some peace and quiet. I miss my wife and children."

José paid no attention to the comment and asked Daniel, "Are you ready to have a look?"

"You bet."

With that, they pushed past the gawking bystanders and stepped over the tape. Around twenty yards toward the beach Daniel got his first sight of the victims, an elderly couple, one man and one woman. As they drew closer he discovered the victims were sitting naked in white beach chairs facing the ocean. Their arms were tied behind their backs and they were securely lashed to the chairs with rope. Large pieces of flesh were gone and teeth marks were scattered everywhere. Cloth gags were in their mouths. Their eyes were frozen open in horror.

Daniel thought he had seen everything.

Not so.

José said, "This couple from Australia thought they'd have a little quiet time on the beach. They both were having a little champagne when they were ambushed. They never had a chance."

Gomez asked, "Do the fingerprints match the other crime scenes?"

"Yes."

"How about the teeth marks? Any evidence of sexual assault?"

"Yes they match and, like all the other cases, no sexual contact."

Gomez asked, "How much longer do you need to complete the forensics collection?"

José cocked his head and estimated, "Another hour or two and we'll have it all wrapped up."

"Good. I'll go to the office and get the paperwork done. I'm going to need another goddamned filing cabinet if this shit keeps happening. Call me when you're ready, and I'll get the bodies picked up and put on ice."

Gomez turned to Daniel. "Have a look around for as long as you'd like, then Tepano will take you into town to rent a car and buy a cell phone. For this investigation, you're going to need to be mobile — these murders are happening all over the island. And, believe it or not, I want you to take tomorrow off and do a little sightseeing. Get a feel for the place before we start working your ass off."

Daniel paused in thought and finally advised, "Gomez, I don't think you can keep this under wraps any longer. I'm not a betting man, but I'd bet everything I have that a number of these murders could have been prevented. This couple would *never* have been out here alone if they had known what was happening. They were easy pickings."

Gomez scowled at Daniel. "If the public knew, they wouldn't be here. And this island would dry up and blow away without tourist money. I have orders from my Chilean superiors to keep this top secret — at any cost."

He lowered his voice to a whisper. "Hawk, you're not here to make judgments on how we do things around here. You're here to solve this mess, so if you know what's good for you, you will keep your mouth shut. Do you hear me?"

Daniel met his steely-eyed stare and nodded.

Gomez turned and walked away, heading for his vehicle. When he departed, the tires squealed in anger.

José informed Daniel, "There're a number of us here who agree with you, but Gomez calls all the shots, and there's not a thing we can do about it."

"I understand, but I'll still check with HQ about this."

"Do what you need to. It'll be a while before I can take you into town, so go ahead and snoop around."

"I will," Daniel said as he looked at the sky, "By the way, what are those large hawk-like birds I see flying around?"

"They're caracaras. They were brought to the island years ago to control the rat population. Whoever had that bright idea didn't realize the rats were nocturnal. Since the caracaras don't fly at night, the rats could care less whether they're here or not."

"Whatever," commented Daniel, "they're beautiful birds, that's for sure. They remind me of the red-tailed hawk back in Oklahoma, my home state. Anyway, I'll check around. Yell when you're ready to go."

Daniel left to examine the dead couple on the beach. He had sensed something earlier but thought better about saying anything. As he moved closer he was sure of it. Even though it was many hours after the actual murders, his fine-tuned sense of smell — the same sense that had helped him track the eastern cougar — picked up a faint, but distinct odor, which he was sure no one else had noticed. He had never smelled anything quite like it — an odd mixture of body odor, campfire smoke and earthiness.

But there was more . . .

Something else besides that macabre blend of odors was completely unique. As he closed his eyes and thought about it, his inner voice told him loud and clear what it was . . .

Evil — pure unadulterated evil.

Later that evening, Daniel drove his newly acquired Suzuki four-wheel drive rental car back to the Te Manutara Hotel. He pulled into the parking area, turned off the ignition, and sat — thinking.

He was, to put it mildly, bewildered. Never had he come across a case that had no immediate answers, no pathway to a solution. For the first time in his life, he began to doubt his skills.

What if I can't figure this out?

The more he thought about it, the more he realized this case would require thinking outside the box — *way* outside.

No quick fix to solving this series of murders. Daniel knew he would have to begin a slow, methodical investigation, and he hoped, like when he sat in meditation, answers would eventually come to him. But this would be no short meditation; rather, one that could last for months.

Daniel also figured he would have to learn the Rapanui language. Yes, he decided, to get at the nuances of the culture, he would have to be able to communicate with the local people. He had the distinct feeling that someone, somewhere, would eventually give him a clue that would set him on the right track.

Perhaps he could find a book that would help him learn the language. His ability to assimilate and retain information was his ace in the hole.

As Daniel stepped out of the SUV and began the walk to his room, he noticed an attractive middle-aged woman, wearing a short dress with a bright red floral pattern, sitting to his right in a lawn chair. He guessed she was Rapanui.

" 'Iorana," she said with a bright smile. "Welcome to the Te Manutara Hotel. You must be the new guest my husband told me about?"

"Well — yes," Daniel answered, surprised. "My name is Daniel Fishinghawk, but everyone calls me Hawk."

She motioned for him to sit in the empty chair next to her. "My name is Alame Koreta." Her smile deepened. "If you don't mind, I'll just call you Daniel." Her mid-length hair was brown and wavy, and her dark eyes smiled at least as much as her face did. She had a youthful and assured presence about her.

"I don't mind at all," he said as he sat down beside her.

"How do you like Rapa Nui so far?" she asked.

"Rapa Nui?"

"Yes," Alame affirmed, "Rapa Nui. It is the name most islanders prefer."

"I see. Well, so far, so good, but I've been so involved with work I haven't had the chance to see much of it."

"To really get a feel for our island," she explained, "you must see what it offers.

The moai — our lovely carved stone figures — and the beaches, the hills — there is much for you to explore. As you come to know us and our history, you will be better equipped to discover the answers to your questions."

Daniel studied her closely. It seemed she and Jack had pretty much figured him out.

"I agree with what you're saying," he said. "In fact, I need a book on the language and a mentor to teach me about your island. Can you give me a recommendation?"

"Let me do some checking, but there is an older woman who lives on Tu'u Ko Ihu who might be willing to help you. She is in her nineties, easily the oldest living Rapanui, and knows much of the history of our island. Besides that, she has taken upon herself to learn English and Spanish. You would enjoy making her acquaintance. As for a book, I'm not a bookish person, but she might know of one."

"Good," said Daniel. "One more thing, please. Tomorrow I've been given a day off to do a little sightseeing. What do you suggest?"

She clapped her hands in delight. "Oh, the hike to Mount Terevaka, the highest point on the island. From there you will have a panoramic view and can see the island from end to end. Drive your car to the trailhead, and you should have no trouble finding the way.

"Afterward you should hike down to 'Anakena Beach, the place where our legendary founder, Hotu Matu'a, first landed on our island. At 'Anakena you may see some of our beautiful moai."

"Sounds great."

"It is," she said. "Do you need a guide for the trip?"

"No. I've got a map, and I really need some time by myself. But, come to think of it, I will need someone to pick me up at 'Anakena to drive me back to my car. Could you arrange that, say, for around seven p.m.?"

"I'd be glad to."

"Thank you, Mrs. Koreta."

"O te aha no — you're welcome. And please call me Alame."

As Daniel rose to leave, he felt Alame's hand on his arm, and her ever-present smile had disappeared.

"One more thing," she added. "Be careful — watch your step. You are being watched."

"By whom?" Daniel asked.

"That, I do not know."

Daniel nodded and walked across the lawn to his room. After he closed the door behind him, he checked it twice to make sure it was locked. Then he checked it again — just to be sure.

Chapter 7

September 3, 2014

The morning brought a chill in the air as Daniel shouldered his navy-colored backpack and walked from his room. A green, manicured lawn spread out before him, divided by a stone walkway. As he strolled down the path to the building, which doubled as reception and breakfast areas, he enjoyed the sweet aroma of flowering shrubs.

He entered the indoor dining area, which was surrounded by large glass windows. The outside was beautiful, and the inside equally attractive. The dining room was well lit and offered tables covered with bright blue tablecloths, while the decorated walls were a brilliant green. Two wooden statues, which represented moai, stoically guarded each side of the entranceway. He sat down at an open table and looked forward to another delicious breakfast.

Daniel was served by a pleasant young Rapanui woman, and he couldn't help but smile as he noticed a pink flower in her hair. A short time later, as he sipped on a cup of Earl Grey tea, he was presented with a large cheese omelet, toast and fresh pineapple, and a matching pink flower adorned the plate. Daniel had just started to eat when Alame arrived to greet him.

"Good morning, Daniel, I trust you slept well?"

"Like a log," Daniel lied. After the warning she had given him, he had slept with one eye open.

She chuckled and said, "Somehow, I believe that's not true. Anyway, I wanted to let you know that the pickup has been arranged, and Jack will be there to meet you today around seven p.m. at 'Anakena."

"Great."

"Also, last night I placed a call to the elderly woman I had mentioned, and she said she would be happy not only to tell you the history of our island, but also to teach you our native language. You know how older people can be — they love to talk about the past."

Daniel couldn't help but think of his grandpa, and how much he wished he was still around to tell him stories about his Cherokee ancestors.

Alame paused for a moment, as if she could read his most precious and personal thoughts. "Anyway, I believe you'll find her most interesting. Her name is Tiare Rapu; Tiare means flower in the Rapanui language. I think you'll agree that her name suits her quite well. She is as colorful of a person as you'll ever meet.

"I've written her name and telephone number on this piece of paper. Give her a call at your convenience; she is anxious to meet you. By the way, I know a little about Native American culture. Is Fishinghawk an Indian name?"

"It is."

"That's what I thought. When I shared my suspicion with Tiare, she said she would like to know more about your heritage."

As a large group entered the breakfast room, Alame said, "I must go. But before I do, I have one more suggestion. Spend some time sitting before the moai when you have the chance. You may discover that they will speak to you — as they speak to me." She smiled. "And do have a good time in your explorations."

"I will," Daniel said. He took his time and leisurely enjoyed the rest of his breakfast. As he was eating, he looked over at one of the expressionless wooden moai and thought:

Speak to the *moai*?

Daniel hiked up the gentle slope toward the highest point in Rapa Nui, Mount Terevaka. He had read that the word Terevaka meant "take out canoes," and it was so named because the early settlers harvested wood from the area to make canoes.

Most of the surroundings had been deforested, except for groves of eucalyptus trees on the hillside that had been planted in hopes of preventing soil erosion and reestablishing the forest.

Daniel shook his head as he thought about it. Just like when the caracaras were introduced to control the rat population, efforts to manipulate nature often backfired. In the case of the eucalyptus trees, it was later discovered they had large tap roots that invade water aquifers, gradually depleting the ground water supply. Equally damaging, the trees used up large quantities of soil nutrients and produced chemicals that suppressed growth of surrounding vegetation, which tended to make the soil around the trees infertile.

Daniel couldn't help but remember the old saying, "The road to hell is paved with good intentions."

Along the way up the mountain he discovered numerous caves. From his readings he knew they were actually lava tubes, conduits for lava flow during the eruption of volcanoes, formed in the island's distant past. One particular cave had a large, flowering hibiscus bush at its exit. While he was a loner, for one brief moment he wished for a woman in his life, one who would enjoy having him place one of these beautiful red flowers in her hair.

Some hours and much sweat later, Daniel made it to the summit and found a lone eucalyptus tree. He paused and looked around to see 360 degrees of ocean. To the southwest was the city of Hanga Roa, sitting next to the ocean. A pair of cinnamon-colored caracaras circled over him.

He was glad to have this moment of peace.

Daniel lay down on the soft soil, put his backpack under his neck and fell into a soft slumber. Before long, he began to dream . . .

He found himself stumbling through a dark cave, hopelessly lost in a quagmire of tunnels, angling up and down with seemingly no end. In his hand he held a flickering wooden torch, barely lighting his pathway. He was searching for something but didn't know who or what it was.

He heard the shuffling of feet from somewhere up ahead — something that felt dark and evil. He had to follow it. Somehow he knew that to stop would be death — and to find that sound might also mean death.

The tunnel began to grow smaller and smaller, and soon he was crawling on his stomach through a tight space. All at once he became trapped. He couldn't move forward and couldn't back up. Then his light went out, and he felt something sticky, warm and wet ooze onto his outstretched hands. He couldn't see anything, but he was sure it was blood — his blood.

He could smell it.

Daniel woke, stifling a scream.

As he jerked upright to a sitting position, he thought: What's my mind trying to tell me?

After a short lunch of trail mix and a banana, Daniel followed his map and headed down the gently sloping hills toward the beach at 'Anakena. After several hours of hiking, from a distance he could make out a number of tall palm trees, along with two groupings of moai, a solo one close to the water and a group of five, along with two statue fragments, farther away from the sandy beach.

Daniel knew from his readings that the single moai was a much older one and was sitting on an ahu — a raised stone platform. This particular one was called the Ahu Ature Huki. In 1956 this moai was the first to be re-erected, and he recalled it took twelve men a total of eighteen days to raise the eleven-foot-tall statue, using a ramp of piled rocks and tree trunks for levers.

Daniel tried to focus on the pristine landscape and smother thoughts of his dream. He was looking forward to the feel of the warm ocean water, the sand between his toes.

As he topped a small hill, he was taken aback as he found José Tepano waiting for him, standing by his police car on the road just before the entry to the beach.

Daniel called out, "José! It's good to see you, but I was expecting Jack."

"I know you were. I phoned him and, when I found out your plans, I came here instead. Hawk, do you have your cell phone with you?"

Daniel came up to him and said, "Yes, why do you ask?"

"Sometimes the cell service on this island is pretty spotty. I have been trying to reach you all day."

Daniel sensed something was afoot. "Why?" he demanded.

"It's Gomez — he's dead."

Chapter 8

September 3, 2014

"What happened?" Daniel asked as Tepano's police car sped down the road toward Hanga Roa.

"Hawk, like you, Gomez wasn't expected to be here all that long, so the Chilean police put him up in the Moana Nui Hotel, just across the street from where you are staying."

Daniel still couldn't believe it. Gomez dead?

"He was last seen alive at the hotel restaurant last night around nine," José continued. "When he didn't show up for work this morning at his usual eight o'clock, his secretary thought Gomez had decided, like he does sometimes, to have a morning phone call with his wife and children. Around nine or so, she started to worry and phoned the hotel. When she learned his car was still there, she called me and I went to investigate. After I arrived, I knocked on his door — no answer. I checked the door and found it was unlocked. Inside — well, you'll soon see for yourself."

"But," said Daniel, "doesn't this make the first non-tourist to be killed?"

"Right. I have no idea why the murderer is killing all those tourists, but the motive for Gomez's killing seems clear. He knew Gomez was on his trail and decided to take him out. And who can tell, maybe Gomez was onto something."

"Well, if he was, we'll never know now," said Daniel.

"One more thing," José added, "I knew the Chilean police would dispatch some-one else from Santiago to head the investigation once they got wind of Gomez's death, so, before he got here and ordered me otherwise, I held a press conference at noon and told the public about the killings."

"You did what?"

"You heard right," José said, "I spilled the whole ugly mess out to the press. That is, except for the details about the crime scenes. We need to keep that close to our vests — for obvious reasons. Besides, we don't need any more hysteria than we al-ready have."

"Agreed."

"This story has been broadcast all over the world and nearly every inbound plane flight and boat excursion to the island has been cancelled — that is, except for the charters from Santiago packed with reporters, who have already started to arrive. The tourists still here will be leaving as soon as they can find a plane. Hawk, you and I both know this was the right thing to do, but the backlash — well — I'll be lucky if I'm not fired."

Daniel nodded in concurrence.

The two rode in silence for the rest of the way until they turned onto the street in front of the Moana Nui Hotel. Seeing no place to park, José drove on a bit farther and pulled into a space.

Daniel asked, "Where did all these cars come from?"

"Looks like the press is now here," José said.

When they walked up to the hotel, they discovered a large crowd, not visible from the street. Someone recognized them and exclaimed, "Look, there they are!"

Daniel tried to ignore the questions as they pressed their way through the crush of reporters. Several microphones were shoved in his face.

"Is it true you're here from New York City to investigate these murders?"

"What's this we hear about the victims being cannibalized?"

"Have all those killed been tourists?"

Daniel and José were finally able to break through the melee and step over the police tape to the front of the Moana Nui Hotel, an inviting, one story, red-roofed hotel surrounded by lush foliage.

"So much for keeping a lid on things," José whispered to Daniel as they walked around the corner to Gomez's room, not far from the main entrance. When they cracked open the door, they discovered a handful of detectives were still inside, dust-ing for fingerprints and gathering evidence.

Before they entered, José said, "Look, Hawk, I'm going out front to deal with the press. See what you can come up with. I'll check back with you when I'm through, and then we'll go pick up your SUV." With that, José turned away.

As Daniel started to walk inside, a policeman at the door thrust a handful of objects in his direction and spoke in English, "Wear these paper shoe covers and gloves — we can't have you messing up the evidence. And here's a flashlight for when you want to take a closer look."

After pocketing the small flashlight, Daniel donned the shoe covers and gloves, then took a few steps inside.

Immediately he noticed the body of Gomez, tied to a heavy wooden hotel chair in the middle of the room. Something about everyone working around a naked body — especially the man who had once been their boss — just didn't seem right.

Daniel tried to put his emotions to the side. What about Gomez's wife and kids? How were they taking the news? While he wasn't close to Gomez, the last time he saw him, he was walking and talking.

Not now.

Daniel refocused his thoughts . . . time to piece together what happened. He scanned the room, putting all the images into his mind, remembering every detail. The room was completely trashed; Gomez did not go down without a fight.

Daniel took a few long breaths through his nose. Just as he suspected, the distinctive odor was once again present.

About five feet past the front door sat a large pool of congealed blood . . .

The killer must have attacked Gomez just after he entered, Daniel reasoned.

Daniel glanced over at Gomez. His throat had two separate cuts, one on each side . . .

Must have slashed one side of Gomez's neck when he came in.

To the far left of the room was Gomez's bloodied gun . . .

Gomez went for his gun, but the killer wrested it from him and threw it aside.

Daniel walked to his right to examine the bathroom, its door demolished. Another large pool of blood . . .

Gomez was bleeding like a stuck pig, but he somehow managed to wrestle himself away and barricade himself in the bathroom. He only had a few moments before the door was broken down and he was cut on the other side of his neck.

Daniel then noticed streaks of blood on the tile floor leading from the bathroom to the chair where Gomez was tied . . .

Gomez was near dead by the time he was dragged to the chair, stripped and tied up. Then he was cannibalized. He couldn't have been alive at that point.

Thank God.

With the fight Gomez put up, it would have created racket galore. He asked the nearest detective, "I'm Daniel Fishinghawk — investigator from the United States. Do you know why no one heard anything?"

He answered, "Our killer is no dummy. There was a rock and roll party going on next door, and it would have taken a nuclear blast to have heard anything. He had kept his eye on the situation and waited for his chance."

Daniel nodded and took a closer look at Gomez. Just like the murders yesterday, Gomez had large patches of flesh missing. Bite marks were all over his body. No gag this time — the killer knew it wasn't necessary.

Now Daniel had a thought . . .

Gomez was an experienced investigator, and if he had a second to spare, he would have found a way to leave a clue about the killer. But when would he have had the time?

The bathroom?

Daniel made his way into the blood-splashed bathroom, careful not to step in any blood. He took his time and meticulously screened the room.

Where would Gomez hide a clue while he was dying?

Where would he put it so his assailant wouldn't find it?

Daniel inspected the shower and tub with its plastic, draw-back curtain. He looked at the bathroom sink and checked every square inch of the room.

Nothing.

He turned to walk out the door and had a final, desperate thought: the shower drain?

Daniel pulled back the shower curtains and removed the rubber plug from the drain. He pulled the flashlight from his pocket and examined the inside of the hole carefully.

Something there . . .

He then reached inside with his gloved little finger and felt a tiny rolled up piece of paper, bent so that it wedged against the side of the drain.

As he carefully pulled it out, he discovered a torn-in-half business card, wrapped around a broken toothpick with blood still staining one point.

Gomez had used this as a blood pen.

This toothpick was one he likely had in his mouth when he came in from the restaurant. Daniel held his breath as he set the bent toothpick on the side of the tub and slowly unwrapped the crumpled card.

On it was scrawled in blood —

HITIRAU

Chapter 9

September 4, 2014

Despite of the gloom of the previous day, it was a beautiful Thursday morning. Daniel had finished his breakfast and walked briskly, headed to the home of Tiare Rapu, the elderly woman who was to instruct him.

Daniel smiled as he discovered all sorts of cur dogs, and an occasional horse, roaming the streets. As he thought about it, he realized he hadn't seen billboards — *anywhere* — since he had arrived. Neither had he seen a stoplight. The main thoroughfares were clean and paved, and a number of colorful shops and restaurants lined them.

As he moved along, his mind went back to yesterday evening in Gomez's hotel room, where he had shown José the evidence he had found in the drain.

"What do you think?" Daniel asked.

José seemed puzzled. "Hawk, Hitirau is an akuaku."

"What's an akuaku?"

"Akuaku are the spirits of the dead, and Hitirau happens to be one from our ancient past. When I was a boy my grandparents used to scare the life out of me with stories about akuaku."

"Sort of like what we in the United States call a ghost story?"

"Exactly. The traditional wisdom of Rapa Nui is full of such tales. But such stories are just that — stories. The question is: What made Gomez think he had seen a spirit? Was he getting so giddy from his blood loss that he began to hallucinate? He knew much about Rapanui folklore; that's one of the reasons he was picked to come here. But he was from Chile, and I'm sure he wouldn't believe such nonsense. What do you think?"

Daniel shrugged. "I've no earthly idea, but I'm determined to find out. By the way, I'm going to call tonight and make an appointment with an elderly woman who was referred to me by the hotel. Her name is Tiare Rapu. Do you know her?"

"Who doesn't know Crazy Tiare? What do you want to see her for?"

"I was told she knows about island history, and if I'm to have any chance to solve these murders, I need to know plenty more than I do now. Also, I'm told she will be willing to help me learn the Rapanui language."

José laughed. "She is truly an ancient relic and will tell you story after story. But I need to warn you to take everything she says — how do you Americans say it? — with a grain of salt."

As he hurried along, Daniel kept glancing at his map of Hanga Roa, which eventually led him to Tu'u Ko Ihu Street. Before long he came upon her home. It was a rather small, rectangular shaped house made of what appeared to be native stone. As he approached the modest residence, he saw wooden carvings of lizards above the door. He knocked and waited.

In a few moments the door opened wide, and a slender, white-haired Rapanui woman appeared, wearing a white blouse with black pants. Her beaming smile made the wrinkles on her face hardly noticeable. She said in clear English, "You must be Daniel Fishinghawk?"

"Yes, and you must be Mrs. Rapu?"

"Yes." She motioned him inside with a wave of her hand. "Please call me Tiare. Everyone does."

"Of course," Daniel replied as he entered into a concrete-floored living area with carved wooden furniture padded with brown cushions. The coffee table was a salvaged shipping crate, and the furniture sat on a large frayed area rug with pictures of moai on them. As he sat on the couch, he added, "Most of my friends back home call me — Hawk."

She smiled at him as she sat on an adjacent chair. "If you don't mind, I'll just call you Daniel — it's such a strong name."

As Daniel heard her words, he recalled his previous conversation with Alame Koreta. He figured: I might as well give in to it.

"While we're on the topic of names," she added, "your last name is most interesting — *Fishinghawk*. Alame tells me it is Native American."

"Actually, it is Cherokee."

"Forgive me for saying so, but you don't look like the Indians I've seen on television in your American westerns. While your hair and eyes are dark, your skin color is much lighter."

"No apology necessary," Daniel said. "Over the centuries, a good number of my tribe have intermarried with those of European descent. Many who consider themselves Cherokees have the appearance of Caucasians. Even one of the best known Cherokees, John Ross, our principal chief in the early part of the nineteenth century, was one eighth Cherokee and seven eighths Scottish."

"How interesting," she remarked. "Since we began interacting with the Europeans, the same has happened with us."

"I noticed the lizard carvings over your front door. Do they have any special meaning?"

"Well, yes," she said. "This is one of our ancient traditions. When my ancestors settled on this island, they often placed carvings of either lizards or crayfish over the entrances to their homes. They felt the image protected them from evil spirits."

Daniel glanced around the room. "You have a very nice home."

"Thank you. In the nineteen eighties the Chilean government built me an asbestos-sheet home on this location. The construction quality was awful, and the material it was built with was even worse. You do know about the association of asbestos and cancer, don't you?"

"I do," Daniel said.

"In the nineteen nineties I had it torn down, and with the little money that I had, I built this one. The native rock was cheap, but the concrete had to be shipped from Chile and was terribly expensive. So much so, that I couldn't afford the bags of sand to mix with it. Fortunately, I knew some strong young men who were aware of my predicament. At night, when no one was looking, they took some loads of sand from 'Anakena, and I was able to complete my home." Tiare smiled and winked at Daniel.

Daniel couldn't help himself — he laughed out loud. "Where there's a will, there's a way, and you seem to have plenty of will."

She grinned and said, "Now, I understand you want to know more about Rapa Nui?"

"Yes," Daniel responded, "and not only about the island. I want to learn the language as well. I would like to pay you for your time."

"No, no — don't be silly. The only payment I require is for you to tell me some things about your Cherokee history. Does that sound fair?"

"You bet it does. That's a great deal — I haven't heard a better one lately."

"Before we go on," she added, "I'd like to learn from you what your motivations are to learn more about Rapa Nui. I must confess I saw you on television last night. You're here to investigate the murders?"

After the broadcast, he saw no further reason for subterfuge. "Yes. I have sought you out because it's my belief that the more I know about your people, the better chance I'll have to solve them."

"Where would you like to begin?"

Daniel leaned forward and said, "First, tell me about akuaku."

Her eyebrows rose ever so slightly, and she cautiously asked, "What would you like to know about them?"

"I've heard they are spirits of the dead."

"That is true," Tiare confirmed, "but there is much more to say about them. We believe that, sometimes, when a Rapanui dies, their spirit may linger and help protect the territory of their descendants from intruders. If the members of their own clan behaved properly, the spirits — the akuaku — were well-mannered and protective towards them and their land. But toward strangers or invaders they could be hostile or even dangerous. Some have even been described as being demonic in nature."

"Really?"

"Oh, yes. So, like almost everything in life, akuaku have a good and a bad side."

Daniel said, "In my country, some believe that people can be possessed by demonic spirits. Do akuaku do that?"

"Not in our tradition. While akuaku can be embodied in animals and natural phenomena, such as landslides and heavy raindrops, they are not known to possess people. They can affect them, though, and cause them to fall down, get bucked off a horse, or even make someone have a heart attack. Even in our modern times, akuaku are still taken quite seriously by many Rapanui."

Daniel decided to take a chance. He leaned forward and said in a confidential voice, "I would like to share some information with you and get your thoughts. Can I count on you to keep this to yourself and tell no one else?"

Tiare grinned, obviously delighted by this turn of events. She brushed her index finger across her closed mouth and promised, "My lips are sealed."

"I'm sure you've heard about the death of Detective Gomez at the Moana Nui Hotel?"

"I have."

"What would you say if I told you the last word he wrote down was Hitirau?"

Tiare paled. "Oh, dear. Hitirau is an akuaku who stays in the area of our island called Puna Pau. Have you heard of it?"

"No," Daniel admitted.

"It is a small crater just outside of Hanga Roa that is the sole source of the red scoria — a type of lava — that is used for the hats of some of our moai. These hats are also called topknots or pukao. Just to be safe, I would stay away from there. Remember, you are an outsider, just as Gomez was."

Daniel cocked an eyebrow at the dear lady and asked, "If we chose to believe akuaku really exist, could one actually be the murderer?"

Tiare paused, obviously thinking. Finally she answered, "Not likely, but certainly one could influence someone — and perhaps even give them special powers — to allow them to do their dirty work."

"Interesting."

"Enough of that for now," Tiare suggested, "let's start learning Rapanui." She then threw back her head and laughed, "Daniel, you don't fool me. You're a smart one, and I know it. A few lessons and you'll be speaking our language like a native."

Daniel was excited about learning the language, but talking about the note Gomez had left behind reminded him of how mutilated the poor man had been. And there had been twenty-six others before him.

Daniel shuddered at the thought.

Chapter 10

September 5, 2014

Daniel and José sat in front of what used to be Alejandro Gomez's desk. The meeting with the new Chilean police head of investigation was set for ten a.m. Daniel and José waited for his arrival

Daniel asked, "Do you know anything about the new appointee?"

"I'm afraid I do. His name is Salvador Diaz, and he was one of the head police in the Pinochet regime. How much do you know about this period in history?"

Daniel listened for footsteps and lowered his voice. "I know about Pinochet being a dictator."

"I'll make this quick," José responded quietly. "Diaz could be here at any moment... Pinochet assumed power in Chile in nineteen seventy-three in a coup d'état, overthrowing the democratically elected government. Pinochet's seventeen years of power were a nightmare; his political opponents were brutally oppressed; thousands were killed and tens of thousands, including women and children, were tortured."

José stood and moved to the open door of the office, and glanced up and down the hallway. He pulled the door closed, sat back down and whispered to Daniel, "Hawk, it is widely believed that Diaz was involved in the butchery, but it could never be proven, so he was kept on the police force. He's very well educated — even got a degree in Criminal Justice at Rutgers before he started his career in law enforcement. He has a reputation as someone who gets the job done, one way or another, no matter the cost — just like when he murdered and tortured his fellow Chileans. If I had my way, I'd put him behind bars and —"

The door popped open, and a man in a black suit with neatly combed silver hair came into the room, looking as if he'd just stepped out of the latest issue of *GQ*. He wore a white shirt and a red checkered tie, and his black leather shoes were polished so highly they could blind anyone who dared to admire them for too long. Following him was a tall, muscular man in a grey suit and sunglasses.

As the silver-haired man sat down behind the desk, he said, "My name is Salvador Diaz, and he—" pointing to the other man now standing behind him, "is my bodyguard."

A deafening silence followed as Diaz studied his audience with cold and distant dark eyes. Finally, looking at José, he said, "You must be Detective Tepano, the one who blew the lid on this investigation and completely screwed things up?"

José's brow furrowed as he admitted, "Yes, I am José Tepano."

"And you," he said, turning to Daniel, "you must be Detective Fishinghawk — the one who goes by Hawk — from New York City?" He sarcastically added, "The prima donna we've all heard so much about?"

Daniel straightened in his chair and met Diaz's stare.

He's trying to intimidate us, Daniel thought. He felt like laughing in Diaz's face. But he suspected that might not be such a hot idea.

Diaz turned back to José. "Young man, after what you've done, if I had a choice, I'd throw you in the slums in Santiago chasing drug dealers, and you'd be dead by the end of the week." Diaz shook his fist at José, a flashy ebony ring on the middle finger of his hand. "How *dare* you bring this case to the public? The only reason I don't get rid of you is because in Chile, you're a hero for blowing our cover. The newspapers would all go crazy if I fired you, and I'd come under public scrutiny. God knows I've had enough of that in my life already. I'm stuck with you, and you'd better work hard or you'll be gone, gone, *gone*. Understand?"

José nodded.

"Good. Now you," Diaz said with a growl, turning once again to Daniel, "I can't send you back home with your tail between your legs for the same reason. I'd get rid of you — our hope and our salvation — but there would be a public outcry. I promise you this, though, the minute this case is solved you will be out of here and back to New York City as fast as I can snap my fingers."

Daniel refused to respond and continued to stare at him.

"So, gentlemen," Diaz continued, "it seems we have an understanding. I have brought in five of my top investigators from Santiago, and I want all of you to crawl under every damned rock on this damned island and find me our killer. I'm telling you — one way or another — in the next month we will have our man. No later. Every second we delay means less money for Chile and this worthless place. If you ask me, we should have left it as it was: an island full of half-naked savages whose only skills were raising sheep, sweet potatoes and carving cheap wooden curios for tourists."

José turned beet red and started to stand. Daniel put his hand on José's shoulder and pushed him back down in his chair.

Diaz pretended not to notice. "Now get out of my office and hit the streets. We've got a murderer to find. And believe me, we will find him." With that he picked up the phone on his desk and waved Daniel and José out the door.

As the door closed behind them, José whispered to Daniel, "He's exactly like I thought he would be — *a real piece of shit.*"

Daniel was worn out after a long day of doing interviews with some of the local population who happened to speak English. He had gathered all sorts of useless information. Daniel knew this was not the way to find the killer, but it was clear that Diaz didn't care to utilize Daniel's investigative skills; instead, Diaz made him do grunt work as a way of putting Daniel in his place.

Daniel glanced at his wrist watch, which showed the time to be 6:25 p.m. He was already running late — he was to meet Tiare at 6:30. He hopped in his SUV and drove to her home.

He knocked on the door. No response. He knocked again; still no response. He was about to try again, when he barely heard her voice.

"Just a minute!"

When she appeared at the door, she was wearing round wire-rimmed glasses that The Beatles' John Lennon might have worn. "Sorry you had to wait so long." She opened the door for him to enter. "I was in the back studying on my computer."

Daniel couldn't believe it. "You're doing what?"

Tiare closed the door and motioned him to sit in the living area. As he sat on the couch, she settled in a chair across from him, removed her glasses and said, "I've already gotten online degrees in English and Spanish, and now I'm working on getting a degree in cultural anthropology. I'm enrolled at Ashford University in the United States. Have you heard of it?"

"No," he admitted.

"Not many universities offer these courses online. It's quite a challenge because our Internet speeds are so slow. Do you know what anthropology is?"

"Isn't it the study of people and their cultures?"

"Close," she answered, "but not exactly. It's actually the science that deals with the origins, physical and cultural development, biological characteristics, social customs and beliefs of humanity."

Daniel could tell she had memorized the definition, and he couldn't help but smile.

Tiare said, "Just because I'm ninety-four doesn't mean I should stop learning. Don't you agree?"

"Absolutely." He looked at his watch and said. "Mrs. Rapu . . . I mean Tiare, I had planned to eat before I came, but I ran late at work. Could I buy you dinner at a place where we could talk privately?"

"Of course you may," she replied with a smile. "I recommend a little vegetarian restaurant called Laguna Azul. It's only a short drive away. Around ten years ago I gave up eating meat when I heard being a vegetarian was healthier."

"Really?"

"Really," she repeated. "And it's better for the environment as well. It takes a lot more water to produce meat protein than it does vegetable protein, and the waste produced by animal production contaminates our ground water. Here on Rapa Nui, where our water is in such short supply, conservation is an important issue."

Daniel smiled and thought: What an amazing woman!

Daniel and Tiare were seated at an outside table at the quaint Laguna Azul restaurant. Original island artwork that hung on the wall welcomed them, and a sea shell wind chime tinkled in the background. As they sat eating their salads, Tiare asked, "Daniel, what's on your mind this evening?"

"Well, Tiare," he said, feeling a little uncomfortable bringing this topic up at a vegetarian restaurant, "I suppose you've heard that all of the murder victims were cannibalized?"

"I have."

"Let me get right to the point," Daniel said, "does Rapa Nui have a history of cannibalism?"

Tiare ducked her head. "Well . . . I . . ."

"Yes?" Daniel asked.

Tiare took a deep breath and looked up at him. "Before I answer, let me give you some background. You see, Daniel, my studies in anthropology have taught me that cannibalism has occurred over much of the world, and in more recent times by those who were starving. Two examples are the Donner Party in the

American west and the crash of the Uruguayan Air Force flight in the Andes in the nineteen seventies.

"Here in Polynesia cannibalism has been practiced in certain places. Fiji, for example, once was known as the Cannibal Isles. Sailors would prefer to land *anywhere* rather than Fiji. There was one Fijian chief, Ratu Udre Udre, who kept a stone for every person he ate. It is said at his gravesite there were eight hundred and seventy-two stones. Hard to believe —"

"Almost too strange to be true."

Tiare added, "I'm sure you know Mark Twain. He once said, 'Truth is stranger than fiction.'"

She was all over the map, and Daniel had to get her back to his question. "Yes, I know Mark Twain. But — what about cannibalism on Rapa Nui?"

"The definitive way that archeologists can determine if cannibalism has occurred in a specific location is to check bones for cut marks, which are actually nicks or scratches made on the bone by a sharp tool as the flesh is removed."

Daniel nodded encouragement.

"These cut marks have been found in excavated sites on Rapa Nui. Yes, I must admit it, cannibalism has occurred here. Sometimes history reveals the dark side of a society, and cannibalism is the dark side of Rapa Nui."

Their server arrived to place before them plates of steamed vegetables on beds of pasta and grated cheese.

"Ah, this looks good," Tiare commented. "I don't eat out often, so this is special for me."

Daniel gazed warmly at her. "Tiare, the sad truth is that every society has places in their history they are not proud of. For America, one of the darkest moments occurred with the Trail of Tears. Have you heard of it?"

Tiare asked, "Isn't that where some American Indians were forced from their homes in the southeast part of the United States?"

"In a nutshell, yes. For the Cherokee tribe, this happened from eighteen thirty-eight through eighteen thirty-nine. Around seventeen thousand Cherokees made the trek to Indian Territory, now called Oklahoma. Of that group, over four thousand died, either in the detention camps or en route."

Tiare sighed. "That's almost a fourth of them."

"So," Daniel said as he patted her hand, "don't be too concerned about your island's history of cannibalism. There are those in my country who have done much worse and on a much greater scale. But about the cannibalism that's happening now. Do your senses give you any idea what the motivation might be?"

The old woman placed her fork aside and said thoughtfully, "I cannot be certain of this, but I have an idea."

"Go on," Daniel urged.

"First of all, I believe the reason for these murders is clear — the killer does not want tourists on this island. And perhaps, if we can believe the note left by Detective Gomez, the murderer may be under the influence of Hitirau. Think about it. What better way to keep visitors away than the possibility of not only being killed, but also being eaten alive?"

"Agreed. What should we do next?" Daniel asked.

"There is nothing we can do. As long as the tourists stay away from Rapa Nui, I feel certain the murders will stop. If, for whatever reason, the tourists return . . . well, we can only wait and see what happens. Then we can choose our next step."

"We?"

"Yes, *we*," she said. "Since I was a little girl, I've always been interested in adventures, and this will be the grandest one of all."

"But this exposes you to far too much risk — I can't take that chance."

"Daniel," she said, "I am certain that the killer is somehow already aware that we are meeting, and I will do all I can to stay safe. But there's no turning back now."

Daniel studied Tiare closely. Their professional relationship had evolved into a friendship, and if anything happened to her, he would never forgive himself. "Very well," he conceded, "but only if you promise me one thing."

"What's that?"

"Keep this close at hand." Saying that, he reached down to his right side, pulled his Beretta from its holster and slipped it under the table onto her lap. "Tuck that in your carry bag — it could come in handy one day."

When she fingered the pistol and realized what he'd done, she grimly said, "Let's hope not."

Chapter 11

September 19, 2014

Daniel and José sat at a table for lunch at the El Tiberon restaurant, which overlooked the small but beautiful Pea Beach in Hanga Roa. Salvador Diaz had been cracking the whip, and they, along with the investigators he had brought with him from Chile, had investigated every square inch of the sixty-three square mile island. Like all the other days, Daniel had gathered up all sorts of data, which was of little or no use to the overall goal of finding the killer.

As he cut into a tasty nanue fish, a local favorite, Daniel asked, "Any news from your side?"

José lowered his voice. "Well, there's an interesting rumor floating around."

"What's up?"

"Seems Diaz has a prime suspect," José said.

"You've got to be kidding."

"I'm not. We should know more in the next week or so, but he's honing in on Roberto Ika. Do you know of him?"

"No," admitted Daniel.

"He's a little old man in his seventies who has a history of mental illness; I believe his diagnosis is paranoid schizophrenia. In other words, he's crazy and thinks everyone is out to get him."

"Besides that," José continued, "he was one of the protesters who occupied the Hangaroa Eco Village and Spa in August of two thousand-ten before being forcibly evicted the following February. The protest occurred because my people believe they were cheated out of the ancestral land the hotel is sitting on. The protest, as you might have guessed, fell on deaf Chilean ears. Unfortunately for Roberto Ika, this makes him an easy target, one Diaz's supervisors would approve of."

"But that doesn't make any sense," Daniel said. "First of all, the evidence is clear that our killer is someone who is physically strong. No way a seventy-year-old man could overwhelm each of the twenty-seven victims, most of whom are younger than he is. And there are the fingerprints. As you know, there are no matches with anyone on the island. Nothing about this fits."

José nodded agreement. "Of course you're right, but Diaz wants someone behind bars to restart the flow of money into Rapa Nui. And he'll stop at nothing, even putting an innocent man in jail."

"That doesn't surprise me in the least," Daniel said. "By the way, do you have family on the island that might be affected by this?"

"Not any more. I was an only child, and my parents and grandparents are all dead."

"It's the same with me. I've got no living family."

"Well, then," José concluded, "we have something in common. Any girlfriends back home?"

"No," admitted Daniel, "how about you?"

"I could only wish. When I returned from Chile after my training at the police academy in Santiago, the one Rapanui woman I was interested in got tired of waiting and married a local man. On this island, good Rapanui women don't grow on trees."

"I imagine Rapanui women might say the same thing about Rapanui men," Daniel said.

José grinned at the dig and grabbed the check. "I need to get back to work. Before we go, tell me, how are things going with Crazy Tiare?"

Daniel was surprised to find himself offended at José's words. "She's not crazy at all, and she has been a great help in teaching me Rapanui. We've been meeting every evening for lessons at her home. After only a couple of weeks I'm already getting a pretty good handle on conversation. Besides that, she's a smart as a whip and seems to have some intriguing ideas about the killer."

"Anything worth repeating?"

"Not just yet, but tonight she is going to share with me some of the history of Rapa Nui. I believe it will be interesting."

"Good luck," José said. "You'll need it to sort out the truth." He threw money on the table to settle the bill, and they both stood and walked out to their vehicles.

That evening Daniel again paid a visit to his now-favorite Rapanui, Tiare. As they sat in the living area sipping hot tea mixed with honey and milk, Daniel asked, "Tiare, why is it that some call you Crazy Tiare?"

Her wrinkled face broke out into a big smile. "Do some still call me that?"

Daniel grinned.

"Well," she said, "I suppose it's because I like to tell stories of old Rapa Nui. These tales must sound crazy at times, but my people often forget that the legends of our culture are ingrained within us, no matter how outlandish they sound today."

Daniel said, "I'd like to hear more."

"Very well, then— I will try to blend the mythology of Rapa Nui with what historians tell us. The tales I have heard when I was a child — and there are many— are mixed in with this telling. Are you ready?"

"I'm listening."

Tiare had a faraway look in her eyes as she related, "Legend tells us that the first chief who led his people to our island was Hotu Matu'a, who lived on what we now believe was Mangareva in Polynesia. His clan had lost a number of battles to a nearby clan, so he asked Haumaka, his shaman, to dream and find a new location they could travel to and live.

"In his dream, it is said that Haumaka saw our unspoiled isle. He told Hotu Matu'a of his vision, and six scouts were sent to find it. Many miles of ocean southeast of Mangareva they discovered their future home and felt it was ideal for colonization."

"When was Rapa Nui actually settled?"

"Sometime between 600 CE and 800 CE—"

Daniel interrupted, "CE?"

Tiare explained, "Common Era. It is a term often used in place of AD by those who wish to be sensitive to non-Christians. Likewise, 'Before the Common Era,' BCE, is used as an alternative to BC. Understand?"

Daniel nodded.

"Our legends state that two large canoes were built, one captained by Hotu Matu'a and the other by Tu'u ko Iho. Historians tell us that these canoes were large enough to hold up to forty people each."

"Pretty big canoes."

"Bigger than I've ever seen," she added. "And in these canoes were all the supplies necessary to begin a new Polynesian society."

"Such as?"

"Many different food plants, as well as paper mulberry — for making barkcloth for clothing. As far as animals on board, the most important was the chicken. Likely there were also pigs and dogs, and even the Polynesian rat, which could be eaten."

"Eat a rat?"

"Obviously you've never tried one. When I was a child there were many times of hunger, but one thing there was plenty of was rats. The rumor is true— they do taste like chicken." Tiare laughed at the look of disgust on Daniel's face.

Tiare continued, "While legend tells us the first landing was at 'Anakena, the early settlers eventually migrated to the southwest part of the island, where bird meat and eggs were plentiful.

"From their Polynesian roots, the islanders brought with them a similar social order. The noblemen were called 'ariki, while the most exalted of this class was the 'ariki mau, who was considered to be a living deity and had absolute authority. The 'ariki mau always came from the royal Miru clan.

"Next in line were the shamans, who were not only respected but also feared because of their spiritual powers. Following the shamans were the masters of stone and wood carving, and last were the commoners, which included farmers and fishermen."

Daniel said, "About shamans. They are also in our Native American culture, though I don't know a lot about them. What exactly does a shaman do?"

Tiare answered, "A shaman is one who acts as an intermediary between the natural and supernatural worlds. They might use magic to cure illnesses or even foretell the future."

"I see."

"And so, as my ancestors populated the island they formed clans, and legend tells us each of these clans have a common ancestor who was supposed to be a son or grandson of Hotu Matu'a.

"Once the island was settled, construction began of ahus — ceremonial stone platforms — and moai, the carved stone figures. From the twelfth to the fifteenth century, the island's entire purpose seemed to be to construct these platforms and statues. As hard as it is to believe, there were almost nine hundred of these moai carved."

"Did the islanders see these statues as gods?" asked Daniel.

"No, Daniel, the moai are not depictions of gods; rather, they represent the living, powerful essence of our ancestors. Nearly every one of the erected moai was placed on an ahu along the coastline, facing inland toward us, protecting us with not only their presence, but also their mana. Do you know what mana is?"

Smart as Daniel was, he'd somehow never heard the word. "Help me here."

"Mana is a supernatural force or power," Tiare explained.

Daniel asked, "Where on the island do you believe that the moai have the most mana?"

"All have some degree of mana, but for me, it is the old moai you have seen at 'Anakena — I feel quite connected to it. Now as to the rest of the mo —"

Daniel heard an abrupt whizzing sound through the open window, then a *thud* as Tiare screamed and fell face-forward from her chair, a spear buried in her left upper back. She lay on the floor moaning, blood pouring from her wound.

Daniel heard footsteps running away from the window and fought back the urge to chase after them — Tiare needed him. He pulled out his phone and speed dialed police dispatch.

The minute the phone was answered, he screamed into it, "This is Detective Fishinghawk — I need an ambulance — *now*!"

Chapter 12

September 19, 2014

Daniel was worried sick.

He sipped on a cup of coffee and paced the beige-tiled hallway of Hospital Hanga Roa. Though he arrived there shortly after Tiare's ambulance, in the hustle-bustle of the emergency department, Daniel was unable to see her before she was whisked away to the operating room.

Tiare had been in surgery for around three hours when a man dressed in green surgical scrubs approached him.

"You Detective Fishinghawk?" he asked as he extended his hand.

Daniel shook hands. "Yes. How is Tiare doing?"

"I'm Doctor Fuentes. She's doing amazingly well, even though the spear almost went completely through her chest. It barely missed her heart but did collapse and form a blood clot in her left lung. I've put a chest tube in to keep the lung expanded, and we'll remove it in three or four days if all goes well. She's lost a lot of blood, but I believe she'll pull through."

"What about the spear?" Daniel asked.

"That's the interesting thing. It's an old-style weapon, a spear with a point of sharpened obsidian. This knife-like tip is what the islanders call a mata'a. It's one of the deadliest weapons I've ever seen; it passed through the tissue of her chest like a hot knife through butter. The minute I pulled it out, I passed it along to a courier from the police department. I might guess by now they've had a few hours to look at it."

"Good. When can I see her?"

"Not tonight. She's just too groggy, and I want her to be as quiet as possible. In the morning you should be able to visit her." He paused in thought and said, "I must share with you that I did speak with her after surgery, and suggested we fly her to Santiago in the morning to get more intensive care. She informed me that she's staying right here, saying something to the effect that 'We've got a killer to catch.' She is the most strong-willed old woman I've ever seen." Doctor Fuentes smiled. "Because of that, I'm sure she'll pull through."

Daniel thanked the surgeon profusely as tears welled in his eyes. The thought of losing his new friend had been almost too much to bear.

"One more thing. What blood type are you?"

"I'm O positive," Daniel said. "Why?"

"It just so happens that our patient has the same blood type, and we don't have any of that in this small hospital. She needs at least a unit to get her by. Do you mind donating?"

"I'd be honored," Daniel said.

"Good. We'll have the blood bank come in and collect a unit. It shouldn't take long to cross-match, and we'll have it in her before the night is up." Before he turned to leave he added, "Don't worry — I've instructed the nurses to keep a close eye on our patient, and I'll be checking on her first thing in the morning."

As the surgeon retreated, Daniel noticed José walking down the hall toward him.

As José approached, he asked, "Hawk, how's she doing?"

"She's tough as a boot," Daniel said. "She nearly bled to death, but the doctor says she'll be fine."

"That's a relief. We're lucky the spear didn't kill her."

"An inch or two in the wrong direction, and she'd be dead," Daniel explained.

"That's what I've heard. I wanted to let you know that we've done a preliminary on the weapon, and the killer's fingerprints match with those from all the other crime scenes. It's definitely the same guy." José then asked, "Hawk, you're the expert imported all the way from New York City. What's your take on this?"

Daniel thought for a moment and answered, "First of all, this is the only murder attempt where our suspect didn't succeed. The question in my mind is whether or not he really tried, or if he just hoped to scare her away from helping us further."

José ventured, "As close as he came to her heart, it would seem to me that he wanted to kill her."

"Remember, José, our murderer is an expert at killing. I believe if he wanted to put it through her heart, he would have."

José shrugged. "You could be right. I just don't know."

"Think," said Daniel, "this is the first Rapanui he has attacked. My best guess is that our killer has his eye on us and somehow knows our every step. The reason he attacked Tiare was because he was afraid she might give us some useful information."

"I agree, but I'll add one more thing. I believe he also wants to scare you away as well. I have to ask you, would you prefer to step away from this case?"

Daniel angrily said, "Not just no, but *hell* no. José, this isn't just a police case anymore — now it's personal." He took a deep breath and tried to calm himself. "But until this is finished, can you give Tiare protection?"

"The best protection I can give her is to fly her off the island till this settles down. Somehow I don't think she's going to allow that."

"No way she'll leave Rapa Nui — ever," Daniel confirmed.

"I had suspected as much. I've already talked with Diaz, and he has agreed to place a guard outside her room twenty-four seven. Don't worry, we'll keep her safe."

A woman in white with a red cross embroidered on her pocket approached and asked in English, "Sir, are you Detective Fishinghawk?"

"I am."

"I'm here to collect your blood," she explained. "Would you follow me?"

"See you later, Hawk," José said.

As he walked away, Daniel grinned and said, "I sure hope so,"

Daniel arrived early the next morning at the hospital and sat in the waiting area, hoping to see Tiare. A white-clad nurse soon appeared.

"Sir, come with me," she said to Daniel. "You may see her now."

Daniel followed closely behind as she walked down the hallway to Tiare's room. Sitting next to the doorway was a uniformed Chilean police officer, who grimly nodded at them as they entered.

Tiare was sitting up in bed, wearing an off-white hospital gown tied behind her. A large plastic tube appeared to be coming out of her left chest, which led to a suction bottle attached to a humming machine. It was nearly half-filled with dark blood.

The nurse closed the door behind her as she left the room. Daniel walked up to the bedside and carefully hugged Tiare.

" 'Iorana, Daniel," Tiare said with a weak smile.

" 'Iorana," Daniel said softly in return as he sat down in a bedside chair.

"Daniel, I understand you donated some blood for me."

"That's true."

She reached out her hand to him. "Thank you. I felt much better about receiving blood knowing it was from you."

He took her hand and squeezed it. "That's what friends are for. Considering what you've been through, you're looking great! I'm so glad to see you alive and kicking."

"It's certainly better than the alternative."

Daniel smiled at her words and asked, "Do you have any family coming to check on you?"

"Yes. My son and daughter, who are both married and living in Santiago. They will fly here tomorrow with their spouses."

"Oh, you must be delighted."

"I am. The doctor says I will be in the hospital for around a week, and my family will stay for another week or so after, until I'm able to make it on my own."

Daniel offered, "After they leave, I'm at your service."

"I don't believe that will be necessary, but thanks all the same. Now," she sternly said, "I want to see you every evening — starting today — to continue our lessons."

"But —"

"Daniel, don't you see? The killer has made it obvious that he's worried about the two of us working together, and to give in would be exactly what he wants. No, we have to keep going. You think a little spear wound can slow me down?"

Daniel couldn't help but chuckle. "Somehow I don't think so."

"Very well, then, I want to see you here at six p.m. sharp, and that's an order!" She added, "I have heard that I would have made quite a good drill sergeant. Do you agree?"

"Sir — yes sir," Daniel said as he saluted, a grin on his face.

The nurse reappeared. "Sir, it's time for you to leave. We need to run more tests."

"Take very good care of my good friend," he instructed her.

After he spoke, he glanced over at Tiare.

She was smiling from ear to ear.

As Daniel drove away from the hospital, he knew there was something he had to do, and he had to do it alone. While he wanted to believe the stories of the akuaku that Tiare had told him, he felt he had to go check it out for himself, and the only way to do that was to go to the alleged haunting ground of Hitirau: Puna Pau.

When he was young he had been taught by his grandfather that the best way to learn something was by personal experience. As he thought about it, all he expected to have was a nice walking tour of the place where the beautiful red scoria topknots — pukao — were mined in Rapa Nui's remote past.

He parked the SUV at his hotel, gathered his backpack from the rear seat and hiked up the road, which gradually wound upward through verdant hills. Before long he came to a parking area, which was absent of cars. At that place stood an ancient, gnarled tree, which looked like it could have come out of a horror movie. Perched in the branches was a pair of caracaras.

Daniel smiled at them as they once again reminded him of the red-tailed hawks from Oklahoma. Perhaps, he thought, I'm feeling just a little homesick. Could be? Here he was — in as remote a location as anyone could imagine — and thinking of Oklahoma. He wondered if anyone visiting Rapa Nui had ever thought of Oklahoma while they were here. Somehow he didn't think so.

He shoved the memories of his home into the back of his mind and began to walk uphill on a graveled trail, which moved in a circuitous manner along the hillside. Soon he began to see the unfinished red pukao scattered along the trailside. Daniel knew from his previous studies that many weighed as much as ten tons, and in the past some had been moved as far as twelve kilometers to rest on the heads of the moai. It boggled his mind to think of how a primitive culture was able to not only move them such a distance, but also to place them on the top of the statues, some over thirty feet high.

Daniel stopped at the top, looked down upon the crater the pukao were mined from and saw several more of them at the bottom. He lowered his backpack from his shoulders, grabbed his water bottle from it, took a long drink and then bushwhacked down into the crater.

When he reached the bottom, he pulled off his backpack and sat on a large boulder. Suddenly the clear sky became overcast with dark clouds and a distinct chill filled the air.

Goose bumps rose up on both of Daniel's arms.

Something about this doesn't seem natural, he thought.

Even the caracaras, which now circled above him, screeched and seemed agitated.

What used to be gentle gusts of wind suddenly became forceful and howling, and when lightning began to strike in the area around the crater, Daniel thought: I'd better get out of here.

He stood to put on his backpack, when suddenly he was shoved down to the rocky ground from behind. He turned around to find nothing. Daniel stood again, and this time he felt something like a club hit him in the back. Again he fell to the earth, only now he felt himself pressed facedown into the dirt, jagged stones scratching his face.

The sky became pitch black and the weight on his back seemed as heavy as an elephant. Daniel began to crawl and stopped when he saw a skeletal form coalesce in front of him, sitting on a boulder. He had a long hooked nose with a dark goatee and earlobes which hung to his neck. He was bent over and emaciated — a nightmare from hell.

He leered at Daniel and spoke Rapanui in a deep, gravelly voice, which was painful to hear. "My name is Hitirau. What is yours?"

Daniel could barely catch his breath, yet somehow said, "Daniel."

Hitirau scowled and croaked, "You are an outsider — you do not belong here. Feel my power."

With that the heaviness in Daniel's chest increased tenfold, and he was frozen in position on the cold ground.

I'm going to die . . .

Suddenly the pressure lessened, and Daniel was able to gradually stand and stumble away. The blows to his back continued, but somehow Daniel found the strength to keep going. As he began to scale his way up the crater walls, the sky slowly cleared and the winds lessened.

At the top of the crater the sunshine warmed his face and a cool breeze blew through his dark hair. Daniel screwed up his nerve and looked back at the bottom of the crater. No sign of Hitirau, and Daniel's backpack still lay on the ground where he had left it.

To hell with the backpack . . .

Daniel hurried away from the crater and down the path as fast as he could run.

Chapter 13

September 20, 2014

D aniel was in his SUV driving to the hospital to see Tiare and couldn't escape the terror of his experience at Puna Pau. Diaz had given him a laundry list of interviews to do that afternoon, but he just couldn't concentrate on anything else for the time being.

So instead, when he returned from his confrontation with Hitirau, Daniel chose to sit in his room at the hotel and focus on his breath, as his grandpa had taught him. With time he began to feel less anxious, though the events of the morning starkly reminded him of how thin the veneer was between life and death. Daniel had no idea what had kept his life from being snuffed out, but whatever it was, he was glad to still be breathing.

At Puna Pau he had entered a foreign world — the world of the unknown, of spirit. His grandpa had often talked of Native American spirituality, but only in generalities. Any doubts Daniel previously had about existence of the ethereal world were cruelly snuffed out. What had happened to him was not vaporous, it was real and substantial.

Promptly at six p.m. Daniel parked his car and entered the hospital. He walked past the uniformed bodyguard sitting outside Tiare's room and discovered her sitting up in bed reading a newspaper, her John Lennon glasses hanging low on her nose.

" 'Iorana," Daniel said as he sat at her bedside.

" 'Iorana," Tiare repeated as she lowered the paper. She stifled a gasp. "Daniel, what happened to you? It looks like you lost a fight with a rabid cat."

"Tiare, I have a confession to make — I went to Puna Pau this morning."

"You didn't!" Tiare exclaimed with a shocked look on her face. "What happened?"

"Let's just say that Hitirau didn't take kindly to me being there, and this," he confessed as he pointed to his face, "is the end result."

"You never should have set foot in his domain. But now, since you have, do you have any doubts about his existence?"

"None whatsoever."

"Good. While it was reckless for you to go there alone, if you've learned from your experience without any permanent damage, then it was well worth it."

"Good way to put it," Daniel responded, feeling a bit foolish.

"Now," Tiare said, "let's put all this behind us for the time being and get on with the history of Rapa Nui. Where were we at?"

"I believe you were talking about the moai."

"Oh, yes," said Tiare. "As far as our moai were concerned, the carving and placing of them on Rapa Nui peaked in the fifteenth century. After that, things began to deteriorate."

"Why was that?"

"Unfortunately, my ancestors were not environmentalists. They adopted the same slash and burn philosophy as their Polynesian forefathers. So, when the forests became depleted, widespread erosion occurred, which led to crop failures and the drying up of the perennial streams.

"Once they were without large trees, they were no longer able to build boats capable of going out to sea where the larger fish were. So they had to rely on fishing close to shore, and soon even that resource became depleted. They were landlocked on an island with not enough food to feed everyone."

"They must have felt trapped," Daniel concluded.

"Indeed. So when there was a lack of food, the social order broke down and moai production stopped. It eventually led to the weakening of the once all-powerful 'ariki mau of the Miru clan and emergence of the warrior class, and as a result frequent clashes occurred between the eastern and western clans. During that difficult time, eventually all of the moai were toppled, and the warriors put forth the ancient god Makemake as a replacement for the mana of the moai. That led to the establishment of the Birdman Cult."

"The Birdman Cult?"

"Yes. A competition put in place by the warriors to establish the Birdman for the year. But there was a darker purpose, that being to take away the religious authority of the 'ariki mau and put it in the hands of the warrior class, represented by the Birdman — the tangata manu — a supposed incarnation of Makemake."

"What exactly was the competition?" Daniel asked.

"In September of each year the shamans of all of the clans selected one or two contestants who they thought gave them the best chance to win. Often this was the warrior leader, his proxy, or both. The competitors first gathered at the ceremonial center of Orongo, and when the arrival of the manutara birds was imminent, they climbed down the one thousand foot cliffs of Rano Kau, the inactive volcano."

Daniel grimaced as he recalled seeing the steep cliff from the airplane. He couldn't imagine anyone in their right mind who would try to climb down it.

"Once at the bottom, they paddled on reed mats packed with provisions to Motu Nui, the islet located southwest of the island, swimming almost a mile through shark-infested waters."

Daniel got a cold chill just thinking about it.

"After arrival, they camped out in caves and stayed there until the arrival of the manutara birds. It has been said that the first to find a manutara egg was the winner. He announced his find to the other contestants and placed the egg in a little reed basket, which was strapped to his forehead before he swam back across the ocean. He then scaled the cliff and delivered the egg to Orongo, where he, or the one he was proxy for, was declared the Birdman.

"While this may be true, I believe it is more likely that many of the contestants would find eggs close to the same time and it would be a mad race to be the first back. I might guess the contestants would try *anything* to be the winner of the competition, even if it meant pulling their opponents off the cliffs or trying to drown them.

"Once the new Birdman was declared, he shaved his head, eyebrows and eyelashes, and his head was painted. He lived a life of luxurious isolation, and, in the year to follow, he was not allowed to bathe himself or cut his nails, which grew as long as the talons of a bird."

"That sounds appealing," Daniel jested.

Tiare briefly smiled and said, "Meanwhile the Birdman's thugs ran amok on the island, terrorizing and plundering all of the clans who were not strong enough to resist. It was organized chaos, and in spite their efforts to unseat him, they never truly took away the religious power of the 'ariki mau, who still ruled as the paramount chief."

Daniel asked, "When did the Europeans first discover the island?"

"The first was Captain Rosendaal, a Dutchman sailing one of three boats commanded by Jacob Roggeveen. The sighting occurred on April fifth, seventeen twenty-two, on Easter Sunday, so it was named Easter Island."

"I had wondered where that name came from," Daniel said. "It's not exactly Polynesian-sounding."

"We islanders prefer Rapa Nui. No one likes the idea of our home being named by a European. Later, many others eventually visited our island, but one of the worst periods for the Rapanui occurred from the period from eighteen sixty-two and eighteen eighty-eight, when around *ninety-four percent* of the population died or emigrated, sometimes by force. Probably the worst example was when Peruvian slavers kidnapped — also called blackbirding — around fifteen hundred Rapanui, and of the twelve survivors that were finally returned to their homeland, one had smallpox. That dread disease nearly wiped out the remaining population."

Daniel said, "My Native American ancestors also suffered greatly from exposure to European diseases."

Tiare added, "As the world shrinks, it would have to happen at some point in time, but that doesn't make it any less painful."

"Not at all," Daniel agreed.

Tiare took a sip of water from a straw on her bedside stand. "That's enough history for now; we can finish up later. I do have some homework for you. Tomorrow I would like for you to go to the Father Sebastian Englert Anthropological Museum. It'll be open in the morning. Have a look around. I'll be interested to hear your thoughts."

"I'll be glad to," Daniel said. His phone then rang and he held it to his ear. "Really? Okay, I'll be there."

When Daniel hung up, he said, "That was Detective Tepano. It seems that Salvador Diaz is holding a press conference tomorrow morning to announce he has captured the murderer."

"Who?" Tiare asked

"Roberto Ika."

"That can't be," she said.

Daniel shook his head in dismay.

Chapter 14

September 21, 2014

Daniel and José sat in the front row of the packed meeting room at the Moana Nui Hotel. At least a hundred were in attendance, most of them reporters. Also present were a handful of Rapanui who somehow managed to slip inside.

Salvador Diaz, dressed in an immaculately pressed grey suit with an equally crisp white shirt and navy paisley tie, moved to a place behind the podium. Standing behind him was his ever-present bodyguard, his arms tightly folded in front of him as he intently looked over the audience.

Diaz lightly tapped the microphone and, when he was sure it was live, spoke in English — the international language. "Ladies and gentlemen, I have called this press conference to let you know some very good news. For over six months Easter Island has been terrorized by a madman who has killed and mutilated many people. Now, due to some excellent investigative work by our detectives, we have our man, and the islanders can relax."

He paused as a muffled gasp went up from the crowd.

Diaz cleared his throat and moved on, saying, "The killer is Roberto Ika, a mentally ill man who just yesterday confessed to all of the murders. He —"

A cry came from an old Rapanui man standing in the back of the room. "It can't be! Roberto is crazy, but he wouldn't hurt a fly!"

Diaz motioned to a small group of Chilean policemen. They escorted the thrashing man outside to a waiting paddy wagon.

"As I was saying, he has already confessed to the murders, and not only that, his fingerprints match those from each of the crime scenes."

Daniel and José glanced at each other.

Then an elderly woman next to José stood and spoke, "I am Roberto's neighbor. He comes home early every night and watches television, and I've seen his lights on during the times the murders were committed. Why would he confess to crimes that he didn't commit? Was he tortured?"

Two more policemen appeared and ushered her to the exit.

José whispered to Daniel, "Do you get the feeling that there are some raw feelings about how Chile has treated the people of Rapa Nui?"

Daniel nodded.

Diaz turned as red as a beet and yelled at the woman as she was escorted out, "He was *not* tortured! That hasn't happened since the Pino —" he abruptly stopped before finishing the sentence. He cleared his throat again.

"And I'm sure he fooled you into believing he was there by leaving the lights on. He is guilty, guilty, *guilty*!" he screamed into the mic, the sound reverberating through the small room.

Diaz quickly regained his composure. In a lower, more compassionate voice, he said, "He is a sick man who needs professional help, and today he is being flown to Santiago for evaluation at a mental institution. Once he is certified insane, he will be locked up in a place where he can never hurt anyone again.

"At this time, I also want to thank all of those who helped make this possible, especially Daniel Fishinghawk, from the New York City Police Department."

A smattering of applause rose from the audience.

He glanced at Daniel and announced, "Thank you, Hawk, for all of your assistance, and I'm glad to say you are no longer needed here."

In other words, Daniel thought, he's telling me to get lost.

Diaz then flashed his biggest smile at the television cameras, his teeth glistening. "For all of you out there listening, you need to know that Easter Island is now one hundred percent safe, and you can once again travel to our Chilean paradise without fear or concern. We welcome you back."

He then glared at his audience, adding, "There will be no further questions."

With that, he and his bodyguard beat a hasty exit from the group of stunned onlookers.

Daniel heard a reporter from behind him grumble, "What do you mean no *further* questions — there were no questions from the reporters — *at all*!"

As the crowd filed out, Daniel and José remained in their chairs.

When Daniel was sure no one was within earshot, he said, "Can you believe Diaz planted the fingerprint evidence? There's no way the ones at the scenes matched with Ika's. And not only that, Tiare's protection will now be stopped, and when the tourists return our killer will be back. Does Diaz believe he'll just go away? What is he thinking?"

José answered, "I can tell you what he's thinking. Like I told you before, the almighty tourist currency is what's on his mind, and he's been told by his Chilean superiors to get the money flowing again, whatever the cost."

"And the cost will be enormous," Daniel added. "I'm going to have to think about what I should do next — I can't leave Tiare unguarded. For some reason, the killer believes she's a link to discovering his identity."

"Perhaps so," José said, "or maybe if you're gone he'll just leave her alone."

"José, I can't take that chance. I'm going to hang around for a while longer just to be sure. And maybe, just maybe, when the killings start again, I can find a way to catch him."

"I wouldn't count on it. Our suspect is craftier than all of us put together. So far he's avoided the entire Chilean police department and the best the United States has to offer. Somehow I don't believe that's going to change."

Daniel claimed, "In my experience, every killer — no matter how smart he or she is — will at some point make a mistake. And when our killer does, I will be on him like a fly on crap."

"I wish I had your confidence," said José

"After what he did to Tiare, I promise you, I *will* find him, one way or another. Right now, though, I'm headed over to the Englert Museum. Would you like to join me?"

"No, I've been in that dusty old place too many times to count over the years, and there's nothing there that draws my interest anymore. But since you've never been, I believe you'll find it intriguing. I'll check back with you later."

"Sounds good," Daniel replied. He was starting to get the feeling that before too much longer he would have some answers to this seemingly unsolvable mystery.

But where would the answers come from?

His instincts quickly spoke to his own question:

Somewhere I'd rather not go.

Daniel climbed into his car and was en route to the museum when his phone rang. A familiar voice spoke:

"Hawk! You ol' son of a bitch! I hear you've solved another case and are headed back soon to your favorite city in the world."

"Chief Kelly! How did you know? I left the press conference only a few minutes ago."

"Seems your new boss, Diaz, had his secretary call my office this morning with the news. What the fuck, Hawk? You've never taken more than a day or two to figure out who done it."

"Well," Daniel said, "there's a little problem you don't know about. You see, the case has not been solved."

"What do you mean?"

"Let's just say the Chilean police needed to make an arrest, and they did."

"Are you telling me this is a frame-up?" Kelly asked.

"That's what I'm saying. I'm sure once the tourists come back, the murders will start again. I need to hang around here until we get the real killer nailed."

"But that's impossible. They don't want you around any longer. In fact, Diaz's secretary tells me your flight out has already been booked for tomorrow. Whatever, I need you back here. I've got a backlog of unsolved murders I want you to sort out."

"Chief," Daniel insisted, "I need to stay here — even if it's in an unofficial capacity."

"Hawk, listen up! The Chilean police don't want you there — period! I don't like doing this, but I must order you to return."

"I don't like doing this either, but you've backed me into a corner."

"What are you saying?"

"I quit," said Daniel

There was a long pause at the other end of the phone. "Damn it, Hawk, are you sure? I'll throw in a big raise and an extra week of vacation just to sweeten the pot. What do you say?"

"Sorry — can't do it."

"Well, shit," Kelly said, "I think you're making a big fucking mistake, but if you change your mind, let me know. I've always got room for you with the NYPD."

Daniel then heard a loud *click*.

Daniel parked his vehicle in front of the museum. It was a bright, sunny day, and the royal blue ocean next to the museum was calm and serene. As he got out of his SUV and strolled up to the front door, he heard the echoing sounds of seabirds.

He entered, paid his admission fee and began to look at some of the objects on display.

The first exhibit to catch his eye was one that contained the hand tools used to carve the moai. He had previously learned that it would take six men around twelve to fifteen months to complete a sixteen-foot-tall moai. Considering the large number constructed, the amount of labor involved for such a feat was astronomical.

He then saw a female moai in the museum, obvious because of its breasts. He wandered over to couple of large wooden planks with symbols on them, one in the shape of a fish, and discovered the inscriptions were representative of Rapa Nui's own unique rongorongo script. Granted, these were not originals. A plaque explained that all those were on exhibit in other museums across the world, but none were here.

Daniel walked over to another case, which from a distance looked to contain five wooden figures propped up on wooden braces. As Daniel got closer he caught his breath.

Hitirau! They look like Hitirau!

All were skin and bones with prominent ribs, goatees and hooked noses. He read the explanation below them, and discovered they were all representations of akuaku called moai kavakava. Daniel found it hard to look at them. They appeared darkly sinister and angry.

He left quickly. Just being in the same area as the carvings brought up memories he would just as soon forget.

It was a busy afternoon. Daniel turned in his car and cell phone and rented another of each — on his own nickel. For the time being, he decided to stay at the Te Manutara Hotel and foot the bill himself, at least until he could make other arrangements.

The only good news about the day was that apparently Gomez had not told anyone about the loaning of the Beretta to Daniel, so he was not asked to return it. Daniel felt better knowing Tiare still had it in her possession. Now, whether or not she knew how to use it properly was an entirely different matter, an issue he would have to address in the near future. But not now. His immediate priority was to encourage Tiare in her recovery.

Daniel entered the hospital and made his way to her room. When he walked through the unguarded door, he discovered two couples, who appeared to be in their sixties, sitting around the bedside. The two men stood up to greet him.

"Daniel!" Tiare exclaimed. "I'm so glad to see you!"

"I'm glad to see you as well. This is your family?"

The closest man smiled and extended his hand, and Daniel shook it. He said, "My name is Eduardo Rapu. I am Tiare's son." He motioned to an attractive, dark-haired woman sitting next to him. "This is my wife, Carla, and on the other side of the bed are my sister, Sofia, and her husband, Pablo."

Pablo reached across the bed to also shake Daniel's hand.

They all smiled and nodded at Daniel.

"Please sit down," Daniel said to the men.

As Eduardo and Pablo took a seat, Eduardo spoke, "As you may know, mother far outlived her husband, our father Ernesto, who died about twenty years ago."

Daniel glanced over at Tiare and thought he saw tears form in the corners of her eyes.

Eduardo didn't seem to notice. "Mother also has eight grandchildren, twenty-eight great-grandchildren, and seven great-great grandchildren. All of them live in Chile, but we can't talk her into moving away from here."

"Why does that not surprise me?" Daniel said with a grin. "Anyway, I don't want to take away from your family time, but I wanted to check in and make sure your mother was doing well."

Eduardo replied, "My mother, as I'm sure you've already discovered, is extremely strong-willed and has told us that when you arrive, we need to leave. I hear you are a student of hers?"

"Yes, she is teaching me Rapanui and the history of the island."

Eduardo said, "We understand that you were one of the investigators for the murders that have occurred here?"

"Yes."

Eduardo added, "Mother has told us that the wrong man has been accused of the crimes. Is that true?"

"Unfortunately, yes."

Sofia then stood and said with a look of concern on her face, "We are worried about Mother's safety. Are you planning to stay until the real man is caught?"

"I am."

Sofia said, "We in the family have talked about this, and we have decided to hire a guard to protect her. We have chosen Felipe Nahoe, who is an old friend of the family and a retired police officer. He has agreed to keep watch mainly during the night, which seems to be the riskiest time. As additional protection, we were hopeful that you would agree to stay at her house."

Tiare blushed. "Children, I know you are concerned about me, but Daniel may have made other arrangements. Anyway, I only have one bedroom."

Daniel said, "I'd be honored to stay with you and keep an eye out. I can sleep on the couch."

"Then it's settled," concluded Eduardo as he stood with all the others. "We'll be here for around two weeks to make sure she's doing well, but you can move in now. Mother had invited us to stay at her home, but it's too small for all of us. We're staying at a local hotel."

Sofia walked around the bed and took Daniel's hand. "We also want to thank you for saving Mother's life. If you hadn't been there when she was attacked, we don't believe she would have lived."

"I'm glad I was able to help," Daniel replied.

With that the four filed out the door of the hospital room.

As they left, a wave of guilt hit Daniel:

Tiare had nearly died — because of me.

Chapter 15

September 21, 2014

As Tiare propped herself up in the hospital bed, she asked, "Daniel, what did you think of the museum?"

"It was interesting to say the least. Did you send me there to see the moai kavakava?"

"That was one of the reasons," Tiare said. "What are your thoughts about them?"

"After my experience with Hitirau, it was hard to look in their direction. I have to admit they had an uncanny resemblance to him."

"There's a reason for that," she explained. "In legend, the original carvings of the moai kavakava were based on an early sighting of Hitirau. These carvings were made of toromiro wood —"

Daniel interrupted, "Toromiro?"

Tiare said, "Toromiro is a species of tree native to Rapa Nui. It is now extinct — gone with the rest of our native trees."

Daniel asked, "What about the symbols I saw on the wooden planks?"

"That is called rongorongo — Rapa Nui's own unique script. As you saw, many different symbols are engraved in the wood. Rather than represent a true language, these designs stand for concepts or ideas. While researchers have made progress in trying to crack the code, the exact meaning remains a mystery."

"Why wasn't the way to interpret rongorongo passed on from your ancestors?"

"Rongorongo could be read only by the 'ariki mau and the elite members of our society," Tiare said. "Remember me telling you about the period that started in eighteen sixty-two, when many of my people were killed?"

"I do."

"Everyone who knew how to translate rongorongo died over those seventeen years."

Tears began to roll down Tiare's face, and Daniel handed her a tissue.

She wiped her eyes. "We not only lost much of our heritage during that time, but also many of our basic human rights. In eighteen sixty-nine the Frenchman Dutrou-Bornier negotiated a contract that converted the whole of Rapa Nui into one big sheep ranch. He brutally ruled the island and treated us as if we were his slaves.

"The final straw was reached in eighteen seventy-six, when he began kidnapping young girls for his own personal pleasure. He was killed by islanders who had reached their breaking point. One year after he died, the population dwindled to an all-time low of one hundred and ten."

"What?"

"It is true," Tiare grimly said. "As I have told you, disease, blackbirding and emigration took their toll. Considering the population was estimated to be five to twelve thousand in eighteen sixty-two, it was a catastrophic drop."

Daniel sat in stunned silence.

"The next landmark event for Rapa Nui was the annexation by Chile in eighteen eighty-eight —"

"Why Chile?" Daniel interrupted, recalling his question from long ago.

"Because the French, who had occupied the Leeward Islands the previous year, seemed content to allow Chile to have possession of Rapa Nui. As you might have guessed, we weren't allowed to choose our conquerors."

"I see," Daniel replied.

"Anyway, in eighteen ninety-seven," Tiare continued, "the Chilean government leased out our island — you guessed it — as a sheep ranch, and all of my people were confined behind a wall around Hanga Roa, much like human livestock.

"In nineteen hundred, when protestors demonstrated about the subhuman conditions, they were rounded up and taken on a boat to be exiled to Chile. They never arrived because they were thrown overboard at sea, and none survived. This reign of terror finally ended in nineteen sixty-six, when we were released from our prison of Hanga Roa and were allowed at long last to roam our own island. Finally, we were granted Chilean citizenship."

Daniel said, "How can you not hate the Chileans for what they have done to you?"

"Hate is a strong word," she said, "though there are many who feel that way, and some in the indigenous rights movement have called for autonomy. But, in fairness and especially over the recent years, Chile has done much for our island. They have helped develop the infrastructure and have promoted cultural tourism. While this is good financially, it is challenging ecologically, with the increase in cars, waste, and demands on our power and water supplies."

Daniel said, "I can't help but wonder if these murders have something to do with those who wish to secede from Chile."

"It's possible, but there is more to it than that. I have had a lot of time to think while I've been lying in this bed. So, let's put our heads together for a moment."

Seeing Daniel's nod, she continued, "First of all, I think we have both agreed that the killer wishes to stop the tourist industry on Rapa Nui. The motivation for this is uncertain.

"And since your experience on Puna Pau and the note left by Gomez, we believe the killer has been influenced by Hitirau. And you have also told me there are no fingerprints which match those of the killer on Rapa Nui, or, for that matter, anywhere in the world. Correct?"

"Correct."

"Now," Tiare said, "two more facts make this even more interesting: One is the cannibalism that is occurring with these murders and the second is the obsidian-pointed spear I was impaled with. Both of these are from Rapa Nui's distant past. Why have these suddenly reappeared in modern times?"

"Could it be that the killer is performing these bizarre acts simply to scare people away?"

"Well, yes," Tiare agreed. "But a piece of the puzzle is clearly missing." She paused for a moment. "What I say next should be kept between the two of us." She lowered her voice to a whisper. "Please close the door."

Daniel stood and pushed it shut.

Tiare's spoke softly. "I believe I have an idea which would explain why the killer wants me dead. You see, my young friend, it is not only my age that connects me to the past. There is something else about me you do not know, and I have purposefully waited until you were ready to hear it. While a few on the island are aware, the knowledge of my lineage has generally faded away as those of my age have passed on."

Daniel sat, waiting.

"You see, Daniel, like a select few of my family before me —

"I am a shaman."

Chapter 16

September 21, 2014

"What?" Daniel couldn't believe what he'd just heard.

"Yes, it is true," declared Tiare, "I am a shaman. While most of my predecessors were men, of the nine children in my family, I was the one, according to my shaman father, who had *the gift*. So, he took me under his wing and instructed me."

Daniel said, "You had told me a bit about shamans before. What exactly do *you* do as a shaman?"

"Most of what my father taught me was of the ways of healing. While in my childhood we were restricted to the Hanga Roa area, when we were able we would sneak over the wall and pick the various herbal plants in the countryside that had medicinal qualities. The quantity was limited because of the deforestation, but my father taught me much about the ones we were able to find. I have treated many an illness over the years.

"Also, in our culture, shamans have a reputation for using dreaming to find answers to challenging questions. Dreaming for us is not falling asleep, but is actually a deep form of meditation, one from where the world of spirit can be entered. In this way, sometimes the waves of the future can unfold before us."

Daniel asked, "Have you dreamed about these murders?"

"I have, many times."

"What have you seen?"

Tiare frowned. "Not as much as I would have liked. Some years ago I began to sense an upcoming evil presence. Any attempt to enter and understand it was blocked time and time again, and I'm certain the entity is aware of me. What I was able to perceive was that it was from deep within the Rapa Nui past."

"Could it be Hitirau?"

Tiare answered, "Hitirau is part of it, of that I am certain. But there is at least one other being involved, and that is where the mystery lies. I am unable to discover who that is. This person sees me, a ninety-four year-old woman, as a threat because of the information I could give you. His first attempt was to try and frighten me away. Since that has failed, the next will be to kill me."

"Not if I can help it."

"Thanks for that. But you should also know, Daniel, if the opportunity arises, he will try to kill you. Because you are younger and stronger, you would not be as easy a target. I'm certain you've noticed that most of his victims have been older — much easier prey."

Confused, Daniel asked, "Why am I that important?"

Tiare sighed, then looked directly at him. "Because, my friend, I have seen you in my dreams, and you are one that is capable of stopping this evil."

"Me?"

"Yes — you."

"Why not someone else?"

"Daniel," Tiare explained, "it is because you are like many shamans; you are able to perceive things that others cannot. Your senses, inner and outer, have been extremely fine-tuned. I would venture to guess that is one of the reasons why you are such a good detective.

"And another thing, Daniel, you should know that to succeed you must go to the source of this evil and confront it. You must pull it up by its roots. Where exactly you will go, I don't yet know. But go there you must."

"How do you know all this?"

"I just do."

"Tiare — will I live through this?" Daniel asked.

Tears came into her eyes as she said, "I . . . just . . . don't . . . know." She covered her face with her hands, as if the future was too much to contemplate, and repeated, "I just don't know."

After a few moments of uncomfortable silence, Daniel and Tiare continued on with his Rapanui lessons. It was hard to believe how well he was grasping the language after such a short time, but his razor-sharp mind, along with his eidetic memory, served him well. Simple conversation was getting to be second nature, and he was even becoming accustomed to understanding more complex sentence structures.

Before Daniel left, Tiare handed him the key to her home, and he was on his way. As Daniel stepped out of her room into the hospital hallway, he discovered a stocky, white-haired Rapanui man sitting in a chair outside the room with what appeared to be a .45 pistol clipped to his waist.

He had a big smile on his face as he spoke in Rapanui, "My name is Felipe Nahoe. You must be Daniel."

"Yes I am. I understand you are here to protect Tiare?"

The smile left his face and he said, "As long as I'm alive, no one will lay a hand on her — *that* I promise you. By the way, the rumor is that you are staying around until the real murderer is caught?"

"That's true."

"The whole community is behind you. Roberto Ika is an odd one, but we all know he is innocent. When the right man is caught, we want Roberto back. Life is a lot more colorful with him around."

Daniel grinned and said, "I'm sure it is."

Daniel's head spun with thoughts of his conversation with Tiare as he drove to her home.

Why me? He kept saying over and over to himself.

It was around nine p.m., and only moments earlier he had stopped at the Te Manutara Hotel and checked out. Daniel had hoped to chat with Alame Koreta, but she was out for the evening.

Daniel pulled into Tiare's driveway, and when he walked up to the front door and started to put the key into the door lock, he caught himself. The faint hint of a distinctive odor emanated from the side of the home. He cautiously walked around the house to a partially open window. It was there that the smell was the strongest, a curious mixture of body odor, campfire smoke and earthiness.

The killer had recently been here, Daniel sensed by the freshness of the odor. Maybe even just a few minutes ago, looking in the window.

Could the killer be in the house?

Daniel had to unlock the front door and step inside; he had to be very alert and careful. He must not forget:

Tiare had warned him.

Chapter 17

October 13, 2014

It was late in the evening, and Daniel sat at an outside table at his best-loved restaurant, El Tiberon. He had just eaten a freshly grilled filet of nanue fish with all the trimmings and was enjoying an after-dinner cup of Darjeeling tea.

Daniel gazed at the beach and smiled as he discovered parents closely following two squealing young children who frolicked in the sand with their toy plastic buckets and shovels. Very soon it would be dark and given the lack of light pollution, unless there was a moon, the surroundings would be pitch-black.

The past weeks had been a whirlwind of activity. Tiare had come home a week after her surgery and seemed as good as new. Her family stayed another week to be sure she was doing well and then flew back to Santiago.

Daniel enjoyed living with Tiare. Since his grandpa's death all those years ago, he had lived alone. It was nice to have someone in the house, someone to talk and share with.

He reflected on the hour he had arrived at Tiare's house, the time when he stood by the window, almost afraid to return to the front door, turn the key in the lock and step inside.

What a chilling experience . . .

Daniel had carefully reached inside the door, groping along the wall in vain for light switch — not there. He then took some moments to let his eyes adjust before he tiptoed through the house, looking into shadows, wondering when, not if, the murderer would strike out at him in a moment of absolute terror.

When he was positive no one but Daniel Fishinghawk was on the premises, he located a light switch, flipped it on and locked the front door as his first line of defense.

Perhaps, he thought, I just missed him.

Daniel sighed — better to move on and leave this memory behind.

He took another sip of his now lukewarm tea, and realized he was feeling closer and closer to Tiare, more so than one might have guessed with the short time he had known her. The longer he thought about it, the more he was certain he had no greater friend in the world. In spite of her life-threatening wound, she had continued to give him Rapanui lessons — as if she were on a mission.

He smiled and thought: They don't make them like Tiare anymore.

Over the past few weeks, though, she had pretty much clammed up about the killer. It's not that she wasn't thinking about the murders; in fact, Daniel was sure she was. If he had to guess, he figured that Tiare wanted to be sure of her thoughts before she shared them with him.

A week or so ago the tourists once again began to trickle back onto the island. Four days ago another older couple, this time from France, were found cannibalized and dead in their hotel room.

Daniel was not surprised.

Salvador Diaz and his entourage had made a speedy return from Santiago, and Diaz held yet another televised press conference.

"Ladies and gentlemen," Daniel heard him proclaim, "the recent unfortunate deaths of our guests was due to another murderer trying to mimic the original killer, Roberto Ika — in other words, a copycat. Soon we will have the new killer behind bars, and our beautiful Shangri-La, Easter Island, will once again be totally safe for those of you who would like to have the experience of a lifetime —"

Daniel grimly thought: or the experience of the *end* of your lifetime.

He had just finished paying the tab for his dinner, when he heard a familiar voice, "Hey Hawk, how's life for the retired detective?"

Daniel smiled as he saw José Tepano approach. "Sit down, José. Can I buy you something to drink?"

"Thanks but no thanks. I'm bushed and just want to go home and stretch out on the couch. Besides, I've got a couple of cold beers waiting for me in the refrigerator."

"I understand. Any news on the investigation?"

"Nothing you wouldn't have already guessed. Diaz brought the same five investigators with him, and he's got them and me working night and day. I believe sometime soon we'll have a new scapegoat."

"No doubt."

José paused in thought, then asked, "Hawk, have you come up with anything?"

"I'm completely baffled and Tiare hasn't come up with any fresh ideas. So I'm just cooling my heels."

"Cooling your heels?"

"Oh, sorry, it's an American figure of speech. I'm just waiting and watching and keeping an eye out on Tiare."

"I don't think you have to worry about her. It would take a battalion of troops to take her out. Tiare will outlive all of us."

Daniel smiled and stood, "You're probably right. Speaking of Tiare, it's starting to get dark — I'd better go check on her."

José also stood. "Good plan. I'll head home as well. Those beers are calling my name."

Daniel grinned and stepped out to his car. He rubbed his arms as he felt a chill in the air. His short sleeved shirt was all at once no longer warm enough.

Daniel wondered: Why has it gotten so cold all of a sudden? With a start he remembered Puna Pau.

Oh, no, he thought. *Oh, no . . .*

Daniel accelerated and sped down the road as fast as his SUV would take him. He honked his horn and swerved back and forth, tires screeching as he avoided pedestrians, dogs, horses — anything that happened to get in his way. There was no time to spare. The wind began to gust and rain sprinkled down on his windshield.

Daniel breathed a sigh of relief as he pulled into Tiare's driveway and discovered Felipe Nahoe sitting in a lawn chair on the front porch.

As Daniel stepped out of the car, he asked, "Hey, Felipe, how are you doing?"

No response.

Daniel walked closer.

"Felipe?"

Daniel flinched as he saw a deep slash mark on the side of Felipe's neck and a large pool of blood under the chair. Daniel quickly checked for a pulse. There was none.

"Tiare?" Daniel yelled as he frantically knocked on the door. "Oh, God! Tiare! Are you okay?"

It was then Daniel heard a scream and two gunshots echo from inside the house. He quickly pulled out his keys, unlocked the front door and burst through it. He heard more than saw the intruder as he exited through the now infamous window.

A trembling Tiare stood by her couch, holding the Beretta at her side. She said, "I am not hurt, but I'm not a very good shot. I'm afraid I missed."

"Are you sure you're okay?" Daniel asked as he saw blood oozing down from a gash on her neck.

Tiare nodded. "Daniel, you must go quickly. And one more thing —"

"Yes?"

"I know," Tiare declared.

"You know?"

"I know where our killer comes from. Daniel, be safe on your journey."

My journey?

Daniel took a deep breath, smelled the singular odor again and said, "Felipe, he's dead." He saw Tiare's eyes well with tears, but there was not a second to spare — his friend would have to deal with this by herself.

He then dashed out the door into the dark night to follow the odor — that awful, evil odor.

Chapter 18

October 13, 2014

D aniel wiped the rain from his eyes as he followed the trail of the killer. He had to be careful; if he ran too swiftly, he might lose the trail. Too slow and he might lose the scent.

As Daniel gradually worked his way out of Hanga Roa, the small amount of ambient light from the city began to fade, and he felt as if he was on the dark side of the moon. He pulled from his pocket the flashlight given to him at Gomez's murder scene and carefully scanned the rocky ground. He could hear no footsteps and guessed the killer was pulling away from him.

Just up ahead was a rare, muddy place.

Daniel shined his light upon it.

Barefoot?

Daniel charged ahead, generally upslope to the northeast, and the rocky ground began to test even his acute tracking skills. Soon all he had was the occasional slight bend in the native grass along with the scent to mark the trail, and even that was fading.

He lectured himself: pick up the pace.

As Daniel scurried along, suddenly he sensed he had lost the trail. He paused in the middle of the blackness for a brief second and inhaled slowly and deeply. He could not find the stench in the air.

It was gone.

The light from the stars through a break in the clouds began to dimly outline the landscape — a stone wall just ahead. He hurried up to and around the wall, breathing deeply, imagining he was a hound on a hunt.

Nothing here.

His shoulders slumped and he managed a vigorous, "Oh, shit!" He turned and jogged back around the wall and along the trail he had followed, looking for something he might have missed.

Still nothing.

He began to question himself and his actions. He shook his head; he was losing his focus. He breathed and brought his scattered mind back to a single point. Tiare and Kip Kelly were right; sometimes answers came to him, ones that didn't follow rules or logic. He asked himself:

Could the killer have backtracked and taken another trail?

No — I would have seen it.

Is there any evidence of a trail beyond the wall?

None whatsoever.

So, where is the trail?

Where else could it be?

It has to be in the wall.

But where in the wall?

He returned to the wall and began to go over it with his hands, inch by inch, foot by foot, crack by crack, boulder by boulder. As he probed, suddenly his hand disappeared into what Daniel thought was a small crevice. He put his face next to it, and there was the scent of the killer. Daniel pulled the overhanging brush to the side, which revealed a small entryway into what appeared to be a cave. Daniel squeezed inside it. The odor hung heavily.

The killer is here.

Daniel shined his flashlight ahead of him and found that the cave widened into a cavern. He listened carefully — no sounds.

He was hypervigilant as he began to stealthily make his way along the damp, rocky floor. While Daniel was nearly certain the killer was far ahead of him, he knew it was not a time to play the odds. He focused his light into every dark corner; he didn't want to risk falling into a waiting trap.

As he moved ahead, numerous brown spiders crawled above him, at his feet and on the walls. Occasionally one would fall on him from the cave ceiling, and some would find their way onto his pant legs. He brushed them off and kept on. Spiders were the least of his worries.

All went well for a short time, and then the cavern abruptly narrowed. Daniel found himself crawling along the floor on his hands and knees, and then on his stomach — like a snake crawling on the ground. Daniel had never been one to be claustrophobic, but the fear of being trapped in the bowels of the Earth began to overwhelm him. His dream when he was on Mount Terevaka rose up to haunt him. He also realized that the farther into the passageway he went, the less likely he would be able to back out.

It was forward or nothing.

He felt pressure from the rocky walls of the cave on his chest and upper back. The sharp points began to dig into his skin. He felt trickles of blood rolling down his side. He couldn't breathe.

Keep moving.

After scraping, inch by inch, along the floor of the cave for an interminable period of time, the space began to widen, and he was once again able to move to his hands and knees.

Soon Daniel stood again and walked along the cavern floor. After another hour or so he began to catch a hint of light from the far distance.

Does the killer have a flashlight?

No doubt the murderer would have some sort of weapon, and Daniel readied himself for a confrontation. Daniel was the best in his class at the police academy in hand-to-hand fighting, and, whether his opponent had a knife, a spear — whatever — he was ready.

To his surprise, as he approached the source of the light, the cavern again narrowed to a small crawl space, and Daniel realized that the light was the exit to the cave. Like the entrance, it was covered from the outside with brush.

Beyond the brush, it seemed to be daylight.

How could this be?

He slowly pulled himself out of the cave into the light of midday, blinded at first. He felt disoriented and lost, and before he could regain his vision he had wandered a good way from the cave entrance.

Where am I?

It was then that he heard the distinct wash of waves upon the shoreline, and farther away a group of women singing in Rapanui. He could understand the words, but the dialect was different from what Tiare had taught him.

Daniel caught his breath as he moved closer and discovered the women were all topless! What . . . what is going on?

Suddenly the singing stopped, and the women began to scream and point their fingers at him. Without warning the all-too-familiar stench almost over-whelmed him.

Then Daniel felt a sharp *thud* on the back of his head.

And everything went black.

Book
Two

Chapter 1

Daniel had a throbbing headache as he began to come to, the bright sun blurring his vision. When his eyesight finally came into focus, he was certain he must have died; an angel from heaven, wearing a lei of white flowers around her neck, was looking curiously upon him.

Daniel tried to move but discovered he was on his back, staked to the ground, stripped naked. A large crowd gathered around him, men wearing loincloths and the women knee-length skirts.

The angel seemed unafraid, keeping her face close to his. Then she spoke in Rapanui, "Look. He's coming around!"

Am I dreaming? Daniel questioned himself. No one could be that beautiful.

Suddenly she was shoved to the side with a shriek, and her face was replaced with that of a scowling, heavily tattooed man. He appeared to be in his thirties, and his tattooed face looked like a skull.

Daniel thought with a start: It's him ... the stench ... that awful, evil, stench ...

"How dare you look that way at the daughter of the 'ariki mau!" the tattooed man said, almost screaming. He pulled his arm high into the air and backhanded Daniel in the face, jerking his head to the side.

That blow was real, Daniel realized as his head swam and his face burned with pain. This is no dream. But how?

The man pulled out a sharpened piece of what appeared to be obsidian, held it to Daniel's neck and said, "I will kill you now, intruder."

"Stop!" a deeply resonant voice boomed from behind the crowd. As they parted, a stout, middle-aged man stepped forward. He wore a white feather headdress and from his neck hung carved wooden ornaments, which jingled as he walked. Walking behind him was a tall man with a smaller headdress.

"Hotu Iti!" the tattooed man exclaimed. "I was about to come and tell you about this man."

"Atamu, I'm sure you were," he said with a look of disbelief on his face.

With more than a hint of sarcasm, Atamu said, "O great 'ariki mau, this man wandered into 'Anakena and was about to attack a group of women. Your daughter was with them. He —"

"Father?" the beautiful angel interrupted.

Hotu Iti looked with love at the young woman. "Yes, Mahina, my daughter?"

"The man did not try to hurt us. He was only walking toward us when Atamu came up from behind and hit him with a rock."

Atamu glared angrily at her. "I was worried about your safety, so I did what any warrior would do. I protected you." He looked back at the 'ariki mau. "The stranger wore very odd clothes that we have removed and burned. And this was in his pants." He produced the pocket flashlight. "See what happens when you press your finger on this place."

Hotu Iti pushed down on the spot and with a *click* the light came on.

An audible gasp went up from the crowd as they at first jumped away, then all moved in for a closer look.

He pressed it again and the light went out.

Once again they gasped.

Hotu Iti handed the flashlight to the man following behind him. "Paoa, as my shaman, I need to know if this is magic."

Paoa held the flashlight, turned it over and over, and answered, "O great 'ariki mau, I don't believe this is magic. We have seen many unusual things since the outsiders have visited us, and I feel certain this can be explained."

"I see," Hotu Iti replied. He knelt down and looked at Daniel.

To Daniel's surprise, the 'ariki mau had a warm smile on his face. "Now, young man, if you can understand me, what is your name?"

"Daniel."

"Dan-iel? That's an odd name. How did you get on our island?"

Daniel thought carefully. What do I tell him?

"Yes?" the 'ariki mau questioned.

Daniel explained, "I came on a boat from a land far, far away. I became lost and drifted at sea. My boat sank far from shore and I swam here —"

Atamu interrupted, "You are lying. Your clothes were not wet when we found you."

Daniel insisted, "That's because I came ashore off to the west. I had been walking for a while and my clothes had dried."

Atamu exclaimed, "You lie even more!" He glared at Daniel. "Your accent is strange, and you know our tongue. How?"

"All languages in these seas are similar. I was taught —"

Atamu shook his head and growled at Daniel, "Say no more, intruder." He turned to Hotu Iti. "I want to kill him. He should not be here. I believe he is a spy trained in our language, sent from across the sea." He brandished his obsidian knife.

Hotu Iti looked at the crowd gathered and declared, "Dan-iel will not be killed. He looks strong and healthy and could be a worthy addition to our Miru clan. Daniel, are you willing to work and earn your keep?"

"I am."

"Very well, then," Hotu Iti said. He looked over at Atamu. "Remove him from these restraints."

Atamu sneered and muttered, "As you say, O great 'ariki mau."

While Atamu was bent over untying Daniel, under the murmur of the crowd Atamu whispered, "Dan-iel, I will kill you the first chance I get."

Daniel grabbed his wrist with a vise-like grip and said under his breath, "I'd like to see you try."

Atamu jerked his wrist free and walked away to join a band of warriors. He, along with them, glared as Daniel stood. Grumbling, the group marched away, their spears with obsidian points clutched in their hands.

Daniel looked closely at their weapons. They were exactly like the one that had pierced Tiare.

Hotu Iti asked into the crowd, "Pakia? Are you here?"

A slender, elderly, white-haired man stepped forward, "I am," he answered.

"Dan-iel needs a home," Hotu Iti said, "and as one of the best fishermen of our Miru clan, would you be willing to let him stay with you and teach him your trade?"

Pakia said, "My wife, Uka, and I would be happy to have him. As you know, our children and grandchildren now have their own hut, so we have extra space. But he will have to work hard."

"I am sure he will." Hotu Iti turned to his daughter. "Come now, Mahina, let us return home. Your mother and brothers will be worried about you." He walked away with Mahina at his side.

After they took a few steps, Daniel saw her briefly turn her head to glance at him.

He had never seen a more attractive woman.

Daniel and Pakia walked a short distance up a gentle slope to the west. Daniel again noticed the distinctive odor, and with disappointment realized the scent was common and not unique to any one person.

When they paused, Daniel looked back toward the east and saw the Ahu Ature Huki, the one that Daniel had visited at 'Anakena, and on it the solo ancient moai. Daniel was shocked to discover the other larger ahu was now barren, the moai lying on the ground beside it.

Daniel asked, "Pakia, why are those moai knocked down?"

Pakia said, "Some time ago the warriors from the east broke through our defenses and pulled them over. But we were able to strike back."

"And?"

Pakia chuckled and added, "And all of the moai at Tongariki were taken down by our warriors. The ahu there now has nothing standing on it except for the shame of the eastern clans."

Daniel was saddened but said nothing.

Before long they came upon a group of thatched huts of varying sizes, which had the appearance of overturned boats. They were at most around three feet high, and there was a central entrance to each of the huts, which faced the sea. The entry was small and looked more like a crawl space than a door.

Daniel asked, "Does your village have a name?"

"Yes, it is called Vai Tara Kai Ua. It is close to the ocean for fishing, and nearby is a natural spring from which we draw water."

Daniel noticed that many of the homes had adjacent stone-fenced garden areas with sugar cane, bananas and yams. Chickens squawked and pecked around the homes.

As they walked on, Daniel's feet became more and more tender. He glanced down at them — huge blisters had formed.

They approached the entrance of a small hut. Daniel looked carefully, and sure enough, there was a wooden carving of a lizard above the entry.

Pakia looked around and yelled, "Uka! Uka! Where are you?"

Over a nearby hill a diminutive, elderly woman came running up to them with a big, toothy smile and more wrinkles than Daniel had ever seen on any one person. She was at least as slender as Pakia, and Daniel guessed the both of them together couldn't weigh more than one hundred eighty pounds dripping wet.

"My Pakia!" she cried out as she excitedly hugged him.

"My Uka!" he exclaimed, kissing her forehead.

She looked at Daniel, her smile widening. "You are a guest in our home?"

"Yes," Pakia answered, "His name is Dan-iel. He is here from a distant land and will be staying with us for a while. You know I can use his help."

"Of course, husband. The loads of fish that you have to carry are far too heavy for an old man." She looked Daniel up and down and said, "We are glad to have you in our home. The first thing to do is to get you a loincloth, and I will make one for you this evening. Second, we *must* do something about your feet. Do you come from a land with no rocks?"

Daniel smiled at her concern. "Where I am from does have rocks, but we cover our feet to protect them."

Uka said, "I see. For now, let's wrap them up with barkcloth. Soon your skin will be strong enough to withstand the rocks."

"Thank you, Uka," Daniel replied, truly grateful.

"Now," she said, "it is getting late, and soon it will be time to sleep. Are you hungry?"

With all that had been happening, his appetite was the last thing on his mind. But, come to think of it, he was famished. "Yes," Daniel said.

"Oh, good," Uka said. "Normally we have plenty of fish to eat, but there was no catch today. So, I have a special surprise. The traps I set out worked very well."

Traps? thought Daniel.

"Follow me," she said.

The three walked over to a steaming rock-lined earth oven, just to the side of the entrance facing the ocean. She carefully pulled out a sizzling bundle wrapped in banana leaves. She sat it on an adjacent rock and slowly peeled it open.

Inside were four cooked rats.

"Help yourself," Uka offered.

Daniel gagged as he lifted one up by the tail and saw it smoldering in front of him, the rat's face contorted in agony.

Daniel asked, "If you don't mind, would you would show me how to eat this? We don't eat rats where I come from."

Pakia and Uka smiled, grabbed two of the remaining rats, bit off the heads, spat them off to the side and began skinning them with their teeth.

Daniel stared in disbelief.

Daniel lay on his back on a reed mat lengthwise in the dark hut. At the other end slept Pakia and Uka, both snoring loudly. Even though he had a splitting head-ache and his feet burned like they were on fire, he had to admit his stone pillow felt surprisingly comfortable. He began to recount the events of the day.

Last night he had been in present day Rapa Nui. In chasing the murderer he had gone into a cave, which he now knew was a portal from the present into the past.

How such a thing could happen he didn't know, but the why of it wasn't as important as his primary mission:

Find the murderer.

At last all the clues fit together. There was no fingerprint match because the killer was from times past, and the cannibalism was also something from old Rapa Nui. The murders had happened during the night, because the murderer's appearance would be too distinctive to attempt killings during the light of day.

Daniel was concerned about Tiare, but knew at this point that whatever happened to her was completely beyond his control. He guessed she was okay; she was a survivor.

As Daniel thought of her, he was ever so grateful for the Rapanui lessons she had given him. Otherwise, he wouldn't have been able to understand what was said here, and if he had been unable to communicate, he'd be as good as dead.

He would search again for the entry to the cave, but he knew it would be difficult to find. He had wandered around for quite some time near-blind from the sun, and after being knocked unconscious, was taken even farther away in an unknown direction. If he ever hoped to get back home, though, at some point he had to find it.

Of course, how could he not think of Mahina, her long dark hair, her beautiful face and her perfectly formed body?

Daniel smiled. He might as well have fallen in love with Snow White or Sleeping Beauty. One thing they and Mahina had in common was that they were fairy tales, completely unattainable.

For now, he had to find some way to get some rest. He knew the challenges he had to face would keep him awake for a while. But in spite of all this, for the moment Daniel grinned.

Like Tiare had said, they tasted like chicken.

Chapter 2

After a breakfast of dried fish and bananas, Daniel and Pakia walked to the coastline to fish. Pakia carried two bundles of fishing line, and Daniel toted a reed basket containing water-filled gourds. Daniel's tender feet were wrapped in barkcloth and he wore a loincloth that Uka had made for him.

As they hiked along, Daniel began wondering how far back in time he had traveled. He asked Pakia, "Tell me about your experiences with outsiders."

Pakia thought for a few moments and replied, "When I was young, white men came in three boats to our island. We were very curious, and when we gathered around them, they pulled weapons to their shoulders which spewed fire and death. Many were killed."

He's talking about the Dutch, led by Roggeveen, who came in 1722, Daniel thought, remembering Tiare's history lesson.

"The next time came much later, when we were visited by two ships with white men who spoke differently than the ones so long ago. They also fired their weapons, but not at us. They played their drums and instruments that whistled when played —"

Fifes.

"— and they were very friendly to us. They also showed us a white tablet, which we were allowed to draw on."

As Tiare had told him, the Spanish came in 1770, and believed they had obtained the land rights of Rapa Nui for Spain with the islanders' "signatures."

"Around a year ago the last ship came, led by a man who I believe was named Cuuk —"

Cook, the British captain who noted the poverty of the island and how some of the moai had been knocked over, came in 1774. Daniel figured it must be somewhere around 1775.

As they reached the shore, Pakia handed one of the bundles of fishing line to Daniel and kept one for himself.

Curious, Daniel asked, "What's this made of?"

Pakia explained, "The line is made of the bark of the hau tree. Your hook is made of stone, while mine is made of human bone."

"Really?"

"Yes. It was taken from the thigh bone of the best fisherman in the history of our island. His name was Kahi, and he died when I was a child. We all called him Kahi because of the large kahi he would catch when he went fishing far out in the ocean. The mana from such a bone is good for fishing."

Daniel searched his memory: Kahi means tuna.

"But the days of kahi fishing have passed. The trees we used to build the boats to take us out to sea were cut down long ago. Now we fish from shore, and the catch is not so much anymore. Maybe today will be different."

Pakia reached down and grabbed one of the small, soft-shell crabs running along the beach and pierced it with his hook. "Watch me first, then you can try."

Next Pakia gathered the fishing line, like he was preparing to hurl a lasso, and swung it over his head faster and faster. He flung the line far into an upcoming wave, and in seconds the line was almost jerked from his hands.

"Ah, the fish are hungry today," Pakia said with a smile. He pulled the line in and, as he landed a small, silvery-grey fish, added, "Wonderful! We have caught one of my favorites, the nanue. We will eat well tonight — unless you prefer rats again."

Pakia laughed at the face Daniel made, unhooked the fish and put it in the reed basket next to the gourds.

"Now, your turn," insisted Pakia.

Daniel baited his hook with another of the soft-shell crabs and awkwardly spun the line above his head and tossed it into the ocean, not going nearly as far out as Pakia's throw. As with Pakia, the line became taut, and Daniel pulled in another nanue fish.

Pakia slapped Daniel on the shoulder. "I think you have good mana for fishing. If you're not careful," he joked, "I'll rename you Kahi!"

They both laughed heartily.

Daniel and Pakia stood on the beach and fished together, and after a long day the basket was full of nanue and many other colorful island fish. They carried it back to their hut where Uka had already stoked up the earth oven in preparation.

Pakia then yelled out, so all could hear, "Friends and neighbors, come share our fish!"

A group of men, women and children gathered around and took portions of the catch. In return, they deposited small piles of taro, sugar cane and yams. Before long, all that was left of the fish were three nanue, which Uka gathered up and, along with a handful of yams, wrapped in banana leaves and shoved the entire bundle into the earth oven.

"Pakia," Uka said, "we have time for the meal to cook. Our new friend should know more of our island lore. Would you tell him the legend of the nanue fish?"

Pakia asked, "Dan-iel, would you like to hear it?"

Daniel replied, "I'd love to."

They all sat down by the earth oven on the rocky soil as the sky began to darken. The sound of soft singing from the nearby huts began to fill the air; a cool breeze brushed against their faces, carrying with it the pleasant aroma of baking fish and yams.

Daniel smiled as he recalled the camping trips with his grandpa and the joy of seeing the flames of an open fire flicker in front of his grandfather's face as the s'mores baked.

Pakia solemnly cleared his throat and began: "Two young mothers went out in the evening to catch fish, and one of them brought along her little boy, Ahina-oioi. The child's mother put her sleeping youngster down and went to the nearby ocean with her friend to catch fish and crabs."

Daniel looked over at Uka as Pakia spoke. She was dreamy-eyed and sat in rapt attention.

"While she was away, an evil spirit named Hiti-kapura came, took the child and tossed him into a nearby pool of water. The child cried and sang this song:

'O mother, my time has come to an end,
The evil spirit Hiti-kapura has me in his grasp,
Reflection of the moon.'

"The mother heard her child singing, and both of the women rushed over to him. When the mother picked up the boy, he became lifeless. Frightened, the mother put him back into the water and he revived. The mother and child both wept and the child sang again:

'O mother, my time has come to an end,
The evil spirit Hiti-kapura has me in his grasp,
Reflection of the moon.'

"The tide rose to where the three were, and a wave washed the little boy off to sea. As he floated away he was changed into a fish. He swam along the coastline until he arrived at Motu Kao Kao."

Daniel asked, "Isn't Motu Kao Kao one of the rocky islets by the town of Orongo?"

"Yes," answered Pakia, looking a little hurt that he was interrupted. He went on. "His mother and her friend followed him there and wept as they watched him swim round and round the rock. Finally, he disappeared into the deep waters and was never seen again. Since that time, the little boy, Ahina-oioi, has been known as the nanue fish."

At the conclusion of the story, Uka rushed over to her husband, held him in her arms and gushed, "Husband, the story gets better every time you tell it."

Pakia smiled and kissed his wife affectionately on the cheek.

Daniel was pleased to see their devotion for each other, and began to wish more than ever that he could find someone with whom to grow old.

The sun began to set behind a bank of clouds on the horizon, and the nearby singing continued to waft along with the breeze.

After their meal, Daniel crawled into the hut and once again lay on his back onto the reed mat, his head resting on the stone pillow.

Immediately his thoughts went to Mahina.

Chapter 3

The sun began to peek over the eastern horizon. Daniel and his adopted family were still sleeping when they were awakened by a voice calling from outside their hut.

"Pakia? Uka? Dan-iel? Are you awake?"

Pakia grumbled from his end of the hut, "We are now." Daniel heard him say to Uka, "I was dreaming that I had hooked the biggest kahi in the ocean. I was about to pull it into the boat when, this!

"I am coming!" he barked to the voice from the outside.

The three emerged to find the shaman Paoa waiting, wrapped in a cloak of bark-cloth against the chill of the morning air.

Daniel looked at Pakia and Uka; they were clearly shaken by Paoa's presence.

"Paoa . . . we were not expecting you," Pakia stammered out. "May I . . . give you food or drink?"

Uka added, "We have . . . fresh bananas!"

Paoa smiled and said in a kindly voice, "No, thank you. I have come to have words with Dan-iel." He spoke to Daniel, "Come, let us walk."

Daniel followed Paoa a short distance from the village. When they reached a cluster of boulders suitable for sitting on, Paoa motioned for Daniel to take a seat, while Paoa claimed the boulder beside him.

Paoa was tall compared to his fellow Rapanui, probably in his late forties, and while slender, appeared toned and fit. His long, straight dark hair was tied behind his head and had some streaks of white. As the sun illuminated his face, Daniel noticed Paoa had a scar that extended from his right forehead into his scalp.

Aware of Daniel's scrutiny, Paoa explained, "A wound from an eastern warrior who decided the shaman of the Miru no longer deserved to live."

"How did you stop him from killing you?"

"Not a problem. I turned him into a rat and stepped on him," Paoa deadpanned.

When Paoa saw Daniel's shocked look, Paoa chuckled and said, "No, no, I'm only joking. No matter what you've heard, shamans can't do that sort of thing. Fortunately, one of our Miru warriors noticed my predicament and put a spear through his head."

"Sounds like a close call."

"It was. Now you wonder why I have asked to speak with you?"

Daniel nodded.

"Dan-iel, as you know, I am the shaman for the Miru, and I work closely with our 'ariki mau, Hotu Iti. While every shaman has different tasks, my main purpose is to assist with healing among my people and to protect my clan from evil."

"Evil?" Daniel echoed.

"Yes," Paoa confirmed, a concerned look on his face. "Which brings me to why I came to speak with you: Over the recent past I have detected a growing darkness on our island, which has become stronger with time. I have not been able to learn how this is so. I believe there is an akuaku, an ancient spirit, involved."

Daniel hoped Paoa did not see his look of surprise.

"Which one, I don't know, but I suspect it may be Hitirau."

Daniel's mouth dropped open, and he couldn't stop himself from blurting out, "How do you know that?"

Paoa asked, "Do you know about akuaku?"

"A little."

"Then you know that each usually stays in a certain area of the island. Hitirau's domain is Puna Pau, and every time I come near there I sense his presence. More lately, it seems he is getting stronger and stronger. So much so, I dare not enter."

Daniel thought: I understand completely.

"Another ability I have as a shaman is to know the truth," Paoa explained. "I heard your words to our 'ariki mau the other day, and I am certain that you were not honest with him."

Daniel broke out in a cold sweat.

"I know what you said about how you got here were lies. But don't be concerned, Dan-iel, I have no need to know where you are from. I do sense, though, that we have the same goal, and that is finding this evil and destroying it. Is that not so?"

Daniel again nodded his head.

"Good," Paoa said. "Dan-iel, I believe we can help each other and there is strength in our union. I also suspect that once you have accomplished your goal, you will wish to go back where you came from, wherever that is. Yes?"

"Yes."

"So, watch carefully for anything or anyone that seems suspicious," Paoa urged, "and I will do the same."

"I will," Daniel replied as they both stood and headed back toward the village.

As they approached the small hut of Pakia and Uka's, Paoa stopped and said, "Dan-iel — you should know that our 'ariki mau is favorably impressed by you, as is his daughter, Mahina."

Daniel caught his breath.

"But beware," Paoa warned, "Atamu greatly desires Mahina, and I believe his interest puts you at great risk. I'm not sure when he will strike, but I am certain he will when he feels the time is right."

"I'll keep my eyes open," Daniel promised. He hadn't forgotten Atamu's death threat.

"You'd better, if you want to live," Paoa said as he parted company with Daniel and slowly walked toward 'Anakena.

Chapter 4

Daniel stood on the shoreline fishing with Pakia, and his mind began to wander. His best guess was that it had been over two months since he had made the transition into the past, and to this point it had been a quiet, day-to-day existence. While the ʻariki mau and his family resided just a short distance away at ʻAnakena, Daniel saw neither hide nor hair of them, and, in spite of what Paoa had said, he began to lose hope of somehow, someway, being with Mahina.

Some days Pakia allowed him to take breaks from his fishing chores to explore the surrounding area, and with each opportunity he tried to retrace his steps back to the time cave. But in spite of searching repeatedly, there was no sign of it. No doubt it was well concealed, like the entrance to the cave from present day Rapa Nui. While he badly wanted to find it, Daniel cringed at the thought of once again crawling through the narrow, tomb-like portion.

At some point he *had* to discover where it was — there was no other option. For now, though, Daniel still knew his main objective was to apprehend the killer, who resided somewhere on the island.

Daniel thought that, by now, the killer would have attempted to murder him. But perhaps he knew Daniel was becoming stronger and stronger. After a couple of weeks of soreness, Daniel's feet had developed tough calluses on them, and he could run, walk or skip over the rocky ground without pain. And the daily, strenuous physical activity made his toned body even more muscular. Daniel could only guess that the killer was biding his time, waiting for the right moment.

Daniel was roused from his thoughts by a familiar voice.

"Lowly fishermen, the warriors who protect you would like some fresh fish for our evening meal."

Daniel didn't have to turn around to know who it was, he could tell by the venom in his voice. He turned to see Atamu at the front of around twenty warriors, the entire group walking toward them.

Pakia turned to face them. "Of course, brave warriors, we have plenty for all. Take what you need."

Atamu spoke to a sullen, brawny man who stood next to him, "Rapahango, take their fish." With that Rapahango stepped forward and grabbed the basket with their entire catch in it.

Daniel gritted his teeth and tried to stay calm.

Pakia said, "But fearless warriors, that leaves nothing for us to eat. Leave but a few."

Atamu sneered and said, "There are rumors that our enemies from the eastern clans will soon come to invade us. We need food to fight far more than you who sit around all day and fish." He smiled a wicked smile and added, "Don't worry, there are plenty of rats around for you to eat."

Daniel finally snapped. He walked up to Atamu and stood toe to toe with him. "How about if we share some rats with you?"

Suddenly the point of Atamu's spear and spears of three of his warriors were at Daniel's throat. Four tiny streams of blood oozed down his neck.

Rapahango said, as he twisted his spear a little deeper into Daniel's neck, "Atamu, as your best warrior, I have earned the right to kill him."

Atamu's eyes blazed with anger. "You have, Rapahango. Dan-iel, the last time you were saved by our 'ariki mau. Now he is at his home in 'Anakena. There is no one here to protect you."

"Please, no!" Pakia pleaded, falling to his knees.

Atamu said, "Ki — "

Before Atamu could finish his command, the howl of a woman echoed from the east.

"Help!" she screamed. "We are being — "

The warriors dropped their spears from Daniel's neck and rushed to the sound of the scream, toward 'Anakena, Daniel running along with them.

A short sprint later confirmed the worst. A horde of warriors from the eastern clans had swarmed over the village, and the first scream they heard was multiplied by manyfold. The Miru warriors were fighting valiantly but were hopelessly outnumbered, falling to the spears and thrown rocks of their enemy.

Daniel gave out a loud roar, and he and the group of warriors plunged into the fray. What a second ago were Daniel's enemies were now his allies as together they tore into their common foes.

Daniel's police training, combined with sheer force of will, made him a fearsome combatant. He killed the first four he faced by crushing their skulls with a large stone, but there were more — many more — to face.

Through the melee he saw Paoa, the shaman, and Hotu Iti himself directing a small group of Miru fighters around what appeared to be the 'ariki mau's home. To Daniel's dismay, in the distance he discovered the enemy had ropes around the sole standing moai. It tottered from side to side as they pulled at it.

"Nooooooo!" Daniel screamed at the top of his lungs. He grabbed a spear from a fallen Miru and sprinted in that direction, killing with swift thrusts any who resisted. Seeing his bravery, a handful of Miru warriors rallied around him and cleared a swath to the moai. They quickly dispatched those who resisted.

The ancient moai was safe — for now.

Daniel heard a piercing scream above the chaos, which came from the area where he had previously seen the 'ariki mau. In a few moments Daniel arrived there, and lying outside a charred home was the 'ariki mau himself. He lay unconscious on the ground, his feather headdress knocked askew, with a large bruise on the top of his head. Next to him lay an attractive middle-aged woman with a broken right leg, the bone protruding through her thigh. She was weeping and pulling at her thick, dark-brown hair.

Daniel squatted down beside her. "Who are you?"

"I am Tavake, wife of Hotu Iti."

"I am Daniel. Where is Mahina?"

Tavake screamed inconsolably, "They have taken her away!"

"Which direction?

She pointed to the east. "That way. Please help her!" Tavake tried to stand, and screamed again as the bone protruded even farther through her skin.

Paoa stumbled up to Daniel and Tavake, his face covered with blood and bruises. "I was dragged away by the enemy and beaten before I was able to slip away." He grimaced as he looked at Tavake.

Paoa turned to Daniel. "I will care for Hotu Iti and his wife and will search for their sons." He quickly surveyed the scene. "The battle is close to being won. But you must go for Mahina before it is too late."

Daniel grabbed his spear and sprinted away to the east, barely making out the tracks of a very large man. When his prey hit a soft place in the ground, Daniel could see that the indentions in the soil were deeper than he might have guessed, indicating that the man he pursed was not only huge, but also carrying someone, probably Mahina.

Shortly Daniel no longer needed to track, as he heard a voice screaming from the far distance, a voice imprinted in his brain.

Mahina . . .

Daniel followed the screams across the rocky terrain, moving swiftly through the fields of rocks. He was certain the eastern warrior and Mahina were very near.

The screaming abruptly stopped.

Daniel accelerated his already rapid pace, and when he rounded a hill he found a gigantic, muscular man, leaning over an unconscious Mahina with a large rock in his hand.

"That'll teach you!" he said to Mahina in a gravelly, threatening voice.

Daniel could see a large scrape on her forehead.

But the giant looked even worse. One of his ears had nearly been torn off, and there were deep, bloody scratch marks all over his back. Carrying Mahina away was not the easy task he had thought it would be.

Daniel used all the skill he could muster as he surreptitiously moved in, silently weaving through the terrain. Just before Daniel was on him, the giant turned and faced Daniel. He was at least six and a half feet tall; his hair was long, black and hung past his shoulders. His physique reminded Daniel of The Incredible Hulk.

"Who are you?" the giant bellowed as he brandished a large rock in each hand.

"I am Daniel of the Miru. I have come for the woman!"

"You shall not have her. She is mine!" the giant said. He bared his teeth and hissed, "Come for her, if you dare."

Daniel locked eyes with him and ordered, "Give her to me now!" He tightly gripped the spear in his hand and boldly advanced toward the giant.

The giant guffawed and said, "Come to your death, Dan-iel!"

Faster than Daniel's eyes could follow, the giant threw the rock from his right hand, which hit Daniel's spear and shattered the shaft. The obsidian point — the mata'a — from the spear tumbled down into a nearby pile of rocks.

The giant then threw the one in his left hand with equal dexterity, hitting Daniel in the middle of his chest with a *thud*, knocking him off his feet onto his back.

Daniel gasped for breath; he felt like he'd been run over by a locomotive. Then he felt the giant's weight on top of him, crushing him, his mammoth hands wrapped around Daniel's neck, squeezing out the little air that was left.

At first Daniel tried to peel the giant's hands off his neck. He quickly realized it was hopeless; the giant was far stronger than he was. He was about to be choked to death, but there was one last hope.

The point of the spear, where is it?

Daniel released his hands from the giant's wrists and began feeling around the rocky ground to either side of him. The pressure on his neck increased.

The sharpened obsidian wasn't there. He tried to grab one of the rocks beside him and strike the giant, but they were too large to pick up.

No luck. I'm going to die . . .

With one last-ditch effort, Daniel reached above his head as far as he could, hoping to find the tip of his spear.

There it is!

From between the rocks, Daniel grasped the obsidian point with his right hand and thrust it with all his might into his opponent's throat.

The giant struggled to his feet and frantically pulled at the spear tip while blood spewed from his neck like a geyser. He sputtered, choked and fell first to his knees and then face forward onto the ground beside Daniel. He didn't breathe or move.

"That'll teach *you*!" Daniel exclaimed with satisfaction as he rose and unsteadily stood above the giant. He raised his arms over his head, clenched his fists and screamed in triumph.

Nearby, several eastern warriors witnessed the fight. When they saw the result, they quickened their sprint toward the east.

Daniel, almost exhausted, turned to Mahina, who was still unconscious but now moaning imperceptible words. He glanced down at his chest and saw a large bruise. He felt his breastbone pop every time he breathed or moved.

In spite of the pain, Daniel picked Mahina up and carried her back to 'Anakena, one step at a time. She remained comatose as Daniel approached the home of the 'ariki mau.

Hotu Iti saw them first.

"Tavake!" he yelled as he ran toward Daniel and Mahina. "Dan-iel has returned with Mahina!"

The 'ariki mau took her from Daniel's arms and walked over to where Tavake lay.

"My daughter!" Tavake cried out as Mahina was gently placed on the grass beside her. As Tavake cushioned her daughter's head in her lap and stroked her head, Daniel could see that her leg had been splinted and the bone pulled back under the skin.

A moment later Paoa appeared with two wiry young boys, who looked like mirror images of their father. They were each holding a plank of wood with rongorongo script on it. Paoa still looked like he had been beaten to a pulp, but the boys seemed fine. Hotu Iti embraced them both. Tears of joy welled in Tavake's eyes as she continued to caress her daughter.

Paoa explained to Hotu Iti, "Kai and Poki were worried the invaders would steal the rongorongo boards, so they took them and hid in a cave off to the west. After I took care of Tavake, I began searching for them, and they came to me when they heard me calling their names. The cave was well hidden in the wall of a cliff. Otherwise I never would have found them."

Paoa looked at the unconscious daughter of the 'ariki mau and said, "Dan-iel, I see you were able to find Mahina."

"I was. Her kidnapper was the largest man I have ever seen. I was able to put a mata'a through his throat."

Paoa first grimaced and then smiled. "You killed the most feared warrior of the eastern clans. His name was Hito of the Ure 'o Hei. Did anyone of the enemy see you kill him?"

"Yes, and they fled."

"Good," said Paoa as he slapped Daniel on the back. "The eastern warriors will now be afraid of the great mana you have. Perhaps this will keep them away for a while."

Paoa saw the large bruise on Daniel's chest and asked, "Thrown rock?"

Daniel nodded.

Paoa carefully palpated the area. "You do know it's broken, don't you?"

"I might have guessed."

Paoa pulled a wrapped up banana leaf from the bag slung around his neck and handed it to Daniel. "In this is some salve. Rub it on your chest twice a day. It will decrease your pain, and the bone will heal quicker."

A few moments later Mahina began to rouse and opened her eyes. "Mother," she asked as she looked up at Tavake, "is everyone all right?"

"Yes, my daughter. Your brothers are fine. Your father and I have been injured, but we are alive and that is what matters."

Hotu Iti walked with his two sons over to his daughter and wife, smiled at all and announced, "Thanks to Dan-iel and Paoa, all of us will be fine."

At that moment, Atamu and Rapahango arrived, both carrying bloodied spears. "Honorable 'ariki mau," Atamu proclaimed with pride, "the eastern warriors have been vanquished, and we are once again safe. I will increase the guard here until we are certain 'Anakena is secure."

Hotu Iti said, "That should have been done long before now."

Atamu scowled at him but said nothing.

Paoa asked Atamu, "Have you heard the news about Hito?"

"No, how many has he killed this time?"

Paoa said, "Actually, it is Hito who has been killed — by Dan-iel."

"What?" exclaimed Atamu. "It is not possible!"

"It is not only possible, it has happened," Paoa said. "Dan-iel also rescued Mahina from his clutches. For years Hito has defeated your warriors. You should thank Dan-iel for what he has done."

"I will never thank Dan-iel for anything. I would have killed Hito myself if I had the chance."

Paoa cracked a wry smile. "Oh, I'm sure you would have."

Atamu seethed and moved toward Paoa.

Daniel stepped between them and warned, "One more step and you'll have to deal with me."

Atamu started to raise his spear, then dropped it to his side. He spat at Daniel's feet and said, "Another time, Dan-iel. Another time." Then he and Rapahango walked away.

Five steps removed, Atamu turned around, glanced at Mahina and asked, "O great Hotu Iti. Is Mahina all right?"

"Yes, because of Dan-iel."

Rage gathered on Atamu's face before he once again turned away.

Chapter 5

The days that followed were spent in recovery. Daniel's main job during this difficult time was reconstructing the burned-out huts. While his chest hurt with every movement, he fought through the pain. Thankfully, the salve provided by Paoa helped.

Along with other coworkers, he replaced the framework above the rock foundation with native toromiro wood, while the thatch was placed in layers of reeds, grass and sugar cane husks. To his disappointment, the huts he was assigned to rebuild did not take him near the home of the 'ariki mau.

In spite of the somber circumstances, every so often he heard the distant giggling of children. Once, when he rested for a moment, he gazed in the direction of the laughter. A large group of children were sitting cross-legged around a woman who seemed to be instructing them.

Mahina? Daniel wondered.

Daniel labored mightily for the hard-working Rapanui people, and he came to care for them more and more. He wished he could somehow save them from their upcoming travails.

The warriors had heightened their patrols, and regularly they would walk by with their spears, on watch for another attack. They kept a wide berth around Daniel, though, and he could sometimes hear them whisper in awe, "Look, there is Dan-iel. He killed Hito."

Daniel smiled to himself. They were afraid of him, and the positive aspect of his newfound fame was that he was not harassed anymore. Daniel didn't hear anything from Atamu, and he was glad for it.

At the end of three days of hard work, Daniel walked back to his new family's hut. For their part, Pakia had continued to fish near their village, and, when he delivered his catch back home, Uka cooked it and served those working at 'Anakena.

It was late in the evening, and all three were exhausted. They sat on the ground and quietly ate the meal Uka prepared: chicken, sugar cane and bananas. They had just finished their food when Daniel glanced over his shoulder and saw two people approaching from the east. As they neared, he recognized Hotu Iti and Mahina.

Daniel stood up, saying, "Pakia! Uka! Guess who's coming?"

When Pakia and Uka realized it was the 'ariki mau and his daughter, they immediately jumped to their feet. From their reactions, a thousand eastern warriors might have been approaching. They both began frantically cleaning up the area around their hut.

Upon arrival, Hotu Iti said, "Greetings, Pakia and Uka! Greetings, Dan-iel! May we sit with you?" Mahina stood by his side, a serene smile on her face.

Daniel couldn't help but stare at her, and he hoped no one noticed.

Pakia shook like a leaf as he said, "Yes, most esteemed 'ariki mau."

Uka's hands trembled. "Come, let us sit down. May I offer you some water?"

"No, thank you, kind Uka," replied the 'ariki mau.

They sat in a circle in front of the hut. The old couple sat as close to each other as possible, trying to find comfort. Daniel sat next to Mahina, who softly smiled at him, sending a shiver up and down his spine.

Hotu Iti said, "First, I must tell you news of Tavake. She is able to get around more and more, thanks to the splint and some wooden crutches Paoa made for her, but the uphill walk to your village would have been too much."

Hotu Iti looked at the large bruise on Daniel's chest and asked, "How is your injury?"

"Much better."

"Good," said Hotu Iti. "Paoa said the salve he gave you would help."

"Please give him my thanks," Daniel added.

Hotu Iti nodded. "We came here to thank Dan-iel for saving Mahina's life. It is my belief that the giant Hito would have defeated any other warrior who might have confronted him. Dan-iel, your mana must be very great to have won such a battle."

The 'ariki mau then looked over at his daughter. "Mahina?"

Mahina spoke with a lilting voice that mesmerized Daniel. She gazed at him with sparkling brown eyes and said, "Dan-iel, I must thank you as well."

"I'm glad . . . you weren't . . . seriously hurt," Daniel somehow stammered out.

Hotu Iti announced, "Dan-iel, I believe such bravery should be rewarded. What boon can I grant you?"

"Nothing. I was just glad to help."

"But you must have something. It is my wish."

Daniel glanced over at Mahina. "Very well, then. Since the reconstruction of 'Anakena is almost complete, I would like for Mahina to guide me around the island and show me some of its beautiful places."

"Daughter, is this agreeable with you?"

"Oh, yes."

Hotu Iti said, "Dan-iel, you may see only the western parts of our island; the eastern are occupied by our enemy. Mahina will know the areas that are safe, so there will be no need for you to carry a weapon. When would you like to begin?"

"Tomorrow," Daniel and Mahina said simultaneously.

Pakia and Uka both smiled at Hotu Iti, and he smiled back. It was as if they shared a secret.

Hotu Iti confirmed, "Tomorrow it will be. Now, Dan-iel I want you to understand some things about us. Perhaps you are not aware that I, as the 'ariki mau, am a direct descendant of the gods. In years past I ruled as a god and had absolute authority."

Daniel nodded and started to understand the apprehension of Pakia and Uka. After all, in their belief system, they were sitting before a deity. How could they not be uneasy?

Hotu Iti continued, "Since the resources of our island have begun to diminish, the warriors have used this as an opportunity to take this authority from me. What happened days ago, the attacking of the 'ariki mau and his family, has *never* happened before and hopefully will never happen again."

Pakia and Uka both shook their heads from side to side and whispered together, "Never again. Never."

Hotu Iti smiled at them. "Atamu and his warriors, as fellow Miru, will continue to protect me and my people and will follow my commands, but like the warriors of all the clans, they no longer respect my supremacy. They have also replaced our ancient sacred ancestors, represented by our moai, with the bird god Makemake. Do you understand?"

"I believe so," answered Daniel, as he recalled Tiare's teachings. "You are saying that some of the people, because of their hardships, have lost faith in the mana of their ancestors, and have been led by the warrior class to revere Makemake?"

Hotu Iti said, "Yes. The ancient ways are changing right in front of my eyes, and there is little I can do to stop it. But enough of this. Another reason we wished to come here was to hear Pakia tell one of his stories. Dan-iel, have you heard any of Pakia's tales?"

"As a matter of fact, I have," Daniel replied.

"Then you already know Pakia is the best storyteller on our island. No one else is so good. Pakia, would you?"

"I would be delighted." Pakia took a sip of water from his gourd and stood.

Daniel grinned. Pakia might have been on stage — about to perform. Daniel waited in anticipation.

"This evening I will tell the story of 'The Woman with the Long Arm.'" Pakia paused a moment, as if for dramatic effect, and went on, "In our ancient past there lived an old woman who had a very long arm. She was quite evil and would capture children with her long arm and eat them."

Daniel flashed back to those cannibalized back in present-day Rapa Nui. Is the killer still moving back and forth between times? Are the murders still occurring?

"After a while," Pakia continued, his eyes bulging ever so slightly, "there remained only two children on the island. One was a boy who she had adopted, and the second was a boy who lived in Hanga Roa.

"One sunny summer day the two boys were playing together. The boy of the Woman with the Long Arm told the other boy, 'Prepare to die; my mother is going to kill you.' The other child said, 'She won't kill me, because I am going to catch the largest kahi in the ocean and give it to her to eat.'

"The next day the adopted child said to his evil mother, 'You should leave the other boy alone. He is my best friend, and he has said he will catch the biggest kahi in the ocean for you.' His evil mother shrugged and said, 'I won't kill him. Tell him tomorrow morning I will fetch a boat, and he and I will set to sea so he can catch Grandfather Kahi for me.'

"That night the two boys met, and the adopted son of the Woman with the Long Arm told his friend of the planned fishing trip. His friend said, 'After we sail off, set up ten heaps of stones around your house.'

"At dawn the Woman with the Long Arm and the boy pulled a boat into the water, and sailed out to sea in search of Grandfather Kahi. Her adopted son, as instructed by his friend, set up ten large rock cairns around her home. When the canoe approached the area called Hakanononga, the boy pointed to the rock heaps outside her house and said, 'Look! There are people standing around your home. They are trying to rob you! Perhaps you can grab them with your long arm.'

"The Woman with the Long Arm smirked and said, 'Of course I can reach them.' When she stretched out her arm over the ocean, the boy saw his chance. He pulled out a piece of sharpened obsidian he had hidden on the boat, chopped off her long arm and threw it into the ocean. The old woman screamed and grabbed for the boy with her normal arm. He twisted away from her, dived off the boat and swam for shore. When he looked back, the Woman with the Long Arm was lying dead in the boat.

"And that," Pakia said, "is the end of the story."

Contented sighs went up from the audience.

Hotu Iti proclaimed, "Good, storyteller Pakia! I've never heard it told better than that, and I've heard it many times before."

Pakia blushed. "Thank you, o gracious 'ariki mau. Your words honor me."

Daniel said, "Pakia, where I come from, after a tale is told we always ask what the moral of the story is. Well?"

Pakia didn't think long. "The moral of the story is this: if you happen to have a long arm, do not stretch it out across the ocean when there is someone in your boat with an obsidian knife!"

They all roared with laughter.

Hotu Iti stood and stretched out his hand for Mahina. "Daughter, we must go. Dan-iel, we will see you in the morning. Pakia and Uka, thank you for the evening. Good night."

Mahina took her father's hand and added, "Dan-iel, please come to our hut at dawn. We have a long hike to do tomorrow." She turned to Pakia and Uka and added, "Good night."

"Good night," Daniel, Pakia and Uka called out to the retreating pair.

Hotu Iti and Mahina walked downhill toward 'Anakena, and Daniel followed them until they were no longer visible. He was bubbling inside and couldn't wait until morning.

All at once, Daniel sensed they were being watched. Someone was spying on them, he was sure of it. Then the feeling disappeared.

The murderer might be still going back and forth between times, Daniel reasoned, but only a few moments ago, he had been close at hand.

Too close . . .

Daniel was in for a restless night.

Chapter 6

The glow of the sun was peeking over the eastern horizon. Daniel was up and excited to spend some time with Mahina. It was going to be a glorious day, perfect for a hike — with Mahina, yes, Mahina. He couldn't get her out of his mind.

As Daniel hurried down the gentle incline and approached 'Anakena, he found it bustling with activity. Smoke rose from earth ovens, men and women were up and about, and children were at play. The sight of Mahina, standing in front of her home waiting for him, warmed him to the core.

"Good morning, Mahina," Daniel called out to her.

"Good morning, Dan-iel, are you ready for our three-day trip?"

"Three days?" Daniel said — surprised.

"Yes, three days. There are far too many wonderful places for you to see in just a day or two, so father said we could take three."

"There's nothing I would like more," Daniel said as he reached her side. "But what about food and water?"

"Dan-iel," she said with a smile, "do you not trust the daughter of the 'ariki mau to think of such things? There are many natural springs along the way, and I know every one. We do not need to carry water. As for food, my people are most generous and will gladly share with us. But to be on the safe side, I will carry a bag with some chicken, bananas, and yams. We will have plenty to eat."

"One more thing," Daniel added, hesitating, "Pakia and Uka expect me back this evening."

"Dan-iel," Mahina said with an exasperated sigh, "must you worry about everything? My brothers, Kai and Poki, have promised to visit their hut this afternoon and let them know you will be gone for more days."

While Mahina spoke, Daniel was at long last able to look closely at her. He guessed she was in her early twenties and tall for a woman, perhaps five foot eight. Her body was a shapely slender to medium build, with her shoulder width closely matching that of her hips. Her Polynesian skin was a fetching light brown, and her soft dark hair hung to just below her shoulders.

She couldn't have been more beautiful.

While Daniel was slowly becoming accustomed to all of the women being topless, Mahina was different — very different. Her breasts were perfectly formed and glistened in the morning sun as he looked at them.

"Dan-iel?" he heard someone say.

"Dan-iel?" Mahina repeated.

"Sorry," Daniel said as shook himself from his reverie. "You were saying?"

Mahina looked quizzically at him.

Daniel couldn't help but wonder if she knew what he was thinking.

"Let us be off," she announced as she turned and walked toward the west.

"Where are we headed?" Daniel asked as he picked up his pace to keep up with her.

"First we will walk along the coastline, and then we will head inland to Akivi, where there are a number of interesting caves. We will spend the first night at my uncle's home."

"Caves?" asked Daniel, his curiosity piqued.

"Yes, caves. Our island has lots of them."

"Are there some close to 'Anakena?"

"In all directions," Mahina said as she raised her arms and turned around in a circle.

He sighed, disappointed. How am I ever going to find my way back home? he wondered.

Oh, well, he figured, now was now, and as he looked at Mahina, he realized there was no place *or* time in the Universe he'd rather be. He smiled at her as they walked across the pristine beach of 'Anakena, leaving behind the solitary moai standing on its ahu, which, thanks to Daniel, was still standing.

They walked for hours in silence along the rocky coastline. They came across scattered groupings of huts, but much of the time the two were alone. Mostly they walked side by side, but when Mahina walked ahead of him he was able to examine her only tattoo — positioned between her shoulder blades.

A number of the Rapanui had tattoos. Many fell short of being an art form, but Mahina's was tasteful. It was white, circular, about three inches in diameter and appeared to be a near perfect representation of the full moon. The detail was astonishing, showing the dark and light portions and many well-defined craters. Daniel knew Mahina meant "moon" in Rapanui, and seeing it move up and down before him as she walked along gave him great joy.

When they reached the northernmost part of the island, Mahina paused and sat on a large rock facing the ocean. Daniel settled down on one beside her. She pulled some bananas from her shoulder bag and handed one to him.

Mahina looked out over the ocean. "Tell me about your home, where you lived before you came here."

"My home is called Oklahoma," he replied, thinking it was wonderful it was to hear that word spoken in this time and place.

"I have never heard of it."

Daniel pointed to the northeast. "It lies in that direction, far across the ocean."

"Is your ocean as beautiful as ours?"

"Oklahoma has no ocean; it is surrounded by land."

"No ocean?" A puzzled look came across her face. "What do you mean, no ocean? Everyone has an ocean."

"Oklahoma doesn't."

"The ocean is our mother," Mahina explained. "She feeds us with her fish and cools us with her wind when the days are hot. And if you sit at her shore, close your eyes and breathe, she fills you with peace. I can't imagine no ocean. It must be awful!"

"It's really not that bad. In Oklahoma, we also have a mother, and she is the rolling hills and plains. Mostly it is very flat there."

"Flat? How is that possible?"

"It is possible," Daniel said. "So flat, that when the sun is setting, you can see far, far away."

"Like when the sun is being swallowed up by the ocean and the light shows everything floating upon it?"

"Exactly."

Mahina asked, "Do you have chickens in Oklahoma?"

"Yes, and many other different animals."

Mahina's eyebrows rose in curiosity.

Daniel grinned at her reaction and said, "In the past, our plains were once inhabited with large herds of buffalo —"

"Buffalo?" she interrupted. "What is that?"

"It's a large furry animal with a big head and horns. Here, let me show you." He grabbed a nearby stick and scratched out an outline in the dirt. "Unfortunately, they were nearly wiped out by hunters, and only a few small herds remain. In the past, this animal was very important to my ancestors for food and clothing."

"What do you do in Ok-la-ho-ma?" she abruptly asked.

"I catch those who do wrong and bring them to justice."

Mahina looked troubled — a long silence followed. When she spoke, she said, "Dan-iel, I have heard that you killed many in the battle at 'Anakena, including Hito."

"That is true."

Mahina asked, "In your work, have you ever killed anyone?"

"No."

"What was it like to kill other humans?"

Daniel thought for a moment. When he spoke, he fashioned his words carefully. "Killing anyone is wrong. But there comes a time when it is necessary. I had to be a warrior and put aside any other feelings — I couldn't think that they had families and others who love them. I knew if I did not kill them, they would kill me. If I were killed, then my people would be harmed."

"Do you consider us to be your people, even though you are from far away?"

"As strange as it may sound, more and more so."

"What you say pleases me, Dan-iel. I must also share that I am grateful for your actions. Because of what you did, I am still here with my family. As for me, I could never take the life of another person."

"I understand."

"Enough talk. If we wish to see the caves before it gets dark, we must go now."

They both stood and swiftly walked along an ill-defined trail inland. Like his grandpa, Daniel had a strong sense of direction and knew they were headed to the southeast. He kept his eyes open for anyone who might be watching them. Still, it didn't matter; Daniel suspected the killer was fully aware of their every step.

After an evening meal of baked chicken and yams, Daniel lay outside of the hut of Mahina's uncle and aunt, Moaha and Kiri. They had eight children and had only enough space for Mahina. It was okay with Daniel, though; he needed time by himself to think.

As he lay on the cold ground outside the hut with his head resting on yet another strangely comfortable stone pillow, he thought about the caves they had explored earlier that day. Several went deep into the mountain, and in many ways they were similar to the time cave. If he happened to find a cave near 'Anakena, how would he know it was the right one? And if and when he was able to ID the killer, what would he do then? How would he bring him to justice?

There were too many questions — and not enough answers.

Chapter 7

Daniel and Mahina were on the trail at dawn, headed in a southwesterly direction. Mahina had assured him that if they didn't leave before everyone else arose, they could be stuck there for a lengthy time. Her relatives seemed to have all sorts of questions about Daniel, and the longer they stayed, the worse it would get.

"Where are we headed today?" Daniel asked as they marched along.

"Today we are going to Rano Kau, the dormant volcano where the Birdman competition takes place. Do you know of this?"

Daniel recalled his conversation with Tiare. "Yes, but tell me more."

Mahina explained, "This is the contest during which the Birdman for the next year is selected. The contestants leave Orongo, climb down the steep cliff of Rano Kau, and swim across the ocean, floating on a bound bundle of reeds called a pora. Eventually they arrive at the islet of Motu Nui, and there they stay in a cave and wait for the arrival of the manutara birds.

"When the manutara lays her eggs and the contestants find them, they place them in their headbands, swim back across the ocean and once again scale the cliff of Rano Kau. Whoever arrives first at Orongo with an unbroken egg is the winner. If the warrior leader himself is a contestant and gets there first, he is declared the Birdman. If his proxy arrives first, he will give the egg to his warrior leader, who is then acknowledged as the Birdman. It is a very exciting competition, and great reward comes to the winner."

Just as Tiare had described it, Daniel thought.

He said, "I have a question for you. While in the village, I thought I saw you with a number of children. Are you a teacher?"

"I am. It is my life's calling," Mahina declared proudly. "Even before I was born, Paoa told my parents that I would be a keeper of the customs of my people and would pass that knowledge on to children. Many feel the ways of outsiders, those who come on ships, are more important than our own, but I know they are not."

She stopped walking, paused in thought, and asked, "May I tell you a secret, one which you cannot share with anyone?"

"Yes."

Mahina moved close to him as if someone might hear. Daniel noticed that she did not carry the off-putting odor that drew him into and through the cavern to the Rapa Nui past. Rather, she had a sweet, attractive fragrance, one that reminded him of flowers.

She whispered, "My father has taught me the secret of reading rongorongo."

"What?" Daniel exclaimed. "I thought that tradition was shared *only* among the elders, and *never* with women."

"That is true, and that is why this *has* to be kept secret. My father wants me to be a strong woman, one who can take care of herself. In spite of what is generally believed, I am certain that women are very much as capable as men, and that goes for interpreting rongorongo as well." Mahina gave Daniel a probing look. "Dan-iel, do you agree?"

Daniel did not hesitate. "I do. My tribe, the Cherokees, has a tradition of strong women. In fact, one of our past chiefs, Wilma Mankiller, was a woman."

"Really? A chief?"

"Yes."

Abruptly Daniel felt a prickly sensation on the back of his neck.

Someone is close . . . too close . . . is it the murderer?

Daniel couldn't hear anything, but his finely-tuned senses screamed to him that something was awry. He put his index finger to his lips and whispered to Mahina, "Be still and listen."

She silently nodded.

Suddenly Daniel and Mahina were surrounded by a large group of warriors, all holding spears pointed at them. A tall, stately man, who appeared to be the leader, stepped forward.

"My name is Ropata," he announced, "and I am the leader of the Marama warriors. You have entered our territory without permission. Who are you and what do you want?"

Daniel stepped forward. "I am Daniel of the Miru, and I —"

Ropata interrupted, a look of amazement on his face, "Dan-iel? The same Daniel who defeated Hito?"

"Yes."

"Then you are my friend and not my enemy. Hito had killed many of my warriors, and I am forever in your debt."

Ropata glanced at Mahina and smiled, "Your face is familiar. Are you not the daughter of Hotu Iti?"

Mahina did not return the smile. "I am," she answered.

"Very well, then," Ropata said. "You may be on your way. What is your destination?"

"Rano Kau," Daniel replied.

Ropata said, "I will send a runner to notify the Hau Moana clan of your coming so their warriors will stand aside. Are you returning to 'Anakena soon?"

"Tomorrow night."

"Good. It is said that in two days the shamans from all of the clans will decide on those for this year's Birdman competition. It will be the largest ever, with two from each clan. I'm sure you will want to be there for the choosing. I hope I am one who is selected."

Before he turned away, he added, "Safe travels, my friends. You will meet no enemies among the Marama."

"Safe travels to you as well," said Daniel.

Ropata and his warriors walked over the hillside and soon they were out of view.

As Daniel and Mahina continued their hike, Daniel hid his concern. He realized that with his growing attraction to Mahina, he had let his guard down. He promised himself:

It won't happen again.

Farther down the trail, Daniel once again thought of the killer he was pursuing. He remembered his previous conversation with Tiare and wanted to know more.

"Mahina, I need to ask you a question, which may be a little . . . well . . . touchy."

Mahina studied him and said, "Dan-iel, when two people are friends, there should be no subject about which they cannot speak."

Her words warmed him. Daniel was a bit more comfortable when he asked, "Is cannibalism part of your culture?"

"Why do you ask?"

"Just curious."

"The answer is mostly no. But it has happened."

"Such as?"

"There have been rare reports of it when people are confronted with starvation, but it mostly occurs in the warrior class for one of two reasons: Either they wish revenge on their rival warriors or they want to become stronger. Warriors believe that when one consumes part of their enemy's body, they also take in their mana. The greater the number of their enemy they consume, the stronger they become in all ways, but especially in battle."

"I see. So if I were looking for one who practices cannibalism, the most likely place would be among warriors?"

"Yes," Mahina said, a questioning look in her eyes.

They trekked on . . .

It was late in the evening when Daniel and Mahina stood at the edge of the sea cliff of Rano Kau, overlooking the ocean. They had first walked through the bustling village of Orongo, where the people prepared for the upcoming Birdman competition.

As they hiked, on nearby trailside boulders Daniel noticed numerous carvings of human figures with the heads of birds. He could only guess they represented the Birdman. Also, he saw engravings of a particular face, mask-like in their appearance, with prominent noses and eyes. From his prior readings he knew they were representations of the Rapanui creator of humanity, the fertility deity Makemake.

A cool wind blew in their faces as the sun sat just above the horizon. Daniel could easily see the three islets — motu — in front of him. The closest was the needle-like Motu Kao Kao, then the flat Motu Iti, and farthest away was the final destination of the Birdman participants, Motu Nui.

Daniel recalled that Tiare had said it was almost a mile swim. He shook his head; it looked a lot farther than that.

Mahina pointed to a breach in the wall of the inactive volcano. "The contestants start from inside the crater, and go over the breach, called Kari Kari. From there they work their way down the cliff to the ocean below."

"Is it dangerous?" Daniel asked.

"Many have fallen to their deaths, not only going down, but also coming back up. There is also the risk of sharks."

Why did she have to remind me? Daniel thought.

"But for now," Mahina said, "let's sit and watch the sun set over the ocean." She took long, deep breaths and closed his eyes, as if meditating.

As they sat, Daniel had a hard time keeping his eyes off Mahina. Over the past two days he had felt more and more attracted and yearned to touch her. But it wasn't the right time — not yet, anyway . . .

Daniel shook his head. He needed to concentrate on the task at hand, that of finding the killer.

Isn't that what I'm here for?

Daniel focused his sharp mind on who the most likely suspect was. Could it be the first person who confronted him — who was somehow close to him when he emerged from the cave? The one who despised him because of Mahina's attraction? The one who hated outsiders? The warrior — the one who wished him dead?

Atamu?

Chapter 8

Daniel and Mahina had awakened early and were working their way back down the steep hillside of Rano Kau, headed toward the southern coastline.

Daniel let his thoughts drift back to last night. After they watched the sun set, they shared from the provisions Mahina had packed. It was not a heavy meal by any means, but Daniel was learning to subsist on smaller portions, far different than what it was like in the United States. Mahina had packed a barkcloth blanket in her bag, and they covered themselves with it and drifted off to sleep.

He enjoyed feeling the heat from her body under the blanket.

By mid-morning they walked alongside the gorgeous coastline. The temperature was comfortable, and the cool wind combined with the rhythmic crashing of the surf felt calming and meditative. Settlements dotted the area, and there was plenty of private time in the space between them.

When the sun was directly above them, Daniel and Mahina stopped at a home and asked for food. They were given generous helpings of fish and taro root. They took their donated lunch and sat on large stones facing the ocean.

After they finished their food, Mahina abruptly said, "Dan-iel, I heard the words you said to my father when you first arrived, but I don't believe it is an accident that you are on my island. So, tell me, why are you here?"

Daniel started to protest then thought better of it. "Mahina," he said, "I am looking for a murderer, a man who has killed many people."

"A murderer, here on our island?"

"Yes."

"How would he get here without my people knowing about it?" Mahina looked confused.

Daniel felt caught. How much should I say? Can she handle the truth?

Finally he added, "Mahina, the killer is one of your people."

She put her hand to her mouth and gasped. "It is not possible."

"It is," Daniel insisted. "And the reason I asked you those questions yesterday about cannibalism?"

"Yes?"

"The killer has cannibalized each of his victims."

"No!"

"It's true," Daniel confirmed.

Mahina studied Daniel with open curiosity, and Daniel could tell she was measuring her words before she spoke. After a long pause she said, "Something is not right. I know there is something you are hiding from me. Do you trust me enough to tell me?"

"I do."

"Well?"

Daniel knew at some point this subject would have to come up, but he wasn't quite ready to talk about it now. After some moments of uncomfortable silence, Daniel blurted out, "Mahina, I am from the future."

Mahina's expression did not change and she calmly asked, "Well, man from the future, how did you get here?"

Daniel couldn't tell if she was humoring him or taking him seriously. "I came through a cave, a passageway from my time to yours."

"Where is this cave?"

"Somewhere near 'Anakena. I had just emerged when Atamu attacked me. I have no idea of the exact location."

"Do you have any thoughts about who the killer is?" Mahina asked.

"Anything I say would be a guess, but after our conversation yesterday, I believe he is likely a warrior."

Suddenly Mahina began laughing, at first a little giggle, then a full-fledged belly laugh. "Dan-iel," she said between bursts of laughter, "I believe you are crazy."

"I am not!"

"Oh, I think you are. What you have said is, well, it makes me laugh. Is this a joke?"

"This is no joke."

Mahina laughed even harder, and Daniel felt his face burning with embarrassment. "Is there anything I can say that will convince you?"

"Not a thing," she answered, wiping the tears of laughter from her face. "Come," Mahina said as she stood, "let us head back to 'Anakena. I promised father I would be home by midnight."

Daniel stood and walked behind her. With that one conversation, his hopes and dreams were dashed. He felt like crying.

Daniel and Mahina had been in complete silence since their conversation earlier that day. He could tell she was deep in thought and chose not to interrupt her.

The dark of night began to surround them as they approached the summit of Mount Terevaka. Daniel recalled now — it seemed forever ago — when he first came to Rapa Nui and how he had dreamed of the time cave in this location as he napped. As far as he could tell, the surroundings were the same as before, except the eucalyptus trees were missing; they had been planted in later years.

Daniel quickly scanned the area with not only his eyes, but also his inner senses. He could detect no other presence, evil or otherwise.

At the peak, Mahina stretched out the blanket on the grass and said, "Dan-iel, lie down and gaze at the stars with me."

In the darkening sky the Milky Way sparkled brightly in spite of the crescent moon just peeking over the horizon. Mahina pointed at the cluster of stars and asked, "What do they call that in your country?"

"It's called the Milky Way. It's beautiful, isn't it?"

"Yes, it is."

"There are stars seen in your sky that we cannot see in Oklahoma."

"Really?"

"Yes," Daniel said. "For example, one such group of stars is just above us, the Southern Cross. Many other stars are here that I don't recognize."

They lay quietly watching as the night deepened, and the stars became brighter and brighter.

"Dan-iel, I have given much thought to what you have shared with me," Mahina said, breaking the silence. "I must be honest. I don't believe you are from the future. No one can go back into the past, and no one can go forward into the future."

"Before my experience in the time cave, I would have said the same thing."

"But just for fun," Mahina smiled and added, "for the moment let me join you in your delusion. Tell me what the future is like."

Daniel said, "I live in a time that is many years in the future, and a number of wonderful things have happened. We have developed engines —"

"What are engines?"

"They are devices that make things move. In this way, we are able to travel without walking, not only on the ground, but also in the air —"

"In the air?"

"Yes. We have invented ships that fly higher than you can see, and some time ago we were able to send a man to the moon."

"That is not possible!"

"Oh, but it is. And many diseases have been healed. Because of that, people live longer and longer."

"It all sounds wonderful. But what about hunger? Is everyone fed?"

Daniel said, "Well . . . no."

"What about water? Does everyone have water to drink?"

"No."

"What about war?"

Daniel was starting to get a little embarrassed. "We still have that."

Mahina said, "Here on our island, we have a strong connection with Mother Earth. Do you?"

Daniel confessed, "I'm sorry to say that most in my world live in cities, and they rarely step on the earth itself."

In the dim light Daniel could see a look of confusion growing on her beautiful face.

"Dan-iel, I'm not so sure your world is as wonderful as you say. You tell me you are chasing a murderer across time from my island. So murders still happen in the future?"

"Yes."

Mahina concluded, "It sounds to me your world has some of the same problems as we have, and perhaps more."

"In many ways, you're right," he said.

Mahina asked, "What about my people? What happens in the future?"

Daniel sighed. "There will be much devastation for your people. You will be afflicted by continued warfare among yourselves, diseases, and you will be horribly oppressed by outsiders."

Mahina's lower lip began to quiver. "What about our traditions. Will they survive?

"Many will, but the art of rongorongo will be lost, as all those who knew how to decipher it will be killed. Most rongorongo tablets will be lost or destroyed, and the twenty-five left are priceless artifacts that are scattered across the Earth."

"None left behind on my island?"

"None."

Mahina stayed silent for a long time, though finally her quivering and her look of concern changed into a soft smile. She lay up on her side and edged close to him. Her pleasant scent surrounded him, and the rising moon lit up her face.

"Dan-iel," she said, "I am certain you are out of your mind, and I'm not sure I believe anything you have said. But I've never met anyone like you. You are strong, wise, and there's something about you that attracts me. If I had to guess, I'd say it's the goodness in you."

Daniel could barely talk. He somehow managed, "Mahina . . . I am strongly attracted to you as well."

"A question?"

"Yes?"

"Suppose, just suppose, that what you've said is true. When you find your murderer, will you go back to where you came from?"

"I will."

"Do you love me?" she asked.

"I do," Daniel affirmed.

"Dan-iel, I love you too. I believe with all my heart that surely, somehow, we will find a way to stay together."

"I certainly hope so," Daniel said.

With that she put her hand on his chest, and leaned over him. At first they kissed gently, then hungrily. As Daniel reached down and slipped off her barkcloth skirt, she did the same with his loincloth. At long last he was able to kiss and caress her soft breasts, a desire he had to repress from the very beginning of his time here.

"Dan-iel," she whispered softly in his ear, "I want to feel you inside me."

"And I want to feel you around me," he whispered back.

As the moon shone down and the gentle breeze cooled them, he rolled on top and gently entered her. They pressed their bodies against each other, sharing each other's passion.

In the moments to come, two breathtaking explosions would occur at the summit of Mount Terevaka — ones that only the two intertwined lovers could hear.

Much later, when the moon was high overhead, Daniel would return Mahina to her home. But at that ecstatic moment, the thought never crossed his mind.

Chapter 9

Daniel and Mahina stood together in the middle of a large crowd that gathered before Paoa the shaman, who was preparing to announce the Miru's two contestants for the Birdman competition. A nervous murmur echoed through the throng.

Hotu Iti was conspicuously absent, but many warriors were there, including Atamu, who stood out with his skeleton-tattooed face.

It was early in the morning, and Daniel smiled at the ever-beautiful Mahina — his love. As they waited, Daniel's mind wandered back to last night.

Daniel returned Mahina to her home shortly before midnight, the moon reflecting in her eyes as he kissed her goodnight. He would have preferred to have spent the night curled up together, but felt it important to keep Hotu Iti's trust and return Mahina by the promised time.

Daniel came back to Pakia and Uka's home shortly after, and they were so excited to see him you would have thought he had returned from the dead. Pakia emerged first from the entrance.

"Uka!" he yelled as he excitedly jumped up and down. "Look who's come home!"

Uka popped instantaneously from the doorway. "Dan-iel!" she shrieked as she leaped into Daniel's arms, hugging him tightly. "We are so glad you are back!"

Pakia added, "We have missed you!"

"Pakia — Uka, I've missed you too." Daniel felt immersed in their love.

A glistening tear rolled down Pakia's cheek, but he managed a smile and said,

"Dan-iel, fishing isn't the same without you. I am certain that the fish bite better when you are around."

Daniel laughed. "It's hard for me to imagine that's true, but since you're the best fisherman the Miru have, I suppose I have to believe you."

"We've been waiting up hoping you will tell us of your adventures," Uka told him.

"Oh, I will."

Uka raised her eyebrows and added, "We must know *everything*."

Daniel smiled to himself; he felt like a teenager coming home from a date. He would let them know the basic facts — but no more.

Certain events of life were not meant to be shared.

Daniel's pleasant thoughts were interrupted . . .

Paoa at long last began to speak.

"My fellow Miru, long we have waited for this moment, the time of choosing of our two contestants for the Birdman competition. As you know, it is a great honor to be picked, and it is my solemn duty to select those who will give our clan the greatest opportunity to win. I have spent many long hours in contemplation and have made my choices."

Daniel began to feel a knot in the pit of his stomach. Surely not . . .

"My first selection is Atamu!"

A roar went up from the crowd.

Atamu screamed at the top of his lungs and shook his spear above him. His fellow warriors responded in kind.

"Atamu, as our warrior leader," Paoa declared, "if you win the competition, you will be the Birdman for the next year."

Again Atamu and his fighters shouted their approval.

Paoa then said, "Atamu, the next selection will be your proxy. If he wins, and you survive the competition, you will still be the next Birdman."

Daniel thought again: Surely not . . .

Paoa turned to Daniel, a slight smile curling at the corners of his mouth.

No! No! No! Daniel thought.

"My final selection," Paoa announced, "Is Dan-iel!"

A loud gasp went up from the crowd. Everyone turned to look at Daniel.

He felt Mahina touch his back in reassurance.

Atamu screamed out, "As the head warrior of the Miru, I reject this choice! Rapahango has earned the honor. Dan-iel is an outsider!" He glared at Paoa, "I demand that you choose Rapahango!"

Paoa sternly ordered, "Atamu, step to the front."

When Atamu came forward, Paoa moved face-to-face with him. Paoa stared at him with an intensity that brought the crowd to silence. In a deep, powerful voice, he said, "Atamu, do you challenge my right as shaman to make this decision?"

Atamu stared back, and they held each other's gaze for what seemed like an eternity. Finally Atamu blinked and answered, "Very well. I will honor the tradition of our people."

Paoa nodded and whispered to him, "I'm glad you've come to your senses." He proclaimed loudly so all could hear, "Dan-iel, congratulations on being selected!"

As the crowd cheered, Atamu glowered and stepped away from Paoa. He walked over to Daniel and muttered under his breath, "Dan-iel, some day everyone will see what a coward you really are. On that day I will laugh." Atamu then marched over to join his fellow warriors.

Stunned, Daniel said nothing. He stared straight ahead with only two thoughts on his mind:

Heights and sharks.

Oh, God . . .

As the crowd diminished, Mahina turned to Daniel. "What is wrong, my love?" She gazed at him with concern.

Daniel said, "I know this gives me the opportunity to check out those who would most likely be my suspects, but there's something about me you don't know." He hated to tell her this; he was afraid it would diminish her opinion of him. "You see," he finally confided, "I have a fear of heights and sharks."

Mahina reached over and hugged him. "Dan-iel, what is the origin of these fears?"

"When I was a little boy I was up high in a tree when a storm hit and I was almost killed. I don't know where the fear of sharks some from, but it's there . . ."

"All fears have some basis," she said quietly. "Yet there is not *one* that cannot be overcome. I will be present at Orongo for the competition and will support you in any way I can."

"Thank you."

"You should know, Dan-iel, that selection to be a contestant in the Birdman competition is not only very risky, but is also a great honor. A victory will bring great mana to the Miru."

He nodded in understanding.

"I must go now. I need to tell my parents the news of the announcement. They will be very happy to hear of your selection." She pulled him close and kissed him.

As she walked away, in spite of the recent turn of events, Daniel couldn't help but smile.

Before Daniel returned to his home village of Vai Tara Kai Ua, he decided to make a visit to the home of Paoa, situated on the outskirts of 'Anakena. As Daniel approached the hut, he found Paoa sitting quietly out front, cross-legged, with his eyes closed. Paoa opened his eyes and turned his head to face Daniel.

"Please, sit down," Paoa requested.

"Why did you choose me?" Daniel asked as he sat.

"First of all, Dan-iel, one of my duties as shaman of the Miru is to select the two who would most likely win the Birdman competition. You were actually my first choice, but I thought picking Atamu first would diffuse some of his anger. Unfortunately, it didn't."

"But —"

"And second," Paoa interrupted, "I wanted to give you the chance to be around a group of warriors from all over the island. While I'm not certain of this, the evil we spoke about so long ago could originate from them. This adventure is not without risk, but I am convinced that at some point during the competition, you will know whether or not the evil you seek is there."

Daniel heard the wisdom of his words. "Paoa, I am grateful."

"Remember," Paoa continued, "we both have the same goal, so when I help you, I help myself. Now, about the competition: Even now, the feasting has started in Orongo, and many of the contestants will join in the festivities. You are welcome to attend, if you wish. In the months to come, the manutara birds will visit Motu Nui and lay their eggs. You must be on the islet to gather one and be the first to deliver it to Orongo. Win or lose, I am confident that you will have answers to your questions once it is completed. Best of luck, Dan-iel. I wouldn't have selected you if I didn't believe you could win."

Daniel smiled at Paoa and stood to leave. After they said their farewells, Daniel walked away in a quandary. The thought of what he would have to do, made him want to scream and run away. But he knew he couldn't.

His was to do ... or to die ... in the trying.

Chapter 10

Daniel stood with nineteen other competitors at the ceremonial village of Orongo, waiting for the signal to begin. It was early in the morning and Daniel had his pora — his reed float packed with provisions — securely attached to his back. He was ready to begin — or was he? How he would react when he arrived at the rim of Rano Kau was anyone's guess.

Shamans chanted in the background as Daniel looked around at the numerous spectators, trying to find the most important one — Mahina. He finally located her in the crowd, yet her bright smile could not mask the look of concern on her face.

Daniel began sizing up his competition and became more than a little concerned. As they stretched in preparation, most looked like human spiders that could move up and down the cliff without any difficulty whatsoever. Daniel was pleased to see Ropata, his Marama warrior friend, who returned his glance with a friendly nod. Daniel then spotted Atamu, standing off to the side, growling and angrily thumping his chest with his fists, as if he hoped to intimidate one and all.

As Daniel waited, he thought about the past two months. How wonderful it had been!

Daniel had spent most days fishing with Pakia; still he felt responsible for earning his keep. After spending the day with Pakia, the two of them would have dinner with Uka. Daniel never tired of baked nanue fish, and the daily catch was always good enough that they never again had to resort to eating rats.

Thank goodness, thought Daniel with a grin.

Evenings, though, were always reserved for Mahina. Over the months, the more

Daniel came to know her, the deeper he fell in love. They walked hand in hand up and down the beautiful Rapa Nui beaches, sometimes in silence, but more often in conversation about their respective days.

If they were able to get an earlier start, Mahina would humor him, and they would scour the area around 'Anakena for caves. Daniel prayed they would somehow stumble upon the right one, but all of their searches were fruitless. Either the cave was too big, too small, or too high or low off the ground.

Gradually, Daniel's hope of finding the cave began to lessen, not that staying here wasn't a pleasant possibility — it was — but it just wasn't home. He never said anything to Mahina, but in his heart he began to wonder whether she would come back with him if he found the right cave. As bright as she was, Daniel was confident she would be able to adapt to the modern world.

Daniel's was truly an idyllic existence. But there remained a killer on the loose, and, like it or not, he still had a job to do.

Suddenly the background chanting ceased and the crowd hushed as the shamans of the ten clans marched silently to the front. Daniel wasn't surprised to see Paoa move before the gathering and speak.

"Welcome all to the Birdman competition, where the winner will be chosen for the next year."

A roar of approval went up from the crowd.

"This year, for the first time, we have allowed two representatives from each clan, and they have been carefully selected by those who stand behind me."

The group of shamans bowed their heads in recognition.

"We have determined that the arrival of the manutara birds on Motu Nui could occur any day, so it is now time for the contestants to leave our company and await the birds there. Once they fetch an egg, the first to return an unbroken one to this place will be the winner.

"Contestants," he boomed out, "do you have any questions?"

"No!" they all yelled in unison.

A murmur of excitement arose as Paoa instructed, "I will raise my arm, and when it falls, you may be off."

Paoa slowly moved his right arm upward, and the participants gathered at the starting line, jostling each other for position as they awaited the signal.

Paoa screamed as he quickly dropped it to his side, and the contestants sprinted as a group into Rano Kau, headed toward the large breach on the southwestern portion, Kari Kari.

Daniel was close to the front and felt his heart in his throat as he neared the rim, knowing that on the other side was a sheer drop of a thousand feet — and he had to climb down it to reach the ocean floor. As he reached the edge, he froze and thought:

I can't do it!

The other contestants weaved around him and scrambled down the steep cliff with reckless abandon, loose rock flying in every direction. Before long they were well past him and moving down the cliff. Daniel had just sat down to catch his breath when he heard laughter from Orongo, starting first as a chuckle or two, which gradually developed into a chorus of guffaws. Daniel heard voices yell out over and over again:

"A coward! Dan-iel is a coward!"

Daniel could handle the scorn of others, but what must Mahina be thinking? He steeled himself and made himself sit on the edge overlooking the ocean. Abruptly he heard a scream from below, and he cringed as he saw a man slip on the rocky scree and tumble down the cliff, yelling all the way — to land with a distant *thump* on the beach. The man was only a tiny dot from his perspective, but Daniel could still see a pool of blood form around him.

A second contestant did the same thing, landing close to the first. The remaining participants at first froze in their positions and then more patiently edged themselves down the cliff.

As he sat and watched his competitors move down, Daniel recalled that he had tried repeatedly over the years to heal from his fear of heights and had no success. He had tried everything, or so he thought. At this point, though, he was desperate.

What to do?

Daniel closed his eyes and slowly breathed in and out, and this time, rather than trying to push his fear away from him, he invited it to be present.

Daniel saw himself as a little boy, perched high in a cottonwood tree overlooking the Illinois River in Oklahoma, screaming as he held on for dear life in the middle of a howling thunderstorm. Somehow Daniel knew that, for him to heal, he had to merge with his fear and soothe it. His grandpa had applied the balm of love all those years ago, though now he had to do it himself. He began silently saying to himself, over and over:

"Breathing in, I am aware that I am fearful.

"Breathing out, I smile at my fear and send it love."

Time no longer mattered as he sat in deep meditation, and the jeering voices disappeared from his awareness. Daniel was holding and reassuring the fearful little boy inside himself, when he had an astonishing revelation:

I no longer need to carry my fear.

It is from the past — and the past is over.

It is time to release it.

When he opened his eyes, he looked over the edge. Many of the contestants had already reached the beach and were swimming on top of their poras, headed toward Motu Nui. Daniel stood, lifted his fist to the sky, and screamed in defiance of the fear that had paralyzed him for so long. He heard an unexpected cry from Orongo, and when he looked back he saw a solitary woman also holding her fist upward.

Mahina!

Daniel waved at her, watched as she waved back, and then began to work his way down the stony cliff. His fear hadn't left completely, but at least now it was manageable. He looked at the sky and discovered it was already late in the afternoon. He had sat longer in meditation than he had realized.

Daniel picked up the pace and before long caught up with a straggler. They were both several hundred feet from the bottom of the cliff face when the other man prepared to leap from a rocky outcropping into the ocean, presumably, Daniel guessed, to save precious time.

The man first threw his pora into the ocean and then dived headfirst into the water. Daniel heard a squishing sound like that of a watermelon dropped to the floor, and the next moment he saw the man floating face-down, motionless, on top of the water. What appeared to be his brains — and his pora — floated beside him.

Daniel grimaced and concluded: rock just below the surface.

Daniel eventually reached the beach and, the minute he arrived, he sprinted to the water, leaped onto his pora and began swimming out to sea. Sure, he was scared of sharks, but this paled in comparison to his fear of heights. Daniel guessed the basis of the fear of sharks had originated as a little boy. Perhaps, he reasoned, he had seen one too many shark movies. Whatever — it also was in the past.

The realization made Daniel grin for a brief moment as he paddled on in the chilly, deep-blue ocean.

The sun was just beginning to set as Daniel dragged himself onto the slippery surface of Motu Nui, exhausted, cold and hungry. When he ascended, he discovered the surface of the islet was larger than he had guessed from a distance, probably around five acres in size. He looked across the choppy ocean at Orongo, which soared high above him. The flames from a blazing fire reached high into the sky.

Before long he heard the muffled sound of voices and discovered a narrow

entrance to a cave, nearly covered by grass. Daniel crawled inside and found the re-
mainder of the contestants huddled around a small grass fire, eating their meager
provisions.

Daniel sat in silence next to his friend Ropata, pulled out a water-filled gourd
from his pora and drank sparingly. There was no water source on Motu Nui and he
had to ration carefully, no matter how thirsty he was. Of course he could drink rain-
water — if it came — but he couldn't count on that.

He grabbed a portion of his dried fish — now soaked with ocean water — and
as he ate he sensed pure hate being directed at him. Daniel didn't have to look at the
source to know where it came from.

The man with the skeleton tattoo on his face.

Atamu.

Chapter 11

Daniel awoke drenched in sweat.

He was miserable; his forehead felt as hot as a bed of coals, and he was coughing and aching all over. He'd give just about anything for a couple of aspirin, some hot chicken soup and a soft bed to lie in. Instead here he was lying on the cold rock floor of a cave with only a loincloth to cover him.

It was early morning, and the sun was just starting to peep through the narrow entrance, bathing the interior with a dim light. Daniel knew a number of caves were on the islet, and this was likely one of the larger ones, measuring somewhere around twenty feet long by twelve feet wide. When he entered the previous night, Daniel had found he couldn't stand to his full height in the cave and guessed it was around five feet tall. Close to the entrance, a primitive painting of a large red face, with black eyes and a white outline, stared blankly at him.

Daniel did a silent head count and discovered all of the seventeen remaining contestants were in the cave, most asleep, some coughing as Daniel was. He wanted to get up and walk outside, but was too weak. He sipped on his water and lay in silence. Soon he fell back asleep, and after a period of fitful, restless slumber, he began to dream . . .

Daniel walked alone on a Rapa Nui beach, carrying a spear in his hand. It was late at night, and a full moon glowed overhead. A warm ocean breeze playfully tousled his hair.

He was headed toward his home in 'Anakena, one he shared with Mahina and their three small children. His family expected him, and Daniel couldn't wait to hold them in his arms.

How could he be happier? He was married to the love of his life and, except for the occasional skirmish with the eastern clans, his existence was peaceful and joyous.

Daniel arrived in front of their oh-so-familiar hut and announced, "Mahina, darling, I'm home!"

No answer.

"Mahina, are you there?"

Suddenly there was a bright flash of light, a sense of spinning and disorientation, and he found himself lying alone on a bed at the Te Manutara Hotel, head propped up on a pillow, staring at the blank wall facing him. No Mahina, no children, no home, no ancient Rapa Nui — no nothing. Where did they all go? Did they ever really exist?

He never felt so alone. His anguish was overwhelming. He began to scream . . .

Daniel felt strong hands shaking him.

"Dan-iel? Dan-iel? Are you okay?"

As he opened his eyes, he saw Ropata observing him with a concerned look on his face. Daniel glanced around the cave — no one else was there.

"Ropata," Daniel said, feeling a little disoriented, "I'm fine. I guess I was having a nightmare."

Ropata said, "Dan-iel, you are very flushed. I believe you have a fever. When I heard your screams from outside the cave, I came to check on you."

"I'll be okay," Daniel lied. Truthfully, he felt like he'd been beaten with a sledgehammer.

"Whatever you say, but if I were you I'd stay here and rest. All of us have fish-hooks and are trying our hand at catching something to eat. I'm sure I'll hook some extras, and I'll be happy to bring some for you."

"Thanks Ropata."

Ropata smiled at him, then walked to the cave opening and lifted himself up and out into the bright sunlight.

Daniel lay for a few seconds before he suddenly realized:

I'm alone.

It was a golden opportunity.

He sat up, looked around and noted all the poras were unattended. Maybe he would find something that would help him solve this case. Daniel looked again at the cave opening.

No one there.

He had to act fast. First he decided to check out Atamu's pora, and as quickly as he was able, crawled over to it and began pulling out objects from the inside. First he removed several articles of food — all soaked. There was an obsidian knife — no surprise.

Suddenly Daniel heard conversation and footsteps coming close to the cave entrance. He had to act fast. In a last desperate thrust, he reached inside one final time. All the objects felt familiar — except one. It was small, rectangular and smooth.

What is it?

He heard footsteps just outside the opening as he pulled the unknown article out. In his hand was a silver cigarette lighter, with the initials *AG* on it. Daniel quickly stuffed it and the other objects back into the pora and made it back to his place just before three others walked into the cave.

AG — Alejandro Gomez.

Daniel had all the evidence he needed. As he had suspected —

Atamu was his man.

The sky was just beginning to darken, and all the contestants were back in the cave sitting around a smoldering grass fire. Daniel had nibbled at the cooked fish Ropata had given him, but he just didn't have much of an appetite.

All in the cave snapped to attention when distinctive screeching sounds were heard from the outside. Manutara birds were landing on the islet. During the night some would lay their eggs.

Tomorrow was the day they'd waited for, and once an egg was the first to be delivered to Orongo, the Birdman would be declared. But Daniel had a lot more on his mind.

Can I make it back to Orongo?

Alive?

How do I deal with Atamu?

For now, Daniel closed his eyes and tried to sleep. In the morning he would face the greatest challenge of his life. Meanwhile, his dream was nagging him, haunting him, pushing him to a point of nausea.

He couldn't imagine life without Mahina.

Chapter 12

At the first light of dawn Daniel, who felt at least as bad as he did the day before, was up and out of the cave along with all the other contestants. Hundreds of screeching black and white birds dotted the island — manutaras. Everyone scurried from bird to bird, brushing aside any that were sitting on the ground, hoping to find an egg underneath. Over his shoulder, Daniel heard a shout.

"I've got one!"

An excited man held out a small white, speckled egg for all to see, then hustled back down to the cave to grab his pora. When he emerged a few moments later, the egg was secured in a small reed basket tied around his forehead. He jumped into the water and began swimming away as fast as he could.

Daniel frantically searched everywhere — no luck. Then another contestant found an egg, then another. Ropata found one and yelled at Daniel before he jumped into the sea, "Hurry my friend, before it's too late."

Before long, many — even Atamu — had found eggs and were swimming toward Orongo.

With a sense of desperation, Daniel scoured the area — over and over again — and finally found an egg on a steep slope, which dropped sharply off into the ocean. He precariously reached over the edge and grabbed it before rushing back into the cave.

Once inside, he discovered his pora had been slashed into pieces. It didn't take much imagination to figure out who had done the deed. Fortunately, the little reed basket was unharmed, and he placed his egg in it, strapped it to his head, ran out of the cave and jumped into the sea, chasing after the others and swimming without the support of his damaged pora.

Daniel was determined. Not only did he hate losing, but more importantly he wanted Mahina — *and* the Miru — to be proud of him.

Fortunately the seas were calm that morning, and he swam with determination and strength. He gradually crept up on the pack that once had been well ahead of him. Soon he was in the middle of it, advancing toward the front. Hope began to well up in him.

The encouragement didn't last long. Daniel heard a loud crunching sound and a shriek from someone to his left.

"Shark! A shark has me . . . Help!"

A pool of blood surrounded the man as Daniel reached for him. The man lurched and let out one last sputter before he disappeared into the water.

Daniel's fear of sharks once again rose up to meet him, and he found himself near panic.

What can I do?

Not a damn thing . . .

The sharks were in a feeding frenzy. Soon a second, a third and a fourth went down, and Daniel felt like he was swimming more in blood than he was in water. Then it came to him — he quickly swam away from the bloody water to clear seas. Daniel reasoned that, if he could set himself apart, he would have less chance of being attacked.

Even more went under, screaming and gurgling as they vanished beneath the water. Daniel lost track of how many. Soon Ropata swam to his side, and together they made a beeline for the shore.

Many anxious moments later they set foot on the beach. Daniel looked back; no remaining swimmers were there — they had been wiped out. Anyone left would be far behind — maybe still on Motu Nui.

Daniel eyed the sheer cliff and counted three contestants ahead. Climbing near each other, they were about a hundred feet up.

Atamu was one of them.

Daniel grimaced as he watched Atamu grab the man next to him by the hair and yank him off the wall. The screaming man fell to the beach and was impaled through the chest by a sharp rock. Daniel paused for a moment to help him, but after a few jerking motions the man died.

What else would you expect from a murderer? thought Daniel.

Daniel and Ropata both leaped onto the cliff wall, chasing after those above.

"I can still do it this," Daniel told himself as he fought back fatigue. In spite of the speed he was ascending, Ropata was faster and began to edge ahead, closing in on the others.

From above, Daniel heard Atamu announce, "I have a present for you."

All at once a shower of rocks rained down on him, a heavy one striking his head and causing him to see stars. Thankfully the rocks had missed the egg so carefully cradled on his forehead, and stars or no stars, Daniel was grateful.

Then he felt something dripping on his arm. When he looked up, he realized the blood was streaming from a large cut on Ropata's back.

"You okay?" Daniel yelled up to Ropata.

"I'm fine," Ropata said, "nothing that beating the shit out of Atamu would not take care of."

Daniel smiled briefly. He felt the same way.

Suddenly another man fell, whizzing past Daniel, screaming all the way to the bottom. While Daniel couldn't see what had happened, he was certain Atamu had also pulled him off.

About halfway up, Daniel felt like he was about to pass out. No doubt he was dehydrated, still had a fever, and the exertion was beyond anything he had ever experienced. But he had to keep moving — he had to . . .

Minutes passed into hours, and as Daniel thought of Mahina he picked up the pace. Daniel began to hear the buzz of the crowd from Orongo and knew he must be getting close to the top. He pressed harder and soon found himself just below Atamu and Ropata, who were standing on a thin rock ledge and shoving at each other.

Atamu said to Ropata, "Marama warrior, are you ready to die?"

Ropata responded, "You first," and hit Atamu in the chin with his fist, nearly knocking Atamu off the edge.

Then Atamu unexpectedly kicked Ropata's legs out from under him, and Ropata fell and clung by his fingers to the thin rim of rock he once stood on.

"No!" Daniel screamed from below.

"Oh, yes," Atamu said as he looked down and scowled at Daniel.

Atamu pulled his obsidian knife from his pora, and with one deep cut sliced off the fingers of Ropata's left hand. Ropata defiantly grunted and held on with his right hand, sweat pouring down his face.

Daniel quickly moved up to secure his friend. Before he could get there, Atamu once again brandished his knife and sliced off the fingers of Ropata's other hand. Ropata yelled out "D - a - n — i — — e — — — l" as he plummeted to his death.

Daniel had never felt such rage in his life, and his pressing fatigue suddenly became a forgotten memory. He crawled up as fast as he was able to the place where Ropata once stood, barely dodging the swipes of Atamu's knife.

Atamu said, "How long I have waited for this moment. Dan-iel, now it is your turn to die."

Daniel answered by striking him with a lightning-fast blow to the chest. Atamu momentarily bent over from the punch, then tried to kick Daniel's legs out from under him, as he had done with Ropata. Daniel sidestepped the kick and once again landed a crushing blow, this time to Atamu's flank.

Atamu groaned and, as Daniel moved in, unexpectedly sliced the air in front of Daniel's face. Daniel leaped back but lost his balance and fell off the edge. It took every bit of strength he had left to catch the rim with his fingers.

Atamu smiled his skeletal grin and smugly said, "Well, Dan-iel, it seems you are in the same predicament as your friend. Let me help you join him at the bottom."

As Atamu leaned over him with knife in hand, Daniel found a last burst of strength and grabbed Atamu's wrist. Atamu's eyes bulged as Daniel yanked him over the brink.

At the last second Atamu grabbed Daniel's hand, Atamu's knife spiraling away. Now Daniel was clinging to the ledge with one hand, while Atamu held on for dear life to the other.

Sheer panic spread across Atamu's face. "Dan-iel! Don't let me die!"

"You scum," Daniel said, "you deserve to die — but not now." As Daniel started to pull him up, their hands began to slip apart.

"Dan-iel, hold tighter!" Atamu demanded.

"I'm trying."

"Nooooooo!" Atamu screamed as he finally slipped out of Daniel's grip, flailing wildly as he fell to the ground far below.

No one could survive such a fall, reasoned Daniel.

Justice is done.

Daniel pulled himself over the edge of Kari Kari. He paused here for a moment, remembering how he had frozen as he tried to go over the edge those days ago. He looked down at the beach and discovered that a handful of stragglers were now ashore and taking a wide berth around the bodies scattered there. As far as he could tell, no one else was on the cliff, and those on the beach had no chance of catching him.

Daniel could barely walk as he stumbled down the trail which led into Rano Kau. After what seemed like an eternity, he struggled out of the dormant volcano toward Orongo, where a cheering crowd awaited. As he grew closer, he saw Mahina — tears streaming down her cheeks.

The group of shamans stood at the front. Paoa stepped forward to greet Daniel.

Daniel said to Paoa, "Where is Rapahango? I must speak with him."

Paoa turned around and called out in a thunderous voice, "Rapahango, step forward!"

From the crowd Rapahango emerged and stood facing Daniel, spear in hand.

"Rapahango," Daniel announced, "Atamu is dead."

A loud gasp went up from the crowd.

"Now as second-in-command, you are the leader of the Miru warriors, so I declare that you are the Birdman for the coming year."

A loud cheer went up as Daniel unstrapped the reed basket from his head, removed the egg and handed it to Rapahango, who dropped his spear and received it with his palms up.

Rapahango screamed at the top of his lungs, and along with the ecstatic crowd, began to dance down the hillside.

"Well done," Paoa said. "I knew I had chosen well." He lowered his voice and whispered, "Did you find the evil you were searching for?"

"I did."

"Atamu?"

Daniel nodded.

"I might have guessed," Paoa said with a knowing look. "I'd like to hear more, but now I have other duties to perform, which will take a number of days. If I don't see you again, safe travels back to your home, wherever it may be."

"Thank you," Daniel said. His heart felt heavy. "I'll miss you and your wisdom."

"And I you and yours." With that, Paoa momentarily grasped Daniel's shoulder, then he stepped away and followed the crowd. He glanced back briefly and nodded his head in approval.

Daniel saw Mahina walking toward him. As they embraced and held each other tightly, Mahina whispered in his ear, "Dan-iel, you are strong and brave, just as I thought you were. I love you with all my heart."

Daniel's exhaustion suddenly hit him, and everything became fuzzy. He barely eked out, "I love you too . . ."

As he passed out, Mahina's strong arms caught him.

Chapter 13

When Daniel opened his eyes, he discovered he was in a small, dimly lit room with Mahina leaning over him. Groggy as he was, he managed a weak, "Where am I?"

"In Pakia and Uka's hut," answered Mahina softly.

"Aren't we in Orongo?"

"My love, that was three days ago. When you didn't wake up after you passed out, I was able to get two of Rapahango's warriors to carry you back here. You have been tossing and turning ever since. I have been worried sick about you and couldn't leave your side. What would I do without my Dan-iel?" Tears pooled in her eyes.

Daniel brushed her tears away. Then he remembered — he had been running a high fever.

Mahina continued, "You were so hot, so terribly hot. But that is now gone. I was hoping you would wake up soon — and you have. Would you like some water?" she asked, a gourd in her hands.

"Yes, yes," Daniel said as he took it from her and gingerly drank.

Daniel asked, "I suppose you heard me say at Orongo that Atamu is dead?"

"I did."

"Before he died," Daniel confided, "while on Motu Nui I found evidence that linked him to the killings. I'm certain he was the one I was looking for."

"Really?"

"Yes."

"So your work here is done?" asked Mahina, a concerned look on her face.

"It is, but I still have no idea where the time cave is." Recalling a conversation from long, long ago, he added, "Mahina, do you believe the moai can speak to those who need answers?"

"The moai are the living essence of our ancestors. It is my belief they possess great powers, and yes, I feel they can and will talk to those who are sincere in their questions."

"Have you ever talked to one?"

"No," she confessed.

"When I am stronger," Daniel said, "I'd like to try. Perhaps one can give me the information I need."

"Perhaps . . . but enough of this. I must tell Pakia and Uka that you're awake. They will be pleased to know you are better."

She turned away, stepped outside and called for them.

As he waited, Daniel was sure he noticed some discomfort on Mahina's face as he talked about leaving. In fact, Daniel sensed that she was actually starting to believe him about the time cave. But, without knowing the cave's location, there was nothing for her to worry about.

At least, not yet.

Three days later, at sunset, Daniel sat on a large smooth stone in front of the solitary moai standing at 'Anakena. While still not at full strength, he felt capable of sitting in meditation and planned to be here till sunrise, if necessary. Mahina had offered to sit with him, but he declined. He knew he had to do this by himself.

Daniel had chosen this particular moai for several reasons. First, it was close and easy to get to. Second, he recalled how both Alame and Tiare had some sort of affinity for it. Finally — and he smiled to himself as he thought about it — since some months ago he had personally been involved in keeping it erect, perhaps if the moai did indeed have some sort of consciousness, it might be favorably inclined to help him.

Daniel again fondly recalled his grandpa, and how he had once told him that, if one needed inspiration, it was best to fast and spend time in isolation to make your mind receptive. And so, since noon, Daniel had chosen not to eat and kept to himself. Strangely enough, he didn't feel hungry.

His grandpa had also told him that spirit and matter were connected through the breath. "Concentrate on your breath," he had said, "and before long you will enter the world of spirit."

Daniel heard the evening chatter of 'Anakena murmur in the background as he closed his eyes and began to focus his attention solely on his breath.

Breathing in, breathing out . . .

Breathing in, breathing out . . .

Breathing in, breathing out . . .

Over and over again. Without being consciously aware of it, his breath gradually became shallower.

In minutes, hours, days — there was no way for him to tell — Daniel's surroundings completely disappeared from his consciousness, and all that was present was his breath. He suddenly felt his mind expand upward to first envelop the moon, then the sun and the planets, and eventually exploding outward to encompass the entire universe, and, for that moment in time, he and all of existence were one.

Daniel was surprised to discover that the universe had a pulse, a rhythm, just like his breath, expanding, contracting, in and out, in and out. He was not only breathing with God, he *was* God.

All at once he found himself walking along a beautiful beach. Daniel didn't recognize it, but he was sure it was on Rapa Nui. He strolled along, watching the waves flow in and out — with a rhythm much like his breath — and shortly he came upon a young boy playing in the sand next to the water.

Daniel asked, "Who are you?"

"Sit down beside me," the boy requested.

Daniel did and felt the cool ocean water wash upon him.

The boy smiled at him. "Here — take this stick and draw with me in the sand."

Daniel grabbed it and began to doodle along with the boy, and they both laughed. Daniel looked closer at the boy; there was something about him that was familiar — uncomfortably familiar.

Finally Daniel asked, "Are you . . . me?"

"You guessed it," the boy said. "I was beginning to wonder how long it would take you to figure it out." The boy giggled. "I am the little boy that lives inside of you. Everyone has one, you know, well, except for women — they have a little girl."

Daniel again joined the child in laughter, and then asked, "Why are you here?"

"Don't you know?"

"No," admitted Daniel.

"I am here to show you the way back home. You do want to get back home, don't you?"

"Oh, I do."

"Good. Now, look at my drawing in the sand. I've put an X where you start; that's where you live now. If you follow this line, you will see that the trail curves around this hill, then around this one. Here you will walk around a rocky area until you come to a small tree. I believe it's called a toromiro."

Daniel looked carefully at the sand drawing, recognized the landmarks and knew exactly where it was. He had walked by it at least a dozen times. Daniel asked, "Why have I not seen the cave before?"

"It is well hidden," the boy answered. "Poke around behind the tree, and you will find it."

"Thank you," Daniel said.

"I'm glad to help. Now, it is time for you to go."

"Before I do," Daniel said, "may I ask a question?"

"Yes?"

"I thought I was coming here to talk to the moai, and I ended up talking with part of myself. What happened?"

The boy responded, "Don't you see? All answers to any questions already exist within you. All the statue did was to help you to know that. Oh, and by the way, the statue thanks you for protecting it."

Daniel smiled. "Tell it — you're welcome."

"You can do that yourself." He stood as did Daniel. "Come see me more often. We can have fun together."

"How do I do that?" Daniel asked.

"Anytime you are like a little child, innocent, playful and happy, we will be together, whether you see me or not."

Daniel closed his eyes for a moment, and when he opened them the boy had disappeared, and he found himself sitting once again in front of the moai. The morning sun was just peeking over the horizon.

Daniel looked up at the moai and respectfully said, "You're welcome."

The moai stared at him silently.

Daniel somehow knew he had heard.

And now Daniel headed toward Pakia and Uka's home.

There was much to do before he took his departure.

Chapter 14

Daniel, with much on his mind, gradually walked up the gently sloping hill from 'Anakena to Vai Tara Kai Ua. He felt confident of the information he had received while sitting in front of the moai and was certain he could find the entrance to the time cave.

Still — thoughts crossed his mind, thoughts that made him doubt whether he really wanted to find it. He could stay here in old Rapa Nui and enjoy time fishing with Pakia, though he wanted to spend most of his hours with his love, Mahina.

But the more he considered it, the more he knew his work here was done. The primary reason he was here was to find the murderer, and he had done that. And as much as he loved this life, he itched to return home. But he couldn't help but wonder:

Will Mahina come back with me?

A sense of melancholy caught up with him as he approached Pakia and Uka's hut. Pakia scurried around the front, preparing his fishing lines for a day of work.

Pakia paused to yell out, "Uka! Come out! Dan-iel is back!"

Uka promptly popped out of the hut with a big smile on her face. She hurried to Daniel and put him in a death-grip of a hug.

"Dan-iel, I must know. Did the moai speak to you?"

"Yes, in a way."

Pakia joined in. "What did it say?"

"I was told how to get back home."

"Honestly?" Uka said, in awe.

"Yes."

A look of concern came over Pakia's face. "When will you be going?"

Daniel's response was harder than he could have ever imagined. After a few moments, he managed, "Now . . . I must go now."

Uka began to sob, "But Dan-iel, you are like . . . family to us. We don't . . . we don't want you to leave!"

Daniel touched her cheek. "Uka, you are like family to me as well, but I must go home. Before I do, I must share that many dangers will face you and your people in the years to come, and I was hoping that you both would join me and come to live in my land."

Pakia and Uka at first looked stunned, and then Pakia put his arm around Uka and answered, "Dan-iel, this is our home, and this is where our family lives. We love you, but we cannot go with you."

A tearful Uka blurted out, "Are you sure you have to leave?"

Daniel fought back the urge to say no. "Pakia and Uka, I love you, too, but I have to find my way back."

Pakia was now crying as well. "Dan-iel, since you are set on leaving, take this with you and think of us when you see it."

He handed Daniel a fishhook — the one from the thigh bone of the legendary Kahi — one that Daniel knew was Pakia's favorite.

"I can't."

"You can," Pakia insisted as he carefully closed Daniel's hand around the fishhook.

Daniel's eyes misted as he turned to leave. "I'll miss you."

Pakia and Uka clung to each other, tears trickling down their faces. Pakia begged, "We'll miss you too. Don't go . . . please . . ."

"I must go," Daniel said reluctantly. "I must . . ."

He took one last long look at his dear friends and headed down the slope to 'Anakena.

He held the fishhook in his right hand for the longest time before attaching it securely to his loincloth.

Daniel walked directly to the hut of the 'ariki mau and found the entire family was gathered in front of the home, eating fresh bananas for breakfast.

Mahina jumped up and embraced him, whispering in his ear, "Did you find the answers you sought?"

When Daniel whispered back, "Yes," he felt her shudder the slightest bit.

Daniel and Mahina sat down together, facing Hotu Iti and his wife, Tavake. At that moment her brothers Kai and Poki ran off to play.

Hotu Iti said in his deep voice, "Dan-iel, we have seen you sitting through the night in front of one of our oldest moai. Were you looking for answers?"

"Yes, and I have learned how to find my way back home."

Hotu Iti asked, "And which way is that?"

"Sir, before I answer, I must share something you don't know about me."

Hotu Iti raised his eyebrows. "Yes?"

Before Daniel spoke, he glanced at Mahina, who had a pained look on her face. How hard this must be for her, he thought.

Daniel cleared his throat and said, "I am not from this time. I came from the future through a cave, which I lost track of. The moai told me how to find it again."

There was dead silence. Hotu Iti and Tavake were obviously astonished, while Mahina closed her eyes in discomfort.

Hotu Iti finally replied, "Dan-iel, what you have said I do not understand. Let me sit in silence for a few moments to ponder your words." He and his wife closed their eyes, while Daniel and Mahina waited.

After a while, Hotu Iti opened his eyes. "I see the truth in what you have spoken. And I must say that I always knew there was something different about you, something special. Now I know why."

Daniel knitted his brow and said, "Hotu Iti, before I leave I must tell you that many difficulties are coming to your island. Times of famine, continued warfare, disease, and many other plagues will come upon you and your people. I would like to offer you and your family the opportunity to escape all this and come with me back to my time."

Hotu Iti responded, "Dan-iel, you are kind to offer, but I have a responsibility to my people. No matter what you say might happen, I must stay and guide them through the upcoming troubles."

Tavake added, "And I stay with my husband."

Daniel had expected that response and went on, "Hotu Iti, Tavake, I understand your commitment to your people. Now about Mahina —" He reached over and grabbed Mahina's hand. As he looked at her, he discovered her face was puffy and streaked with tears. "You both must know that I love your daughter with all my heart. So I must ask if Mahina may come with me."

Hotu Iti did not seem surprised. "Dan-iel, Tavake and I have raised Mahina to be a capable woman. I have always wanted her to be self-sufficient and able to make her own decisions. You must already know that."

"I do."

"And so this choice must rest with her. I suggest you ask her, and I will abide with whatever decision she makes."

Tavake said, "And I as well."

Daniel nodded, turned to Mahina and took both of her hands in his. "Mahina, I love you and I want to share my life with you. I want us to marry, have children and grow old together. Will you come with me?"

Tears freely flowed down her face. "Dan-iel, I love you too and want to share my life with you. Before I make my decision, I must ask a question."

"Yes?"

"If I come with you, will I be able to return to visit my family?"

Daniel's face dropped. "No, when I return the time cave must be closed permanently. To leave it open would be too risky."

Mahina turned and looked at her parents, then back at Daniel. "Then here is my decision: I cannot leave my parents, my brothers and my people. If hard times are coming, they will need me." She clutched Daniel's hands even tighter adding, "You must go on without me."

Daniel felt his throat closing; he could barely speak. "Mahina, are you sure about this? Once I leave, you will not be able to find the time cave without my help, and we will never see each other again."

Mahina gazed at him silently, confusion troubling her beautiful face.

Daniel thought quickly. "You could at least walk there with me. Perhaps you will change your mind."

Mahina said, "There is no reason for me to come with you. I will not change the decision I have made."

Hotu Iti said, "Then it is done. Dan-iel, I wish you well in your travel back to your time. May you find happiness. We will miss you. You have brought much honor to your people, the Miru. For many years to come we will speak of how you defeated the dread warrior, Hito, and how you came to win the Birdman competition."

Daniel responded, "Thank you for all the kindness you've shown me. I will always be grateful."

Daniel then grasped Mahina's hand, and both stood. He softly asked, "Are you sure?"

Mahina had no words; she merely nodded.

One last look and he released her, turned and slowly headed out of 'Anakena, southwest toward the time cave, hoping she would find it in her heart to change her mind and come with him.

Daniel turned and looked back over and over again, and with each glance there was no one in view. When 'Anakena disappeared from his sight, he bent over at the waist and wept uncontrollably.

When he was finally able to straighten up and walk again, he knew he had lost her forever.

No words could describe his pain.

Chapter 15

Daniel sat beside the toromiro tree and took a few moments to rest. He hoped at any moment he would hear Mahina in the distance, calling his name in the way that only she could.

Finally Daniel sighed and began to carefully search the wall behind the tree. He relied on his sense of feeling rather than his eyes, knowing the entrance was well concealed. Before long, behind a dense layer of brush, his hand disappeared into what appeared to be solid rock. The hole seemed to be just large enough for him to wiggle through. Daniel marked the spot and went back to the toromiro tree, hoping to hear or see Mahina hurrying to catch up with him.

He waited and waited — and waited . . .

It was not to be.

With a heavy heart he slowly returned to the cave and crawled through the opening, fresh tears forming in his eyes. The cavern beyond was pitch black, and Daniel wished he had a flashlight to steer his course. When his eyes adjusted, though, he could see well enough — if only barely — and once again he encountered numerous spiders. As before, he brushed them off and moved on.

Daniel picked his way ahead carefully, and as the entry grew larger, he discovered that walking on the wet rocky floor was easier this time. All those months living barefoot had been good for his balance. Other than that, he felt numb all over — his senses had completely shut down — and it was all he could do just to put one foot in front of another. He couldn't think about what he had left behind — but he did. With every step he thought of Mahina.

Before long the light completely faded, and he had to rely on touch rather than vision, deliberately making his way. After an hour or so, just as he remembered, the cavern began to narrow, and all too soon Daniel was crawling on his hands and knees. He eventually found himself flattened out on his stomach, caught between sharp stones above and below. He didn't remember it being this tight on the way in, and as his ability to move forward became even more painful, he realized he had no doubt muscled up living the life of a fisherman. He groaned and fought to breathe as he paused to rest.

He tried to reorder his thinking, pull himself together.

So what if I become all cut up — I have to get out of here.

With that thought, he pushed himself forward, and as he wedged deeper and deeper into the passageway, his arms out in front of him, he discovered he was stuck. He couldn't move, not even an inch.

Panic threatened to overwhelm him as he realized he might never get home again.

I'll die and rot in this godforsaken time cave.

He tried to pull a deep breath of air into his chest and couldn't do it.

Yes, I'm going to die here.

It was then he remembered what the little boy — the boy that was him — said as he sat in front of the moai: Answers to any questions could be found inside him.

In spite of the situation, Daniel focused his mind, and before long a question, not an answer, came to him.

What can I move?

What can I move? he echoed to himself.

He kept repeating those words, and then there it was — the answer.

My fingers and my toes.

At that point, rather than shifting his body from side to side as he had been doing, he began to dig his fingers and toes into the floor of the narrow cave. After a few moments Daniel noticed a tiny bit of movement. He also realized he was not getting enough oxygen — he could no longer think clearly and felt any second he could pass out.

Once again he recalled the dream he had on Mount Terevaka . . . when he was trapped in the cave.

Keep going, he thought . . . keep going.

He kept going, and the blood produced by the rocks digging into his skin began to act as a lubricant, and he began to slowly slide along the cave floor.

Some time later, he could take deeper inhalations.

He breathed a sigh of relief.

I'm going to make it.

The passageway expanded, and he could now crawl on his hands and knees.

And as he looked ahead, a slight increase in light revealed an open cavern just ahead. Once there he could once again walk upright.

The intensity of nearly dying had shocked him back into an intense awareness, and as he inhaled deeply, eager to take in all the air his lungs could hold, he was shocked to discover the odor — that wretched, evil odor — stronger than ever.

What? It can't be!

The minute he popped his head out into the cavern, a male voice purred in Rapanui:

"Dan-iel, it's so good to see you again."

Before Daniel could turn to see who it was, a chemically-soaked rag that smelled sweet — like sugar — was roughly placed over his face.

Daniel grabbed at the hands holding it.

Too late . . .

He found himself slipping into oblivion, insane laughter echoing in his ears.

Chapter 16

Daniel awoke and found he was seated against a large boulder, hands securely tied behind his back. His legs were lashed together at the ankles and above his knees, and around his chest ropes secured him to the boulder. He tested the restraints; they were tight to the point of being uncomfortable. He couldn't move a muscle.

How did this happen?

Daniel glanced around. He was still inside the cavern. At that moment, footsteps echoed from its depths.

When the footsteps arrived, Daniel's unknown assailant sat down on a boulder near him, face obscured by the dark. A male voice said in Rapanui, "Dan-iel, I see you're finally awake. Chloroform acts very quickly, but it took longer for you to wake up than I would have guessed. "

"Who are you?" Daniel demanded.

"Before I tell you, I must share with you how joyful I am. For longer than you can imagine, I have waited for the chance to kill you, and now it is finally here. I feel like crying I'm so happy."

Daniel wished he wasn't tied up so he could help the mystery man with the crying part. He tugged again at the ropes and bitterly said, "Oh, I'm sure you are. Who are you?"

A clicking sound followed and light flooded the cavern.

Paoa sat before him.

Daniel was bewildered. Despite his ability to capture knowledge, digest it, remember it and make sense of it, he was completely surprised at who sat before him. His eyes went to the source of the light — and then he remembered.

Paoa laughed and said, "Your flashlight. Hotu Iti gifted to me, and it has made my travels through the cave much easier." As Paoa spoke, the light eerily lit up his face. "Before you die, I have much to share with you. You're the kind who wants to know everything. Yes?"

Daniel nodded.

"You see, Dan-iel, many years ago when I was a young shaman, I discovered I had the gift of being able to see into the future, and I saw the devastating events that were ahead for my people. I'm sure you've read the history books. Need I say more?"

Daniel didn't respond. He decided to let Paoa ramble on.

"As I looked into the future, I could see a brighter time, a time of more abundance. I also saw that my people were under the yoke of an oppressive nation. Yet there was hope, as during this time, there would be a rare opportunity for freedom. And, Dan-iel, that time is now."

Daniel said nothing. He was thinking — thinking of ways to free himself, ways to turn the odds of living in his favor.

"The problem was this," Paoa droned on. "Since I lived in another time, how could I affect the future? So I went to Puna Pau, the home of Hitirau, and sat there quietly, hoping he would come to guide me. Before long he appeared.

"When I told him of my vision, he informed me that in the old magic of our ancestors, from long before we were on our island, there was an ancient way to create a gateway into the future. But as my vision of what lay ahead opened up before me, I could see a problem."

Daniel found his voice and asked, "And what was that?"

Paoa stared at Daniel and pointed at him. "You," he replied. "You were the one person who had the greatest opportunity to stop me."

Daniel was dumbfounded.

"So, together, Hitirau and I schemed to create such a channel into the future, but we chose a time when you were younger, so we could kill you well before you had a chance to interfere."

Daniel didn't dare show his emotions. He had made a decision — play it cool and confident.

"How long ago was that?" Paoa marveled at his own genius. "Around ten years? You see, Dan-iel, we knew we could place the exit to the time cave wherever we wished, and once we discovered where you were at that time, we put it into a place you might know. Okla-homa, I believe it is called?"

Daniel was taken aback. Oklahoma? The man knew nothing of Oklahoma. How could this be?

"I see you know exactly what I am talking about. Anyway, I came out of the cave into a river bed —"

The Illinois River?

"— and I walked for a while, hiding myself from others until I came upon a small house, the one where you lived."

Oh, my God . . .

"No one was there, and I hid in the bushes in front, when an old man with long black-and-white hair appeared."

Grandpa . . .

"I came up behind him, intending to cut his throat. But he fought like a wild animal and for a moment I thought he was going to overcome me. Finally I was able to put my knife to his throat and cut it. He bled to death right in front of me."

"No . . ." Daniel's breath had left him.

Paoa laughed his evil laugh. "How does it make you feel, knowing the old man, I'm guessing he was your grandfather, died because of you?"

Daniel clenched his teeth in rage, but said nothing.

"As a shaman, I could tell he had great mana — something I needed for my quest. So, like all those on the island I have killed, I enjoyed his flesh."

Daniel recalled how mutilated his grandpa had been. He had thought it was only the animals. Daniel couldn't hold his loathing back any more.

"Paoa — I'll see you dead," he said in a voice of quiet determination

"Oh, will you now? I believe you've forgotten who's tied up. No Dan-iel, soon it will be you who will die. By the way, do you recognize this?" He held up a large green flint arrowhead, one that appeared to have an engraved brown hawk in the center.

Daniel inhaled deeply. How could he forget?

"From your face I see you remember. I've kept it in my possession since that time." Paoa then placed the arrowhead on the boulder beside him.

"Now to finish my story. After I killed your grandfather, I planned to wait and do the same to you. But then the oddest thing happened. I heard loud screeching and out of nowhere two large birds attacked me. Remember that scar on my head?" Paoa pointed at his scalp. "That wasn't from any eastern warrior; that was from those birds. They hit me over and over again with their sharp talons, and I thought they were going to either kill me or at the least put my eyes out."

Birds?

"I knew then I couldn't stay, so I ran back to the time cave, beating the birds back as I ran. After I came back to the past, I decided to wait until you, as my vision told me you would, came to my island. Here I wouldn't have to worry about those vicious birds.

"So, while we were unable to move the time, it was easy enough for Hitirau and I to change the exit for the cave to the island, and it has been here ever since. But then I had to wait for ten full years for the right time to begin the murders, which I hoped would lead to our island's independence."

This is a mad man, Daniel decided, but he is a mad man with a purpose — and that makes him dangerous. I have to keep my wits about me.

"What about Tiare?" asked Daniel.

"The old woman?"

"Yes."

"She was one I didn't want you to have at your side. She knew too much about our island and its history, and was too valuable an ally for you. But since she was a fellow shaman, rather than murder her, I first tried to scare her away. When that didn't work, I intended to kill her, when you unexpectedly showed up. When you followed me into the past, I knew there I would have the best chance to kill you."

"Is that why you selected me for the Birdman competition?"

"It took you this long to figure it out? You saw how many died trying to bring the egg to Orongo. I couldn't believe it when not only did you survive, but you won."

"What about the cigarette lighter I found in Atamu's pora?"

"I was hoping you would fall for that. Just before the competition, I gave it to Atamu. The way he looked at the flame as it came forth, I knew he would keep it in his possession at all times. While you were on Motu Nui, I was hoping you would find the chance to search his pora. I guessed it would throw you off track, and it seems it did."

Now that Paoa was talking, he couldn't shut up. Daniel didn't care; every word Paoa said gave him more time to think about how to get out of this mess.

Paoa babbled on. "In our discussions Hitirau and I both reasoned that by killing and cannibalizing the outsiders on our island, we could frighten them away. Not only that, when I ate part of the victims and absorbed their mana, I would become stronger. All I had to do was call the name of Hitirau, and the magic worked."

Gomez had written Hitirau on the card. Now it all made sense.

So what? Daniel cautioned himself. I'm still tied up.

Paoa boasted, "From what I could tell our plan was working, at least until you showed up. But I don't believe you ever suspected me. As you may recall, soon after you set foot into the past, I tried to strike up a friendship with you, pitting us both against an unknown evil. How could you know that I was the evil?" He chuckled at his wit, and then sneered at Daniel. "You think you're so clever, so strong."

"Well, I guess I was wrong about you," Daniel replied cautiously.

"I will be done with you soon," Paoa said. His voice grew even more sinister. "And with you out of the way, the killings will increase. Chile will realize keeping control here won't be worth the trouble, and we will once again be a free island."

Daniel asked, "What about the cave?"

"The magic of the cave will exist as long as I'm alive. And who knows, once we've claimed the island for our own, I might just live in your time. I'd love the conveniences of modern life. But enough talking. I have a special surprise for you. Would you like to know what it is?"

Daniel said not a word.

"Well, then," Paoa said, "Dan-iel, before I kill you, I am going to enjoy eating your living flesh. Your mana is great, and I will be even stronger than I am now."

No, no, Daniel told himself, keep him talking — it was his only hope.

"How does it feel to kill people and eat their flesh? I want to understand," Daniel asked.

It was as if Paoa could not hear as his eyes glazed over with an unearthly, hypnotic stare.

"Now, it is time." His voice changed to a guttural hiss — sounding like it might have risen from the pits of hell. "Hitirau! Hitirau! I call on you!"

Paoa breathed deeply, in and out, and the muscles in his chest and arms began to bulge. His face contorted into an evil grimace, and his teeth became elongated and pointed. His ears grew and became elfin in appearance, and in the darkness of the cavern his eyes emitted a faint red glow.

The transformed Paoa then growled, "Now, Dan-iel, your mana is mine!" With those words, Paoa walked over to him, his drooling mouth opening over Daniel's face.

Daniel could smell and feel the fetid vapor.

He closed his eyes.

Suddenly Daniel heard a loud *thump* and Paoa's movement toward him stopped. Daniel opened his eyes and discovered a spear was protruding through Paoa's open mouth.

Paoa let out a death gurgle as he twitched and crashed to the floor. Standing behind him was Mahina, holding her hands to her face in shock.

"Dan-iel!" she yelled as she ran past Paoa's motionless body and dropped to her knees to hold Daniel tight.

"Mahina..."

Chapter 17

After Mahina removed the ropes from Daniel, they held one another for the longest time — neither wanted to pull away from each other's embrace. Finally Daniel asked, "Mahina — how did you find me?"

Mahina wiped the tears from her eyes saying, "There is a story to tell. Would you like to hear it?"

"I would."

Mahina said, "After you left, I realized I couldn't go on without you. I confessed this to my parents, and they told me to follow my heart. As I left, my father insisted that I take his spear; somehow he knew I would need it. Then I asked him to do something for me which I must keep secret for the time being."

Daniel nodded.

"I hurried off in the direction I saw you take. For a while there were signs of your path, then, after a long stretch of rocky soil, any trace disappeared. Then the most amazing thing happened. An elderly man, not of this island, walked up to me and said, 'Is your name Mahina?'

"I said, 'Yes, it is.'

"He said, 'Then I know something that is important to you.'

"'And what is that?' I asked.

"He said, 'I know how to find Daniel. Follow me.'

"I'm not sure why, but I trusted him. He led me a good ways from where I was to a toromiro tree. He walked behind it and showed me the entry to a cave.

"'Are you sure this is it?' I asked.

"'Oh, I'm quite sure,' he said. 'Now go on, Daniel will be in need of your help soon.'

"I said, 'Won't you tell me your name?'"

"He said, 'Daniel will know who I am. But go now! There is no time to waste.' So I entered the cave, and you know what happened after that."

Daniel's curiosity was piqued. "Tell me what the man looked like."

"Well, he was tall, a little darker than you, and had long black-and-white hair, which was tied behind his head. Oh, and one more thing: He had a strap around his waist —"

"It's called a belt."

"— and on it, in a silver circle, was a man with long hair like his, and that man was surrounded by six of those animals that you drew on the beach. What were they?"

"Buffalo?" he questioned.

"Yes," Mahina confirmed. "Buffalo."

Grandpa . . .

"Do you know who that was?"

"I do," Daniel said, still amazed at what he had heard.

"Who?"

"Someone who keeps his word — I promise I'll give you an explanation later." Daniel took a deep breath, paused for a moment with the wonder of it all and finally added, "By the way, I'm sorry you had to kill another human."

"Dan-iel, when I saw you tied up with Paoa about to harm you . . . well . . . it was an easy decision."

"Thank you — otherwise now I'd be dead. One more thing: I had no idea you could throw a spear like that."

Mahina said, "As time goes by you will discover more and more about me that you didn't know before. I hope, through our lives together, I will always find ways to surprise you, in good ways of course. Now, shall we go? I'd like to see what my new world is like."

Daniel couldn't think of anything he would rather do.

He picked up his grandpa's arrowhead from the boulder and sighed as he held it to his chest. Then he grabbed the flashlight, and he and Mahina walked together toward the cave exit.

It was dark when they emerged from the cave into the brisk night air. Holding hands, they picked their way across the rocky ground. Mahina inhaled deeply in surprise at the array of lights that marked the city of Hanga Roa, and

Daniel enjoyed seeing her reaction. Before long they walked up to a home built of native rock.

Daniel knocked, and a few moments later a familiar voice asked, "Who's there?"

"Tiare," Daniel said, "it's an old friend of yours."

The porch light came on, the door burst open and Tiare jumped from the threshold to hold him tightly.

"Daniel," she said, "it's been almost five months. I have been worried sick about you."

Then Tiare noticed Mahina, and she gasped.

Daniel said, "Tiare, I would like to introduce you to my love, Mahina."

Tiare looked back and forth at both of them, and at once she understood. She embraced Mahina, saying in Rapanui, "Welcome home, sister."

Everyone was all smiles as they walked into Tiare's home.

There was much to share, Daniel thought, but that could wait for later. For now, he just wanted a hot shower, something he desperately missed, and a soft couch on which to cuddle up with Mahina.

And Tiare had both.

Book Three

Chapter 1

March 7, 2015

Daniel sat alone on the rim of Rano Kau at Kari Kari, overlooking the ocean. It boggled his mind to think that in 1775, two hundred and forty years ago, he had participated in and had won the Birdman competition. To him, though, it was only a little over a week ago.

As he looked over the edge, he recalled how many had died during that contest, including Ropata. Daniel closed his eyes for a few moments and silently thanked him for his friendship.

Daniel then remembered his fear of heights, which had vanished into the ethers. His aversion to sharks was a totally different matter, however. After his Birdman experience, Daniel had no plans that included sharks any time in the near future.

Daniel smiled as he thought about the time that had passed since he and Mahina had arrived into the present. The first morning was spent with Tiare, who cooked up a delicious breakfast of scrambled eggs, hash browns and toast. As they sipped hot tea, Tiare was all ears as they told her the whole story in great detail. No convincing was necessary; Tiare had suspected beforehand that, somehow, there was a breach in time that the murderer had exploited.

Tiare scrounged up some clothes her family had left behind over the years and gave them to Mahina, knowing she couldn't very well stroll topless down the streets of Hanga Roa.

Hand in hand Daniel and Mahina walked the little city, enjoying the sights. Daniel enjoyed seeing Mahina's amazement as she discovered cars, horses, eyeglasses, motorcycles, bicycles — well, nearly everything was new and interesting for her. Mahina caught on quickly, and Daniel was certain with time and patience, she would adapt well to her new environment.

After their return, Tiare insisted Mahina begin to meet the Rapanui community, including Alame Koreta from the Te Manutara Hotel. A select few, including Alame, would be told the truth of how Mahina had traveled across time, but otherwise the story would be that Mahina was a Maori visitor from New Zealand, one who happened to know much about Rapanui culture.

Daniel couldn't help but chuckle as he thought about it. He suspected that within days everyone on the island would know all the details. In a small community such as this, there were few, if any secrets.

Just an hour from now, he had scheduled a meeting with Salvador Diaz. The fact that Daniel had resurfaced after being missing for almost five months had stirred up more than a little interest for the investigator. Especially since, as Daniel had learned, twelve more murders had taken place while he was adventuring in the past.

Like it or not, Daniel planned to tell him the whole truth of his experience, and Diaz could do what he wanted with the information. For now, though, Daniel needed some time by himself to think.

While Daniel was pleased that all seemed to be going well, there were some details that stuck in his craw. Normally when he solved a crime, all the pieces of the puzzle fit together nicely. Oh, there might be a red herring or two, but all the major themes blended together coherently.

Not this time.

For example, Daniel didn't understand how Paoa got his hands on chloroform. Daniel supposed Paoa could have sneaked around during the dark of night and found it, but how would he know about it in the first place?

And the logistics didn't fit. To kill a total of forty-two people without being caught would require legwork — lots of it. Was Paoa capable of emerging from the cave in the dark of night, finding his victims and killing them all by himself? Did he use his shaman magic to assist him?

No, something is missing, Daniel thought.

It was then that he heard footsteps walking on the rocky soil behind him. He looked back over his shoulder and discovered a trim Rapanui man approaching. He wore sunglasses, navy slacks and a long sleeved, white, dress shirt. Daniel grinned when he recognized him.

"José! I've been meaning to call you."

José removed his sunglasses, put them in the front pocket of his shirt and reached out his hand. "No problem, Hawk. The grapevine tells me you came out of hiding just yesterday. I understand it's been a little busy for you."

Daniel shook José's hand. "Very much so. How did you know I was here at Rano Kau?"

José sat down and explained, "I ran by Tiare's this morning, and she told me."

"How have you been?" Daniel asked as he gazed across the water.

"Just fine, until I found Paoa dead in the cave."

Daniel quickly looked back at José, who held what appeared to be a Taser, pointed directly at him.

"José — what are you doing?"

José grimaced and said, "Hawk, I knew before too long you would realize Paoa needed someone on this side of the cave to help him, so I thought I'd better take care of business before you got too close."

Daniel was astonished — yet he asked, "José, how?"

"You really want to know?" Seeing Daniel's incredulous nod, he continued. "It all started last year when I was out hiking and saw a man wandering around half-naked. I thought he had to be crazy, wearing only a loincloth and a feather head-dress. When I talked with him, he explained he was from the past. Naturally, I didn't believe him. But as he went on — you know — I began to wonder if there was any truth to his words.

"To prove his point, he took me through the time cave to old Rapa Nui. God, was that awful or what? I barely made it through, but after just a brief glance at the people and their living conditions, I was convinced. Getting back home through that narrow place was at least as bad as going in."

Daniel sat silently and thought while he listened: How can I get the weapon away from him? There must be a way . . .

"When we returned," José went on, "Paoa explained to me that the purpose of his time travel was to take advantage of an opportunity to rid our island of its oppressors. To do that, he needed someone to keep an eye on things in the present time and help arrange the attacks. I didn't mind the killings so much, but the cannibalism? When he let me know that he needed the mana of his victims, I understood. Besides that, what better way to scare off the tourists, and eventually Chile?"

"But José," Daniel asked, "aren't the conditions under Chile gradually getting better? Why were all those killings necessary?"

José turned angry. "Because we want them out now! We can't put up with them and their so-called help any longer. For a top investigator, you ask the stupidest questions," Jose continued. "Now shut up and listen. Paoa had told me about his visions and how you could mess up our plans, so I expected you when you arrived from the United States and have personally had you under surveillance."

Alame Koreta had said I was being watched, Daniel recalled.

"Paoa also told me that you had taken a fancy to the daughter of the 'ariki mau, and while I can only guess what happened in the cave, I figure that if you hadn't unexpectedly brought that bitch back from the past —"

Daniel bristled. "What did you say?"

José ignored him. "— Paoa would have killed you in the cave as he planned to do. Now it's up to me to do the dirty work. You do know, Hawk, once you're dead, the killings will continue. First I'm going to take out Diaz, so no other Chilean investigator in his right mind would want to come here, and then I'm going to keep killing anyone who doesn't have at least a trace of Rapanui blood. Every foreigner will be gone in no time, and Chile will be out of here within the year."

"Why the Taser?" Daniel asked as he eyed the weapon. I must play for time, he thought. I have to find a way out of this — *another* mess.

"First, Hawk, this is not a Taser. Like a Taser, it's a conducted electrical device, but this one has an adjustable setting, so at the least it will knock you out cold. Once I shock you, I'll pull the probes out and push you off the edge. I'll explain to Diaz that you and I were having a little chat when you slipped and fell. When they find your body, I can't have them find a bullet hole in you, can I? Two little holes in your chest will never be noticed next to all the scrapes and bruises you will have."

"But José, don't you think —"

"Hawk, you might as well quit stalling. I've figured out all the angles, and you are as good as dead." He aimed the weapon at Daniel. "Oh, and one more thing: I saw your lady friend when I was at Tiare's, and she's pretty hot. I know at first she will be upset over your unexpected death, but after a little grieving time I will take her under my wing. Once she gets to know me, she'll come to appreciate how wonderful it is to be with a *real* man. Goodbye Hawk, it's been great to —"

Suddenly a *whoosh* of wings was upon them.

"What the hell?" José exclaimed as a pair of cinnamon colored caracaras streaked out of nowhere and swooped down on him. José flailed wildly as they darted in and out, scratching his face repeatedly with their talons. José screamed and soon his face was covered with deep gashes.

"I can't see!" José shouted as he stumbled close to the edge of the cliff, blood pouring from his forehead into his eyes. "I can't see . . ."

"Watch out!" Daniel yelled.

The caracaras hit José again, and he slipped on the loose rock at the precipice and fell away.

Daniel stood up and looked out over the edge. José tumbled head over heels down the cliff face, shrieking every time he bounced off the rocky wall.

When José hit bottom, he didn't make a sound.

He was dead.

Daniel quivered as he backed away from the rim. He sat on a nearby boulder and gazed at the sky around him. His caracara rescuers had disappeared.

A few moments later he heard the flapping of wings, and the two caracaras settled on a rock five feet away. Both of the birds stood erect and eyed him.

Daniel could sense intelligence in their gazes. As he watched in disbelief, a whirling vortex of brown, gold and white swirled around them, obscuring the birds from view. Daniel stared as the vortex became larger and larger. All at once the movement stopped and the air cleared. The caracaras had disappeared, and two people, a man and a woman, stood in their places.

An astonished Daniel stood and carefully studied them. The man was approximately six feet tall, Native American, with short dark hair, wearing blue jeans and a long-sleeved blue plaid shirt. The woman was Caucasian, had long, straight, brown hair hanging to her shoulders and wore a beige, loose fitting, full length dress. Both of them looked to be in their late forties and had tears in their eyes.

The man spoke. "Daniel — it's good to see you again."

The woman added, "It's been far too long."

Daniel was puzzled. Both of them looked familiar . . . he reached into his eidetic memory — no help. Finally he asked, "Who are you?"

The man said, "I am your father, Daniel Fishinghawk."

The woman added, "I am your mother, Jenny Fishinghawk."

Daniel stared in shock. He took only a moment and ordered, "Go away and leave me alone." He hated them as much as anyone could.

His father asked, "Will you hear us out?"

Daniel turned his back on them and shook his head.

"Please?" his mother begged.

Daniel turned around. In spite of his loathing for them he folded his arms, sat back down and answered, "If you must."

His father looked at his mother. "May I speak for us?"

"Yes," she answered.

"Daniel," his father said, "twenty-six years ago, when you were only two years old, your mother and I were killed in a car accident. You may already be aware that we were both high on alcohol and drugs."

"Oh, I know *all* about that." Daniel glared at them.

His father winced. "Then you also know there was no excuse for our behavior. Your mother and I were both twenty years old — young *and* stupid. If we had only thought for a second about the consequences of our actions, the car accident and our deaths would have never happened." A pained look came over his face.

His mother was barely able to say, "We are *so* sorry . . ."

Daniel's heart began to soften.

His father continued, "After our deaths we both floated above our bodies and were relieved to see you unharmed in the back seat. Our hearts were broken, though, because we knew we wouldn't be able to care for you as normal parents would.

"Before long we were approached by two beings of light. One stood before each of us and beckoned us to join them. I said to the one facing me, 'Are you my creator?' I heard no answer, but in my mind I heard a 'yes.' Your mother asked the being that faced her the same question, and she got the same answer.

"I spoke for both of us. 'We are not ready to join you. We are parents of a little one who needs us. May we stay behind?'

"One voice came from them, and we again heard in our minds, 'It is time for you to come with us.'

"I said, 'We cannot. We wish to stay.'

"We stood together for the longest time in silence, when the lights pulsated and became even brighter. 'Very well. Since you have lost your human identities, what form do you wish to take?'

"Your mother spoke. 'We wish to be birds of the air.'

"'As is our name,' I said.

"The voice said, 'Permission granted — with one condition: When your child no longer has need for you, then you must come with us.' The light faded, and we found ourselves flying in the Oklahoma sky as hawks."

How much they must have loved me, Daniel reasoned.

"And so," his father went on, "for the next twenty-six years we stayed close to you, watching for any help you might need. Around ten years ago, though, we detected an evil presence at your grandfather's home. We left your side at school and flew there as quickly as we could, but arrived too late to help. We saw the murderer lurking around the house and guessed he was waiting for you. So we attacked and drove him away."

Daniel recalled Paoa's story. At last he understood.

"We shared your pain as we circled overhead at his funeral, and when you came to Easter Island, we assumed the form of the caracara, watching you every moment of the daylight hours.

"While we were in our spirit forms, we were able to see brief glimpses of what lay before you, so that time when you napped on top of the mountain, we gave you a dream of the cave, hoping we could forewarn you of the coming dangers.

"Daniel, do you recall when you went to Puna Pau — the home of the akuaku Hitirau?"

I could never forget that nightmare, Daniel thought.

"We saw you were in great danger, and we carried the spirit of love into the area, breaking the spell of evil. We were almost certain he would have killed you had we not been there. But this pleased us greatly, because, as your parents, we were able to help you."

Daniel could feel their love more and more.

The area began to fill with an unearthly light, and his father explained, "We also were told by our creator that today would be the last time you would need our presence. It is time for us to go."

Daniel began to tear up. "Dad, Mom — I don't want you to go."

"But we must," his father said. "Don't worry. We will have plenty of time to catch up when you make your transition. But don't be concerned, that will be many, many years away — that is, unless you do something stupid." His father smiled.

Daniel returned the smile. "Before you go, may I hold you?"

"We were hoping you would ask," his mother responded.

Daniel rushed over to them, and they all tightly embraced. Daniel was astonished at how solid and warm they felt.

Daniel said, "Mom and Dad, I love you — I love you both. Everyone makes mistakes, and I forgive you. Even though you were only in spirit, you were the best parents anyone could have." Daniel was pleased to see the look of joy on their faces.

"One more question?"

"Yes?" his father said.

"Do you ever see Grandpa?"

"All the time," his father answered. "He told us he enjoyed meeting your girlfriend."

"Because he did, she was able to save my life."

"Like us, he wished to help you. Remember, just because your loved ones are in spirit, doesn't mean you aren't deeply connected."

Daniel added, "And I'm glad for that."

"As we are."

"One more thing," his father said as the light brightened around them, "We can see that in the years to come, you and your *wife* will have many happy years together — and many children."

Daniel heard the emphasis on the word wife and grinned at the thought.

His father winked at him as the light became unbearably bright. When it faded, his parents were gone, yet there was a sparkle in the air and a residual sense of cleanliness and purity.

Daniel felt as light as air. It amazed him how heavy hate was; it felt like a ton of bricks. He never again wanted to carry such a load.

As he gazed down at the rock on which his parents had perched, he discovered two flawless cinnamon-colored feathers. He picked them up and put them in the front pocket of his shirt.

Daniel looked at his watch. He had to hurry. It was time to meet with Diaz. But for the moment, he stopped and looked high up in the sky. An amazing thing — a miracle — had just happened.

Daniel was a strong man, but like when he thought he had lost Mahina, the feelings he had were too powerful.

He bowed his head and quietly sobbed.

Chapter 2

March 7, 2015

Daniel and Salvador Diaz, along with Diaz's bodyguard and a two-man team of forensic specialists, entered the cave that held the body of Paoa. After Daniel told him the story of the past five months, Diaz looked at him like he was crazy and said he wanted to see the evidence for himself. After a walk up to the cave, they found themselves in its depths, flashlights probing the dark recesses.

Daniel looked over at Diaz and couldn't help but grin. After squeezing through the narrow entryway, the normally dapper Diaz's dark suit was smeared with mud, his red silk power tie was askew, and his usually neatly combed silver hair was in disarray. His leather shoes kept slipping on the damp floor of the cave, and Daniel kept wondering when, not if, he was going to fall.

Diaz's bodyguard appeared to be a nervous wreck; he held his gun out in front of him and jerked it from side to side as they walked along. At any hint of movement, Daniel was sure the bodyguard would fire off a volley of shots.

It was an odd feeling to again be in the cave — the cave that had changed his life. As he thought about it, had it had not been created, his grandpa might still be alive, and the murders would never have happened. Yet at the same time, Mahina would not be with him — they would have never met — and she would only be part of the past. Daniel shook his head from the paradox. The cave was much like life: in many ways a double-edged sword.

Shortly they came upon the body of Paoa, exactly as Daniel and Mahina had left it. There was no smell of decomposition, though, and Daniel could only guess that the cool air of the cave had preserved it to some degree.

After a brief inspection, Diaz directed his forensics team, "Okay, let's get started." With his words, they descended on the corpse and began gathering evidence.

Diaz said, "Hawk, I'd like to speak with you — alone. Come with me."

They walked to an isolated recess in the cave.

"Hawk, as crazy as your story sounded, from what I can tell by what we see here, I have to believe you."

"There's really no other way to explain this series of murders," confirmed Daniel.

Diaz smoothed his tie in place, as if to declare order out of chaos. "I know, but I can't present such a crazy story to the public. The Chilean police will look like idiots, and I'll be the butt of jokes for years to come. My career as an investigator will be over the minute this story breaks."

He paused and polished one of his muddy black shoes on the back of his other pant leg, as if that were his most important accomplishment of the day. "So, Hawk, we're going to play it like this. Assuming the forensics matches this man to the previous crimes — and I'm sure they will — any evidence that links him to the murders will be destroyed and replaced with that from José."

Daniel nodded his understanding.

"We've already retrieved José's body from the foot of Rano Kau, and it will be a simple matter to make the switch. I'll hold a press conference tomorrow and blame all the murders on him, and, as far as I'm concerned, the body in this cave and our presence here never happened." Diaz squinted at Daniel. "You say now that the shaman is dead, the cave no longer connects to the past?"

"That's what he told me."

"I can't take any chances on that. Today after we leave the cave, I'll have it dynamited, burying the body so it will never be found, and eliminating the possibility of any more crazy men from the past coming over and killing people."

"Good," Daniel agreed.

"You do know, Hawk, this will make you a hero. I will tell the media that for the past five months you went undercover — under my direction of course —"

"Of course," Daniel replied sardonically.

Diaz disregarded the interruption. "— to solve these murders. Now," he whispered softly, "What will it take to buy your cooperation?"

"Not much," Daniel replied, noticing a sense of relief on Diaz's face. "You remember I told you a woman from the past came back with me?"

"Yes."

"I want papers drawn up that give her not only a permanent ID, but also full Chilean citizenship."

"Done."

"Second," Daniel asked, "is Roberto Ika, the man you originally blamed for the killings, still in a mental institution in Chile?"

"He is."

"While he may be crazy, he had nothing to do with these murders. He is to be released immediately and returned to Rapa Nui."

"Agreed."

"Next, I want a five acre tract taken from the Rapa Nui National Park, somewhere close to 'Anakena."

Diaz's eyes shifted a bit, "This one will be a little harder, but I'm sure I can make it happen. What do you want this for?"

"I've got an idea, but I'm not ready to share it just yet."

"Fair enough. Anything else?"

"Yes," Daniel said, "I want the Chilean government to train a number of Rapanui to be policemen, and when they are prepared, you must withdraw all Chilean police from the island. I expect this to be completed in no less than two years. The Rapanui police then would be under the direction of the local government, not the Chileans."

"Impossible!" Diaz blurted out. "Why would you ask this?"

"Most Rapanui believe the Chilean police are oppressive and treat them as less than human."

"That's not true!" Diaz countered.

"Oh, but I hear it is." Daniel paused for a moment to let Diaz calm down. "This is the last of my requests. If you grant them, you will have my full and complete cooperation."

Diaz growled, "Okay, Hawk, the last one will be the toughest of all, but I believe I will have enough influence to make it happen, especially since these murders will have been solved on my watch."

"Good enough. Shall we shake on it?"

Diaz stared at Daniel as he shook his hand. "You drive a hard bargain, Hawk. But yes, it's a done deal."

"Good. Now that's settled, did you know there are spiders in the cave?"

A pained look swept over Diaz's face. "Spiders? I hate spiders."

"Well, it seems they really like you." Daniel pointed to at least a hundred of them crawling all over Diaz's suit.

Diaz looked down at them, his eyes widened and he screamed, "Help! Help! H — e — l — p!"

Diaz slipped and fell with a loud *thump*. He quickly jumped back up, screamed even louder and stumbled over to his bodyguard, frantically brushing the spiders off the sleeves of his jacket.

"Get them off me! Get them off me!" he demanded.

Together, Diaz and his bodyguard wiped them off; all the while Diaz shrieked and jumped up and down like a little boy throwing a temper tantrum.

Daniel fought back the urge to laugh out loud.

Late that same day Daniel and Mahina took a stroll up toward the summit of Mount Terevaka. Their feet were still callused from living in old Rapa Nui, so they shed their shoes for the hike.

Daniel enjoyed the feel of the earth under his feet. He had never before realized how strong a connection he felt with Mother Nature when he removed his shoes. From this point on, he promised himself, calluses or no, I'll go barefoot at least every now and then.

As they walked hand in hand up the grassy incline, Daniel said, "Tell me how your day went."

Mahina answered, "It was lovely. All the people who I met knew I had come from . . . what do they call my island now?"

"Rapa Nui."

"Yes, Rapa Nui. Anyway, they knew I had come from Rapa Nui's past and were bubbling over with questions. By the way, until we can find a place of our own, Alame Koreta offered to let us stay at her hotel at no charge."

"How nice of her," Daniel replied.

"Truthfully, I believe she just wants me close at hand so she can ask as many questions as she would like."

Daniel laughed. "That doesn't surprise me in the least."

"Also, I met several school teachers, and they asked if I would be willing to start giving classes to their students on the customs of old Rapa Nui, and naturally I told them yes. The pay would not be much, but this way I can continue to teach."

Daniel pulled her close and asked, "My love, are you happy here?"

Mahina's eyes misted. "I am. I miss my family very much, but since you told me the magic of the cave died with Paoa, I would not have been able to return anyway, even if the cave were not destroyed.

"But I must share with you that even though my loved ones are long since dead,

I still feel strongly linked to them; it is as if I had never left them. I believe there is one force that transcends death, and that is love. My family will always be with me, of that I am certain. After what you have told me about what happened with your parents and grandfather, I'm sure you understand."

Daniel felt his eyes mist as well. "I do."

Mahina asked, "How are you feeling about José?"

"I'm sorry he died. I know he was passionate about freedom for his people, and unfortunately that passion pushed him to do things he shouldn't have. But I do understand how his mind became twisted.

"Perhaps someday," Daniel continued, "in a nonviolent way, what José dreamed for will come true, and the Rapanui people will have more autonomy and control over their own destiny."

"We can only hope," Mahina said. After a brief pause, she added, "By the way, you haven't shared anything yet about your meeting with Diaz. How did it go?"

"Very well. He wanted to see the cave and the body of Paoa for himself. Once he was convinced that what I said was true, he agreed to my demands to keep silent about the time cave."

"What did you ask for?"

"Several important things. For now, you should know that one was to create an identity for you. In this day and age, people don't just pop up out of nowhere."

"I see."

"Another request I made was to have a plot of land given to me somewhere close to 'Anakena."

"By my old home?"

"Yes."

"What for?" she asked.

"I have no idea how we'll pay for it," Daniel answered, "but I was hoping to create a foundation for the Rapanui people, one that can work on the problems that face them."

"Such as?"

"Well, there are many issues to deal with, but one of the more important ones is to decide how to best proceed with reforestation. It would require a huge amount of effort, but if the proper trees were planted, Rapa Nui could again become the island paradise it once was. Also, it must be determined how best to protect the environment and preserve the moai and the many sacred places on the island.

"Besides, the institute could be a place of teaching. If you wished, you could instruct there, perhaps teaching the art of interpreting rongorongo. I might guess that professors from all over the world would come to learn."

Mahina said, "I would love such a place. And, I just might have an idea how to pay for it."

"How?" Daniel asked.

"You'll find out tomorrow morning. Tiare must be with us."

They continued to walk up the slope, and before long they were on the grassy summit of Mount Terevaka. All sorts of wonderful memories flooded Daniel's mind as they lay down on the grass next to each other like they did back in 1775 and looked at the beautiful array of stars starting to appear overhead.

Daniel said, "Mahina, there's something I need to ask you."

She looked at him curiously. "What's that?"

"Do you recall when we were in this same place, and we said for the first time that we loved each other?"

"How could I ever forget?" Mahina answered.

"And you thought I was, well, crazy?"

Mahina chuckled. "I do."

"Well," Daniel said, "I couldn't think of a better place to remind you once again how much I love you and want to spend my life with you. Mahina — will you marry me?"

Even in the last light of day, Daniel could see the love in her eyes. "Dan-iel," she murmured, "I have come across time to be with you, and I want to be with you as long as I can breathe. My answer is *yes*."

Daniel reached over and kissed her moist lips. "Do you remember what happened the last time we were here?"

Mahina pulled Daniel on top of her. "I remember *all* the times we have been here, each and every one."

"Good," Daniel said as he kissed her neck. "We'll have more clothes to take off this time. Think we can manage it?"

"I believe we'll find a way," she said as she wrapped her arms around him.

After their lovemaking they fell asleep intertwined in each other's arms. As the night passed, the bright stars silently moved in rhythm above them. They awoke to the sun peeking over the eastern Rapa Nui horizon.

"Are you ready for a surprise?" Mahina said as she snuggled her head on his chest.

Daniel kissed her. "I love surprises."

"Then put on your clothes. First we must tell Tiare the news of our engagement, and then let's all go to 'Anakena."

A short time later they were hiking down the mountain, headed to Hanga Roa.

Chapter 3

March 8, 2015

"What?" Tiare exclaimed. "You're getting married?"

"Yes!" Daniel confirmed.

Mahina nodded and was all smiles as she sat next to Daniel on Tiare's couch. She had changed clothes and wore a recently purchased, white, short-sleeved, knit shirt with beige shorts.

"We talked about it on our hike, and we plan to have the ceremony in a month or so," said Daniel.

Mahina said, "We'd like to have our wedding in front of the Ahu Ature Huki. Not only is it near where I used to live, it is also where Dan-iel was given the inspiration to find the cave."

Tiare said, "I am so delighted for the both of you. This pleases me greatly."

"And one more thing," Daniel added, "do you know of a Rapanui who could marry us?"

"I know the *perfect* person — a wise, powerful shaman who has wedded many here."

"And who would that be?" Mahina asked.

Tiare stood up in mock indignation, "Why me, of course!"

Mahina shrieked with excitement, jumped up from the couch and hugged her. "Dan-iel, she would be perfect! What do you think?"

Daniel stood and wrapped his arms around both of them. "I can think of no one I would rather have marry us." He paused for a moment. "Now that's taken care of, Mahina has informed me that she has a special surprise for us. Would you like to come with us and see what it is?"

"I'd love to."

With that, they left in Daniel's just-rented SUV.

The three intrepid hikers walked along the coastline west of 'Anakena. Even at ninety-four years of age, spry Tiare had no problem keeping up with them. Daniel had the distinct impression she could leave them in a cloud of dust if she wanted.

A short time later, Mahina led them to a place high above the water, with a sheer drop off into the ocean.

"This is it," she proclaimed.

Puzzled, Daniel asked, "This is what?"

"Oh, you'll see in a moment. If you'll both wait here, I must climb down some distance. I'll be back shortly."

Mahina scaled down the cliff, clinging to the rock wall as she descended.

"Be careful," Daniel yelled out as he watched her execute the precarious vertical face. In moments she disappeared from view.

Thirty nerve-wracking minutes later, as he looked over the edge, Mahina emerged from the cliff face far below, carrying two large, flat objects in one arm. When Mahina got within reach she handed him the items, which appeared to be wrapped in barkcloth, and then she hoisted herself over the edge.

"What are they?" Daniel asked as he carefully laid them on the ground.

"That you will discover in a few moments, but first I must share a story with you."

The three sat down beside the objects of interest.

"Dan-iel," Mahina said as she lovingly took his hand, "do you remember when the eastern warriors attacked our village, and how my two brothers, Kai and Poki, were later found hiding in a cave?"

"I do."

"That was their secret cave, one very few knew about. And that is where I just was."

"Really?"

"Yes. It is far down the sea cliff and very difficult to access. And so," Mahina went on, "remember when we were on our walk in the past, and you told me of the present day scarcity of the rongorongo boards?"

"I do."

"It broke my heart that there was not even one remaining on our island. So, just before I began my search for you, I asked my father if he would gift me a pair of very special ones. After he agreed, I asked my mother to wrap them up carefully that they might stand the test of time. Then I asked my brothers to hide them in the deepest, darkest corner of their secret cave so they wouldn't be found until I came back for them. Now let's take a look!"

Daniel and Tiare watched in rapt attention as Mahina first removed the bark-cloth, then another layer of dried reeds, placed to buffer the boards from the dampness of the cave. Everyone gasped when the first one was completely unwrapped; it was shaped like a turtle and was in pristine condition. Mahina handed it to Tiare, who held it as carefully as a mother holds a newborn infant.

The second was at least as beautiful as the first and was in the shape of a large fish. Mahina handed it to Daniel, and he admired the intricate, detailed workmanship.

Mahina said, "I would like the turtle board to stay here on Rapa Nui —"

"Mahina," Tiare interrupted, "I know you've been told they are scarce, but has Daniel informed you that before you brought these two into the future, only twenty-five existed in the world? They are priceless beyond measure, and I would guess that none are in as good of a condition as these are. We don't have a rongorongo board here on Rapa Nui because we are a poor island."

"Dan-iel has told me," Mahina confirmed. "I believe, though, it is most important for the spiritual wellbeing of my people to have at least one. Speaking of spiritual wellbeing, has Dan-iel told you that I know how to interpret rongorongo?"

Tiare looked stunned. "No. How?"

"My father believed in strong women, and he taught me the sacred art. So, while I hope to eventually teach others, I must ask you: Would you like to be my first student?"

Tiare's eyes welled with tears, and she appeared unable to speak. She reached over to Mahina, held her in her arms, and stammered out, "I'd . . . be honored."

When Tiare stepped back, wiping her tears from her face, Mahina went on, "Now, as for the other board: Tiare, remember the land we told you about that Dan-iel will be getting near 'Anakena, the land where we want to eventually build an institute?"

"Yes."

"Well," Mahina said, "the second board I would like to sell, and we can use the funds to finance it. What do you think?"

Tiare cried even more and somehow managed, "That is a wonderful idea."

Daniel simply held Mahina tightly.

He was speechless.

Chapter 4

April 5, 2015

A glorious Sunday afternoon greeted the large crowd that gathered around the Ahu Ature Huki, preparing for the wedding ceremony of Daniel and Mahina. Tiare had informed the happy couple that this would be the social event of the year, and a buzz of excitement filled the air.

Daniel and Mahina both roamed the crowd, greeting the many who had gathered. As Daniel had predicted, every Rapanui on the island seemed to know of Mahina's connection with the past and wanted to speak with her about it.

It was an informal affair, and many in attendance either sat on the ground or in lawn chairs. A large buffet table stacked with home-cooked food, supplied by the Rapanui community, was set up near the beach.

Mahina had chosen to wear a long, white, cotton dress, one sewn by a local seamstress. She had a red hibiscus flower in her hair, which Daniel had placed there, and a bright, multi-colored, floral lei adorned her neck. Daniel dressed simply and wore khaki slacks along with a long-sleeved, white shirt. He was barefoot, as was Mahina.

Daniel stepped away from the growing crowd for a few moments and felt the leather bag hanging from his neck underneath his shirt. That morning he had placed precious objects in it.

First he had put in the fishhook Pakia had gifted him. As he held it, he thought of Pakia and Uka, the couple who had shown him much love and kindness while he lived in the past. Daniel had yet to try it, now that he was back in the present, but he was certain it would have the same magic of catching fish as it previously had.

The second item he placed was his grandpa's green flint arrowhead, which Daniel had rescued from the grasp of evil. It brought up all sorts of memories of the times he had spent with him, tracking animals though the rolling Oklahoma hills.

The last two objects in the bag were the caracara feathers left behind by his father and mother. Daniel was certain that, without their continued protection, he would not have lived to see this moment.

After he returned to the crowd, a familiar voice called out to him, "Welcome home, Daniel."

He looked up to see Alame Koreta. "Alame, it's good to see you."

"I wouldn't have missed your wedding for anything in the world."

Daniel said, "I've been meaning to thank you and Jack for allowing us to stay at your hotel. We've finally located a rental home, so we shouldn't have to inconvenience you much longer."

"The pleasure has been all ours. Getting to know Mahina has been a wonderful addition to my life."

Daniel smiled at her, saying, "And to mine!"

Alame smiled back and asked, "Do you remember long ago when I advised you to sit before our moai and listen?"

"I do remember, and yes, I did."

"What did it say?"

"Let's just say that the moai helped me to discover the wisdom I already had within me."

"My experience was very much like yours," Alame replied. " I am certain our best guides exist inside us, not outside."

"Absolutely," Daniel agreed.

At that moment a bare-chested older man with long, grey, disarrayed hair and a wild-eyed stare approached them. He looked like a Rapanui version of an aging Albert Einstein. He stared at Daniel and muttered under his breath, "You Daniel Fishinghawk?"

"I am."

"Let me shake your hand. My name is Roberto Ika, and I've heard that because of you I've been let out of the crazy house in Santiago. Is that true?"

"Well, yes, I suppose so."

Daniel glanced over at Alame, who had a grin on her face.

Tears filled Roberto's eyes. "I can't tell you how grateful I am to be back. I may be crazy, but I'd rather be crazy here than anywhere else in the world. By the way, have you looked around at the crowd?"

"I have."

"Well," Roberto added, "Don't know whether you've noticed or not, but I'm positive there are Russian — or is it Chinese? — agents mixed in that want to take me back to their homeland and torture me. I know a lot of secrets they'd love to have."

"Oh, I'm sure you do," Daniel responded, trying to look serious.

"And if I'm able to escape them, I want you to come to my home sometime so I can talk to you about the things I can see that others can't." He lunged at Daniel and gripped him in a bear hug, "I love you, man . . ."

Daniel hugged him back. "I love you, too, Roberto."

Alame grabbed Roberto by the arm and pulled him away. "Roberto, come with me and we'll check out the food, okay?" She looked over at Daniel and said, "Looking forward to the ceremony."

Daniel gave her a thumbs up.

Mahina arrived at his side. "My love, it is time to begin."

Daniel kissed her. "I can't wait."

Slowly they strolled hand in hand to the ahu on which stood the ancient moai. Tiare stood in front of it and beamed as she saw Daniel and Mahina walk up before her.

Tiare held her hands up and the crowd gradually became silent. She boomed out in a most powerful voice, "My friends, today is a very special day, the marriage of Daniel and Mahina. All of you here know the love they share, not only for each other, but also for the island."

There was a bit of applause, and Tiare paused for a moment. "They have chosen to draw up their own vows, and they will repeat each sentence after me." She looked lovingly at Daniel and Mahina and whispered, "Please turn and face each other. Are you ready?"

Daniel and Mahina both nodded. They joined hands, faces glowing with anticipation.

Tiare began:

I promise to love you
    As long as my eyes see the sunshine
    My feet feel the earth

And my hair is blown by the wind
I promise to love you
  When you are healthy
  When you are ill
  And when you are less than perfect
  Through all the joys and sorrows of life
I promise to raise our children
  With respect for your native traditions
  And for the Earth that nurtures us
I promise to support your spiritual path
  Wherever it leads you
  However difficult it is
  And someday when death separates us
I promise to hold a place for you in my heart
  Forever

Tears were in Tiare's eyes as she turned Daniel and Mahina to face the audience. "I would like to present to you, Daniel Fishinghawk, Jr., and Mahina Rapanui Fishinghawk, husband and wife."

With that, enthusiastic applause greeted them, with Roberto Ika leading the cheers from the front.

Daniel and Mahina kissed to an even bigger roar.

"Let's greet our friends," Daniel said.

"Let's," Mahina replied

They walked into the crowd and received lots of handshakes and many more hugs. At that point, in the traditional Rapanui way, a group of musicians began singing songs as they clapped rocks together in rhythm. As if on cue, a group of manutara birds circled overhead and screeched along with them.

Very few days are perfect, Daniel thought.

But this feels like one of them.

Chapter 5

A little over a month had passed since Daniel and Mahina's wedding, and Tiare smiled as she thought about it while she puttered around the house. She had spent most of the morning cleaning and wanted her home to be tidy before she left. She sat on her couch for a moment and thought . . . Yes, the time is now right.

The floor had been swept; the refrigerator and the oven had been cleaned. No, she couldn't think of a thing left to do other than to write a note to Daniel and Mahina. Sometimes, she thought, it was best to express oneself in writing.

She pulled a pad and pen off the shipping crate which doubled as a coffee table, contemplated for a moment, and began to write:

Dearest Daniel and Mahina,

Today I have an important shaman duty to perform at Puna Pau, but before I leave, I have some words to share with you.

I am in a reflective mood, and as I look back on my life, I realize it has been as full as any ninety-four year old could hope for. I have the respect of my community, and I am proud of my children and the lives they have made for themselves.

Yet — the icing on the cake of my life was helping Daniel solve the recent murders on our island. Never before have I experienced such exhilaration and excitement! You clearly did most of the legwork, but I feel I was a worthy sidekick — at least that's what they call my role in the American westerns I have seen.

If I have any regret, though, it's that the last twenty years of my life were spent without my husband Ernesto. I don't talk a lot about him, but we were as close as any couple could be, and I missed having him by my side.

Now the important part: As I'm sure both of you know, the older generation always has advice for the younger, and I am no different than most. If I would share any words of wisdom with you, it would be to make you aware that you are both bright flames who unselfishly share your light with the world. Together, without giving up your individuality, you can produce a radiance far more brilliant that either of you could have alone. Not only will this benefit others, it will also encourage your own personal growth.

Seeing your love, I have a renewed hope for the Rapanui community. Together you will make a difference. I know — after all, I am a shaman.

Much love,

Tiare

Tiare nodded with approval as she reread the letter. She folded it, stuffed it in an envelope, addressed it, and then walked out the front door to the post office. Once the letter was mailed, she headed toward Puna Pau.

She carefully ascended the upward slope, and before long she was walking among the red scoria topknots. She saw the crater open before her and picked her way down the slope.

Tiare sat on a boulder at the bottom and watched her breath move in and out. As she entered a deep state of relaxation, she became aware of a presence. When she opened her eyes, sitting on a boulder across from her was a grimacing skeletal man with a long, hooked nose, dark goatee and long earlobes.

"Sister Tiare?" he said.

"Hitirau?"

"Yes."

"How did you know my name?" Tiare asked.

"I know all the elders in the Rapanui family." He grimaced even more. "I also know that you helped the outsider Dan-iel ruin my plans for our people to have their freedom."

"That is true," Tiare replied. "But your schemes were evil and had to be stopped."

"But the deaths of the outsiders were necessary."

"I see you believe that. But there is another way, a peaceful way, where innocent people do not have to be killed."

Hitirau looked puzzled and scratched his chin. "Do you believe I am evil?"

Tiare smiled at him. "No one is truly evil, but their actions might be. But I am here for another reason."

"And what is that?" Hitirau asked.

"I have come to take you home. Are any of your fellow akuaku still here?"

"No," he answered, "they have all disappeared, one by one. I am the last."

"You see, they have already found their way."

"But I thought this was home."

"Oh, but it's not," Tiare said. "If you'd like, I can take you there."

"But I am comfortable here."

"I know you are, but your comfort is a trap. And you have been trapped for far too long."

"What about Paoa?" Hitirau asked.

"All eventually make it back home — even Paoa. But he is not ready yet."

Hitirau sat for a long time on the boulder, and Tiare could tell he was thinking. Finally he whispered, "I am ready."

"Give me a moment," Tiare requested. With that, she closed her eyes and took a few more deep breaths. A shimmering light being, which looked much like the Tiare that she was, arose from her body.

Tiare looked down on her aged form, which now sat quietly in meditation. She smiled at Hitirau. "Take my hand."

Hitirau was shaking as he grasped it. "I'm scared," he said.

"I know you are. But I am about to take you to your true home, and once you are there, you will discover that it is far more familiar than our island ever could be."

Together they walked toward a luminous spirit that waited to greet them. Tiare placed Hitirau before it, squeezed his hand one last time and turned to head back. It was then she heard her name called.

That voice . . . could it be?

As she spun around, standing in front of her was a radiant presence, wearing the biggest smile she had ever seen.

She gasped as he recognized him.

"Ernesto," she whispered.

He took her hands in his and said, "My love, how wonderful to see you again. I wish we could spend some time together, but you must go now and return to your earthly existence. When your moment of transition comes, I'll be waiting for you."

Tiare asked, "Darling, how long will that be?"

He murmured softly, "When the time is right, not before, not after."

They slowly separated, and Tiare walked back to her sitting body, frequently glancing back at him.

She closed her eyes for a moment, and when she opened them, she was once again sitting on a boulder at Puna Pau.

Even though tears were flowing from her eyes, Tiare couldn't stop smiling.

Chapter 6

October 9, 2015, Tahlequah, Oklahoma

D aniel and Mahina walked hand in hand alongside the Illinois River just east of
Tahlequah, Oklahoma. It was a lovely fall day; the sky was perfectly clear, and
a light breeze cooled them.

It came as no surprise to Daniel that Mahina looked just as beautiful in
Oklahoma as she did in Rapa Nui. Daniel didn't believe it was possible to love another person as much as he loved Mahina. The amazing thing was that he felt at least
as much love from her.

Daniel listened as the mockingbirds and scissor-tailed flycatchers made sure
their songs were heard. Fall in Oklahoma was glorious, and Daniel was certain there
was no better place in the world when autumn rolled around.

As he heard the sound of the river flowing by, Daniel remembered the call from
his old detective chief, Kip Kelly, when the story first broke about how he had solved
the murders. Daniel recalled, word-for-word, how the conversation went:

"Hawk, you ol' son of a bitch," Kip Kelly said. "It took longer than I expected
for you to clean up that fucking mess down there. But you did — and now you're a
hero. Go figure!"

"Chief, that was the hardest case I've ever investigated."

"I'll show you hard. Come back to New York City and get back to investigating
some genuine murders, not some crazy wacko Easter Island detective who's gone off

his rocker. I'll get you some *real* cases to figure out. What'd you say?"

"Chief, I don't think so."

"Listen, Hawk, I've already talked to Commissioner Walsh, and he's agreed to *triple* your salary if you'll come back home. We need you, Hawk. No one ever will come close to figuring things out the way you did."

"Sorry, Chief, New York City is not home, and I'm not coming back."

"But Hawk —"

"I'm sorry, sir."

Then Daniel listened and listened, until Kelly ran out of words. Finally, Kelly said, "Someday, Hawk, you and I will meet again. Meantime — I'll miss you," and the line went dead.

From Daniel's point of view, there was no reason to listen further anyway. Daniel had already rented a small space in Hanga Roa for his own business. While they were on vacation in Oklahoma, one of the local woodcutters was preparing a sign for his office. It was to say:

Daniel "Hawk" Fishinghawk, Jr.
Private Investigator
of the
Strange and Mysterious

Who could tell what kinds of unusual cases would present themselves? He smiled as he pictured the sign in his mind and seeing the "Jr." — as Tiare had announced at their marriage — that was now part of his name. It felt healing to embrace his heritage, not push it away.

As for the rongorongo boards, the one shaped like a turtle was joyfully accepted at the museum on Rapa Nui, while the second was sold through Sotheby's in New York City. Because of its pristine condition, it was auctioned off for the unbelievable price of $20 million US to the Te Papa Tongarewa Museum in Wellington, New Zealand. After their vacation, plans were to be drawn up for the institute.

With all that was happening on Rapa Nui, Daniel and Mahina made the joint decision to live on the island and raise a family there. Daniel reasoned it was only fair; she had given up everything to be with him — now it was his turn.

His only request was that, at least once a year, they return to Oklahoma for a vacation. There was something about Oklahoma that grew on a person, and the thought of never returning home was just too much to bear. The best way to describe it was like a deep itch that had to be scratched every now and then. Besides, every so often Daniel needed to connect with his roots — and his roots were here.

After an hour or so of walking, Daniel and Mahina finally reached their destination: a cottonwood tree that stood well over one hundred feet high, right next to the river. Its leaves had already changed from summer green to bright yellow.

"Are you ready, my dear?" Daniel asked.

"Dan-iel, you have told me of this place, and it is far more beautiful that I ever could have imagined. Yes, I'm ready."

With that they began to shimmy up the tree trunk, Daniel first, followed closely by Mahina. The higher they went, the more they were able to smell the fragrance of the wild honeysuckle bushes that grew along the river's edge.

Before long the trunk branched and they continued to climb, side by side, until they had gone as high as they were safely able. The branches they clung to swayed side to side in the gentle breeze.

Daniel and Mahina both laughed with the exhilaration of it all, and any residual pain that Daniel had carried from his previous experience there vanished with the wind that moved them.

Finally the breeze blew their branches close to each other so that they were able to wrap their free arms around each other. As they held each other tightly, they passionately kissed.

Daniel said to Mahina, "A-da-do-li-gi."

"A-da-do-li-gi? What does that mean?"

"It's something my grandpa used to call me. It's Cherokee and means blessing. Mahina — you are my blessing."

They kissed once again and Mahina repeated, "A-da-do-li-gi. Dan-iel, you are *my* blessing."

"My love, we bless each other."

Mahina said, "As we should."

With that they released each other, and the wind playfully rocked them to and fro through the clear Oklahoma sky.

Acknowledgements

In March of 2012 my wife Sheridan and I took a vacation to Easter Island. Actually our first choice was Patagonia, a wilderness area in the far south of Chile, and we were making preparations for the trip when Patagonia was closed due to a devastating fire.

Fortunately, the lodge we had been scheduled to stay at had a sister hotel on Easter Island, and we switched to that location. While I was initially disappointed, my wife was delighted, as Easter Island was a place she had always wanted to visit. You might say God works in mysterious ways.

Once there, we both fell in love with Easter Island, which the islanders prefer to call Rapa Nui. The people were extremely friendly and while the island was deforested, there was an inherent beauty and a non-commercialism that was instantly attractive. Besides that, there were the magnificent moai and ahus, remnants of a past shrouded in mystery and turmoil.

There are many to thank in the formation of this book. First I must thank my wife Sheridan for her adventurous spirit and willingness to travel to faraway places. After we arrived back home, she was most supportive as I disappeared for hours on end feverishly researching and writing this book.

I want also to express my appreciation to our Rapanui guide, Yoyo Pakomio, for his explanations and patience as he led us on treks over a good part of the island. Through his assistance, we were able to view the island from the perspective of someone whose roots belong there. Only those with Rapanui blood can truly understand the visceral pain and difficulties their people have suffered through.

I owe a huge debt of gratitude to Georgia Lee, one of the founders of the Easter Island Foundation (EIF). Shortly after I began writing, I realized I needed a mentor to help me with my many questions, and I phoned the EIF asking for help. A few days later she agreed to assist me and has been an invaluable asset as I put together this book. I later discovered she is an archeologist who had spent over six years doing field work there and has written multiple books and papers on Easter Island. While I am responsible for any historical inaccuracies found in this book, her advice has helped me to be as precise as possible.

Finally, I want to thank my editors, the late Betty Wright and Betsy Lampe, who formed an indefatigable team with me as we worked on this novel. Hillary Clinton once authored a book, titled *It Takes a Village*, and that is certainly true in the construction of *Murder on Easter Island*.

About the Author

Gary D. Conrad lives with his wife, Sheridan, and their dogs, Inky and Karma, in Edmond, Oklahoma. Gary is an emergency and integrative physician, and his interests include Tibetan rights, meditation, the music of Joséph Haydn, organic gardening, choral work and wilderness hiking.

Gary's first book is the award-winning visionary fiction novel, *The Lhasa Trilogy*. His second is an autobiographical collection of memoirs in short story form, *Oklahoma Is Where I Live: and Other Things on My Mind*. He is currently working on a sequel to *Murder on Easter Island*.

Gary can be reached through his website at GaryDConrad.com.